DRUMBEAT
NOTES FROM BOSTON #3

A. M. Leibowitz

Supposed Crimes LLC • Matthews, North Carolina

Published in the United States.

ISBN: 978-1-944591-51-9

www.supposedcrimes.com

This book is typeset in Goudy Old Style.

THANKS

As always, I am indebted to my excellent beta readers. Without their support, insight, and critical eyes, I'd be lost.

Heartfelt thanks to my family, particularly for supplying me with ideas. I'm fortunate to have a pair of the most creative kids a parent could ask for. In particular, I'm grateful to my daughter for making sure everyone else leaves me alone to write in peace.

Thank you to my dance instructor not only for teaching me what "threes" and "sevens" are but for many an impromptu Irish history and culture lesson. Thank you to my son for encouraging me to try it out despite my protests that I have two left feet.

And of course, thank you to my readers, who have stuck with these characters and tasked me with answering some important questions. It means the world to me.

May you have the hindsight to know where you've been, the foresight to know where you are going, and the insight to know when you have gone too far.
~Irish proverb

Chapter One

Jamie Cosgrove yawned as he slid his key into the lock on his apartment door. It had been a long night, and all he wanted was sleep. He'd endured a table full of drunk women, one of whom grabbed his crotch. Despite being blitzed, the woman had recognized him, and not from the band. She had taken it as license to feel him up and check whether it was "real." When he backed up and asked her politely to keep her hands to herself, her friend threatened to tell the manager he'd sexually harassed them. Not one of them left him a tip. He did succeed in talking to his supervisor before any of them had a chance to complain, and fortunately, she was on his side. Still, the end result was the same—he was out the money from their tip and left feeling violated.

When he turned the key, the lock was already popped. One of Jamie's roommates was home. He was surprised. Nate spent at least a few nights a week at his fiancé's place, and Mack supposedly had a date and wouldn't be home. Jamie didn't really care, as long as neither of them wanted to have an in-depth conversation about anything. He opened the door quietly.

He stopped dead in his tracks, the door still ajar. Greeting him was the sight of Mack's naked butt, rising and falling rhythmically. Jamie couldn't see who was under Mack on the living room floor, and he didn't need to. It was probably Amelia, his friend-with-benefits, but it could have been someone else. They weren't exclusive.

As quietly as possible, Jamie shut the door. Neither Mack nor whoever he was screwing noticed. Jamie tiptoed past them to the bedroom, glancing down long enough to see that Mack's partner was a slender blond man. Their grunts followed Jamie down the hall, mostly muffled once he had the door shut.

He stripped off his clothes and left them draped over the back of his desk chair. A shower would have been nice, but there was no way he would go back out there anytime soon. He contemplated waiting until he heard the inevitable exit of Mack's date. The times he had someone over besides Amelia, it never lasted more than a round or two before he was shuffling them off home. Amelia always stayed, but she'd known Mack for at least fifteen years, maybe longer.

Jamie wasn't surprised Mack had a guest, only that they'd been in the living room. Mack had a pretty wide range of tastes, and it wasn't unusual for him to bring home anyone who was willing. He and Jamie had even tried things out once, the first time Mack rescued Jamie from his ex. They'd been at a party, Sage was at his usual best, and Mack had had enough. He'd brought Jamie home with him, and they'd kissed against the door to his bedroom. They couldn't even blame alcohol—neither of them had touched a drop. They'd made out for exactly long enough to decide they weren't into each other, choosing to sleep off the bad experience in separate beds instead.

It was neither here nor there. The important thing was that tonight, Jamie smelled like fish and garlic and couldn't even wash it off. He debated about whether to leave the bedroom and confess to having witnessed their moment or stay inside and wait until morning to pretend he'd gotten home after Mack was asleep. The pros were smelling clean and...well, that was the only pro. The cons were having them still going or, worse yet, having them finished but the stranger still hanging around. The sort of people Mack usually picked up were the type to be familiar with Jamie's other work. He wasn't in the mood for round two of that game.

He dragged on a fresh T-shirt but didn't put anything on over his underwear. As he flipped down the covers, he almost groaned. He'd have to wash his sheets because they would end up smelling like seafood too. Just as he was about to slip into bed, he heard the apartment door slam. He cringed, hoping their neighbors wouldn't be too mad. From the sounds of it, Mack's guy wasn't too pleased at being given the boot. Jamie didn't blame him, although he was sure Mack had clearly explained his rules ahead of time. He was casual, not cruel.

Before Jamie could make up his mind about whether it was safe to come out yet, there was a knock on his door. He crossed the room to open it.

"Hey," Mack said.

"Hey."

"Sorry about that."

Jamie swallowed a snotty reply. "No problem. Who was he?"

Mack shrugged. "Some guy I picked up in Starbucks."

"What?" Jamie couldn't stop himself. He giggled helplessly.

Giving Jamie a playful shove, Mack said, "He was finishing his shift. I suggested a more adult-friendly activity."

"And just like that, he came home with you?"

"Nah. I told him I'm in a band." Mack grinned. "Some people are into the whole 'tortured artist' thing."

"And you're among the most tortured." Jamie laughed.

"Gotta keep up appearances."

"Why the hell were you in the living room, anyway?"

"We got talking, and he said he was looking for a new apartment. We're looking for a roommate. Win-win. So I brought him back here to interview him."

Jamie gaped at him. "By fucking him in our shared space? I thought we wanted someone to pay rent, not for you to hook up with."

"Didn't think anyone would be home yet. He wasn't a good candidate anyway."

"That's what you said about the last three." Jamie was tired of having every single applicant sabotaged by whatever perfection Mack was looking for. "We need someone, Mack. Trevor's already gone. Nate barely lives here now either, and even when he does, he struggles to pay the rent. We've both covered for him, but I can't do it anymore. He said the minute we have a new roommate, he wants to move in with Izzy."

"I know, I know. I promise, we'll find someone." Mack craned his neck to peer around Jamie at the clock on the dresser. "Damn, I'm sorry. It's later than I thought. I should let you get some sleep."

"It's fine. I need a shower anyway." Jamie made a show of sniffing himself. "I smell like crap."

"God, I cannot wait until we don't have to work there anymore."

Mack gave Jamie's shoulder a squeeze and turned around. He called "good night" over his shoulder.

Jamie agreed with Mack's assessment. The restaurant was generally a decent place to work, but Jamie could have done without the constant food smell, the inconsistent tips, and tonight's crotch-grabbing patrons. He was also well and truly over having to turn up his charm to a ten. For once, he wanted a job with less false front. Story of his life, really. Even being in the band meant he had a certain image to uphold. Aside from the typical rock star persona, it was mostly due to Jamie's influence that they'd started getting real gigs at all. People's memories were long when it came to who they liked to watch while jerking off, and many were brand-loyal. Jamie's career had been comparatively short but significant.

He grabbed clean clothes and headed for the bathroom. The world's fastest shower later, he was sinking into bed with a contented sigh. His mind wandered back to the scene in the living room, and he squeezed his eyes shut against the replay. That was an image he would need to scour from his brain. He supposed it was better than if Nate had walked in on them; he might have been more bothered by it than Jamie was. Not because Mack was with a man—Nate was as gay as Jamie. But Nate came across as pretty sex-shy to Jamie. Until he met his fiancé, he'd always seemed closed off and embarrassed by everything.

Some of that might have been all the trouble between Nate and their friend Trevor. Nate's years-long crush on Trevor had only ended after things blew up spectacularly between them. Nate had outed Trevor on some guy's blog, and it may or may not have been on purpose. Jamie gathered that a big part of the problem had been some kind of casual bro-jobs arrangement the two of them had, which stopped when Trevor met his current boyfriend. Things were good between Nate and Trevor these days, though Jamie doubted they went back to hooking up after The Incident, as he referred to it.

Thinking about all that brought Trevor to the forefront of Jamie's mental meanderings. Jamie understood perfectly why Nate had pined after him. Trevor was one of the nicest people Jamie knew, and it didn't hurt that he was hot. Even alone, under the cover of darkness, Jamie flushed thinking about him. He'd tried so hard not to develop any feelings for him, but he couldn't help it. Trevor was solidly spoken for; he had a boyfriend and a girlfriend, not to mention a five-month-old baby.

Still, every time they were together, Jamie had that fluttering feeling, the longing to have Trevor closer. Jamie had given up on denying himself the pleasure of imagining Trevor's lips and hands on him. The way Trevor looked at him sometimes made Jamie wonder if he thought about it too. He'd said recently that he and his partners were open, and he'd tried being with other people a couple of times. He'd also said it was unsatisfying and had only left him disappointed and frustrated, so he'd stopped. Jamie gathered that Andre—Trevor's boyfriend—had a girlfriend as well. Marlie, Trevor's girlfriend, seemed mostly wrapped up in her career.

As exhausted as he was, Jamie was reacting to his racing thoughts about Trevor. He rested his hand on his thigh, contemplating whether or not it would relax him to relieve some tension. His fingers gripped and released the fabric of his pajama pants, and he swallowed. Excitement had turned into nerves, and not because he was thinking about jerking off over his friend. Before he could catch himself and stop the thought, it popped into his head.

Better not. Sage wouldn't like it.

Jamie rolled over and buried his face in the pillow, shaking. Months after their final breakup, Sage still had the ability to invade his thoughts. Jamie curled into a ball on his side. He kept his eyes closed, trying to think of anything else. Mack's bare ass. Trevor. Sweet baby Aidan. The leftover spaghetti he'd forgotten to throw out. It wasn't working.

I'll never be free of him.

Then his mind snapped to the other thing he could do to fill the growing hole. He'd promised Mack he was better, but that was before. Tonight he had too much on his brain to stick to his commitment that he wasn't going to hurt himself this way.

He thought he might still have food in the bin under his bed that he hadn't thrown out at Mack's urging. He shifted so he was half hanging over the side of the bed and reached down. Slowly, so he wouldn't make noise and bring Mack to his door again, Jamie pulled the bin out. Yes, just enough was left in there to numb his mind with the ache in his gut. He would deal with the guilt of giving in another time.

###

An angry face. Something heavy, Jamie couldn't see what it was. The man swung but missed. Jamie yelled over his shoulder, "Mama, go!" She didn't move, but neither did Jamie, staying in between her and the man. Jamie shouted at her again. He said he'd find her. She turned and fled. The man lunged, and his whole face changed, morphing into a monster with endless teeth. His mouth opened wide, wider...

Jamie sat bolt upright, his heart racing and his lungs heaving. He tried to shake off the dream while simultaneously puzzling out where he was and what had woken him. The days all ran together since walking in on Mack and giving in to another binge. After his blackout the other night, he didn't know how much time had passed outside work; he tried to avoid thinking about it.

He blinked and looked around at the darkening apartment, trying to remember. Right. He'd fallen asleep on the couch after returning from his lunch shift. His gaze landed on his phone, which vibrated against the coffee table one last time. That must have been what roused him. He picked it up and instantly wished he hadn't.

Sage.

Why he hadn't blocked the number was beyond him. He should have, especially since he'd meant it to be for good this time. At the very least, he should've blocked it when the phone calls started a few weeks back.

Always before when they'd broken up, they'd been back together within six weeks. It had now been nearly five months, and so far, Jamie's resolve had remained firm. He hadn't returned any of Sage's phone calls, and he hadn't contacted him. He could do this, managing on his own. He didn't need Sage.

Except when he did, like now. The dream had rattled him, and Jamie pulled the thin afghan around his shoulders. It happened sometimes, the nightmares of getting away from Mama's—what number boyfriend was it again? More than five, less than ten. Jamie had lost count. That man was the only one who ever hit Mama. They'd planned their escape for weeks, and even so, he'd nearly caught them. Jamie was lucky he got out with only a black eye and a few bruised ribs.

He'd looked for Mama for ages after that, but no one would tell him where she'd gone. She'd been too afraid to give him her whole plan just in case something slipped. Months of searching for her, then searching for his father. Surviving any way he could until he got to the Lighthouse, so sick he could hardly stand and afraid it was more than just the flu. He was damn lucky it wasn't.

Only Sage knew all of it. He was there many nights when Jamie woke, drenched in sweat from reliving the terror of that time. He knew and didn't judge, just held Jamie until he stopped shaking. Sage wasn't the same kind of monster. He'd never hit Jamie, no matter what the others thought he was capable of. Even that last time, he'd shoved Jamie, but Jamie had pushed him, too. If he'd ever beaten him, Jamie would've been out the door sooner. Or so he liked to think.

That kind of violence wasn't Sage's way. Everything he did was softer, gentler. The kind of thing that lulls a person into feeling secure. Even when he touched Jamie in ways that made him uncomfortable, it was always that same tenderness, almost a vulnerability. All fake. Jamie had nightmares about that too.

He didn't call it assault. He'd worked with a man back when they were in the web series together. The guy had been raped more than once—twice by men and once by a woman. He'd said the first time was violent and painful. The second time, he was too drunk to remember anything but waking up to it. The third time, she'd given him an uninvited blow job. Jamie hadn't even known that was possible. In the end, Jamie's friend had said the only time he felt safe having sex was on camera where there was someone to watch and keep it under control.

Then there was Sage. With him, there were no harsh, jagged edges or force. He'd never held Jamie down or attacked him. Never hit him or threatened him. He'd whispered beautiful, cruel things, gently touching him even when Jamie tried to pull away. Sage had kept it all so painfully sweet, wrapping Jamie in his arms and doing what he wanted until Jamie gave in and pretended he was into it until it was over. No bruises. No blood. Nothing violent or angry. Jamie couldn't count that. Not when he'd been awake and sober and hadn't said no. Not when there were countless times he said yes. Not when afterward, there were whispered reminders Sage was the only one who truly loved him. Every couple had times like that, right?

Jamie missed Sage even though doing so made him feel guilty. He hadn't realized he was almost crying, clutching his phone so tightly it hurt. The pain brought him back to his senses. That was what he needed—something to remind him why he stayed away from Sage. He rose from the couch, shedding the afghan, and padded to the kitchen.

He opened cupboard doors, looking for food. After the other night, he had hardly anything left under his bed, but he figured there had to be something out here. He was trying, he really was. He hadn't gone out to buy anything new. If he ate their shared food, maybe he wouldn't overdo it this time. He finally found a bag of popcorn kernels. Perfect. If any of the others showed up, he would have a believable excuse. They wouldn't question what he was doing. It was a good compromise too. He could eat it without a whole lot of guilt; it wasn't dense or heavy, and it would take a lot before it made him sick.

In no time, Jamie was back on the couch with the bowl next to him. He flipped on the television and found something to watch. Whatever it was didn't make a whole lot of sense, but he didn't care. It was good enough, and he settled in.

Jamie wasn't paying much attention to the movie or to what he was doing aside from that. The movie was nearly over—and still not making any sense—when he heard voices in the hallway. A moment later, Nate and Trevor tumbled in, laughing about something. Trevor kicked the door shut and set a bag on the kitchen table. Jamie turned to look at them. Nate waved and ducked into the bathroom.

"God, it smells fantastic in here," Trevor said. "Ooh, Jay, did you make popcorn?"

"Uh...yeah." Jamie looked down at the empty bowl and thought about the half bag of kernels he'd popped. He'd been too busy going over every detail of Sage's messages and had barely noticed that he'd eaten all of it. Somehow, it was both enough and not at the same time. An embarrassed prickle crept up his neck at the thought.

"I can make more."

"Cool." Trevor took a couple of containers out and put them in the fridge. "Marlie sent some stuff. Homemade soup of some kind."

"What are you guys doing here, anyway?" Jamie was sure he sounded as grouchy as he felt in spite of the seed of warmth at Marlie's caring. He'd been enjoying having some space.

"Andre's home, bonding with the baby. I had a date with Marlie, and now she's out seeing some chick flick with Nia. Apparently, they're bonding too." Trevor sounded tense. "Izzy's doing...something, I can't remember what, so Nate asked if I wanted to hang out here."

"Oh."

Jamie stood and returned to the kitchen to make more popcorn. He thought it really might make him sick if he ate any more, mostly because of the interruption and the fear they'd find out what he did on bad days. He didn't know how he would explain it to them. They wouldn't understand. Jamie didn't understand it himself. Why couldn't he do what he'd promised Mack? He'd said he could stop, that being away from Sage would make it easier. Only it didn't, and his friends wouldn't get it. Mack would be upset and disappointed in him. Trevor and Nate would be confused and worried. Sage had said as much before, and he was surely right.

"You okay?" Trevor asked, nudging Jamie with his shoulder.

Jamie swallowed. He didn't know how to answer that. He glanced into the living room at his phone on the coffee table. Sage. The dream. His conflicted feelings about being in the same space with Trevor. It was more than Jamie wanted to talk about right then.

"I'm fine. Long shift, though."

"Diners still giving you shit?"

"Nah. Just busy. There was some business lunch there." He grinned, hoping to put Trevor off the scent. "You know, men in suits—lots of eye candy."

Laughing, Trevor squeezed his shoulder on the way past into the living room. Jamie swore he could still feel the press of Trevor's fingers long after he let go. He tracked Trevor's motions, envious and a little turned on by how comfortable he seemed in his thick, gorgeous body. It made Jamie feel hollow, and he thought about taking his phone into the bedroom and returning Sage's call. Sage would know better than Jamie what to do. He would talk Jamie out of these intense feelings for Trevor and whatever it was Jamie was thinking of doing about them.

Jamie gripped the counter. No. He was better than this. He wouldn't call Sage, no matter what. He would manage his problems himself. If he could be strong enough to leave Sage for good, he could be strong enough to eat properly and wrangle his crush on Trevor back into submission. In the morning, he would start over.

"Hey," he called into the living room. "Butter and salt?"

"Yeah, but not too much, okay?" Trevor answered. "I don't like it too salty."

"You got it," Jamie said.

CHAPTER TWO

CIAN TOOMEY led his students through their stretches and warm-ups. This class was a group of seven-, eight-, and nine-year-olds. He didn't start them until then, so these were his beginners. Since they were recreational, it didn't matter what age they learned. Cian had a whole class of people age sixty plus. There were some who felt that he, as a performer and certified teacher himself, should have had his students competing. This was especially true of those who wanted him to show off his deaf students to prove they were as capable. It pissed him off, and his stance had cost him a few families, but it was worth it. He would not use his deaf students, or any of his other disabled kids, as inspiration.

He counted for them, using a gold-topped cane and signing to visually mark time for the class. In their line, they practiced their forward skip-steps to the beat he kept. They were all in soft shoes, and their feet landed in muffled thuds. Without his hearing aids in, Cian felt rather than heard the difference against the wood of the studio floor. He also felt the vibrations when they intentionally slammed into the opposite wall from where they began; he had to bite the inside of his cheek not to laugh.

"Good, good!" He both spoke and signed to them when they turned around.

This class only had one deaf pupil, unlike his intermediate group. Cian felt that regardless of how many students needed him to sign, he would do it anyway. Besides ASL, he made liberal use of the white board the studio's owner allowed him to install. He wrote each lesson's notes and steps. By the second month of class, his pupils could communicate their basic needs—*bathroom, drink, show me again*—and read his shorthand for the steps. By the end of their first year, his hearing students picked up not only skill as dancers but a significant amount of ASL as well. He tried to do it in a way which didn't feel forced, simply a natural consequence of seeing him do it—like a language immersion class, in a sense.

One of the girls stumbled a little, and three others giggled at her. Cian gave them his stern teacher look, and they stopped. One of the reasons he kept to recreational dance was so he could allow a wider range of ability. The girl who had tripped was on a different developmental curve from her peers. Not that Cian would explain it to the others. It was their job to keep dancing, not mock her coordination.

When he felt they had practiced the steps for a sufficient period, he changed the music. This time they didn't dance. Cian had them lay down on the floor, their hands against the wood palms-down. They all assumed the position and looked up at him.

"Feel the vibrations," he instructed. "Try to pick out the beat."

The music played through a speaker on the floor, and he had the volume up. He'd have been able to hear it reasonably well with his hearing aids in, imperfect though they were, but he preferred to dance without them. Taking them out also made a good barrier to students stopping every two minutes to ask a thousand questions. He lay down facing his students in the same position. He had chosen a traditional melody he was familiar with, as interpreted by a modern pop band. Cian felt the thrum in his chest and counted out the opening in his head, his eyes on the kids as he waited for them to pick up the meter.

The first one to get it was the girl who had tripped earlier. She kept her hands on the floor and counted out the beat by drumming her toes in time with it. The others began to join in as they caught the rhythm. Cian added his own taps, counting out loud for them.

At the end of the song, the children sat up and Cian went to turn the music off. He faced the class. This time, he only signed, knowing they would understand because he asked the same question every week. *Ready to practice your recital dances?*

Excited, they moved into their positions. For the rest of their hour, Cian led them through their performance dance. This group had come a long way, probably farther than any beginner class he'd had to date. He wished some of his older students shared their dedication and enthusiasm for the craft. When they were through, he sent them all to change into their street clothes while he tidied up the room for the next class.

It was too bad he only got to spend a few hours a week at the studio. They rented space, and he was limited in which days he could be there. He had to cram eight classes into a handful of open slots, and he'd had to create larger classes than he preferred to do so. He'd been at it for about three years, and he wasn't ready to take on his own space and make it full-time work. On top of his performing schedule and his day job, he hardly had time for much else.

He opened the studio door to let parents in and students out. After he waved goodbye to them, he welcomed the next crew, his intermediates. A lot of them were older siblings of the first set, and he'd been teaching most of them since the beginning. He didn't need to speak out loud to them, which was nice. Not that he minded talking, but he preferred the ease of signing in this situation. Fortunately, his pupils were adaptable.

There were only six of them, two boys and four girls. Truth be told, this was his favorite class, although that might have been because his own thirteen-year-old half sister was in the group. Her two younger siblings didn't have any interest, but Cadence had joined the moment Cian started teaching.

The students began to arrive. The twins, Patsy and Lyra, showed up first. Patsy was hearing; Lyra was deaf. As soon as they were in the door, they began a steady flow of signed chatter with Cian, all about a talent night at their middle school and could he help them put something together. He told them he would talk with their parents after class. It probably wouldn't be difficult for them, as they were his quickest learners. He might be able to adapt their recital dance for just the two of them if he shortened the song.

The boys and the other girl arrived, and Patsy and Lyra were soon distracted and left Cian to interact with them. At last Cadence showed up, along with Cian's father. She bounded into the room, and Cian came over to give her a hug. He lifted her a few inches off the floor, and she squealed until he let go.

Cian, don't! Cadence signed. *I'm too big now.*

He laughed. *Never!*

She developed an odd look on her face—embarrassment, maybe, or worry—and slipped into the bathroom to change. Cian greeted his father warmly before sending him out to the waiting area and shutting the door. It was usually easier for the kids if he didn't allow anyone to watch them during a lesson. He turned to the class, all of whom were now lined up except for Cadence. Cian shook his head.

Where's Cadence? he signed to Lyra.

Still changing? she answered, shrugging her shoulders to indicate her uncertainty.

Cian sighed. Ever since hitting puberty, Cadence had become so body-shy in class. He thought they'd been over this, and none of the other students saw it as a big deal, but something new must've happened at school. Cian would talk with her later and find out what was going on. For now, the best he could do was get started and hope Cadence joined them.

Go see, please, he told Lyra.

She popped into the back while Cian welcomed the others and got right down to work, still stealing an occasional glance at the bathroom door. At last Cadence emerged, looking happier than she had a few minutes ago. She and Lyra joined the rest of the group, and Lyra made no indication she'd learned what was wrong.

For the rest of the hour, they worked diligently. Afterward, Cian told the twins to hang around so he could speak with their mother about a few extra lessons after the recital. He caught sight of his father again and waved, trying to communicate that he wanted him to stay as well. Either he misunderstood or Cadence was highly persuasive when she pulled on his arm because his father only waved back and let her drag him out the door.

Cian sighed. He'd try to find out what was going on the next time he had dinner with his family. For now, he turned his attention to Patsy and Lyra's mother.

School talent show? he signed, and before he knew it, he was wrapped up in a long conversation about the school, the talent show, and whatever it was the girls wanted to do.

###

Two more classes, a shower, and a shave later, Cian was on the road to Springfield to see friends. Or, more accurately, his three partners. He didn't go often, only a couple times a month. When he'd lived in Springfield briefly after college, they'd seen each other regularly, and it had been spontaneous. Now he only made the drive when they had arrangements. It was fine, as long as everyone kept their expectations casual. He'd never been a full-time part of their triad relationship.

He turned down their street and parked in front of their two-story house. The lights in the windows were inviting, and Cian was glad to be back in their company. As he got out of the car, Nell opened the door. The light framed her softly, her slightly rounded belly silhouetted in the doorframe. She waved, and Cian answered her greeting. He pulled his backpack from the trunk and came up on the porch to give her a proper hello.

Nell kissed him on the mouth, long and full. He put his hands on her protruding abdomen, loving the flutter under his fingers. The baby wasn't his; it was her other male partner's, but Cian had been their occasional lover for so long, he had affection for the children they and their woman partner had. Their life together extended to well before Cian had returned from college in New York.

Cian wondered where the older two kids were that night. He assumed with a sitter or grandparents, or their family wouldn't have invited him. Nell had been off-the-charts horny since hitting her second trimester, so no doubt Eric was worn out. Skye, too, for that matter. Cian was looking forward to reconnecting with all of them for the evening.

He followed Nell into the house. She flipped her long, dark hair over her shoulder, and her body swayed as she walked into the kitchen ahead of Cian. Her balance had been more off than was usual for her as the pregnancy progressed. Skye was cutting slices of chocolate cake while Eric poured coffee from the pot into four mugs. Skye stood and came around the table to give Cian a hug. She was less affectionate than Nell had been, but she pressed her lips to his cheek.

Cian helped Eric carry the mugs to the table, and the four of them kept up a lively signed conversation while they enjoyed the cake and coffee. In the same way Cian appreciated his older students, he loved spending time with these friends. He didn't need to worry about expressing himself with them because they knew each other so well. Except for Skye, they'd all been friends for years, along with a few others—two of Cian's occasional backup dancers, his best friend Brandon, and Brandon's fiancée, Gemma. Skye had come into Nell's life while Cian was away at school, and her relationship with Eric had grown out of that.

These evenings with Eric, Nell, and Skye always flowed naturally. Coffee, catching up, and then renewing their physical bond. Almost the minute he had finished his drink, Eric pulled Cian to his feet and kissed him. Cian tasted the chocolate and coffee on his tongue when he opened his mouth for Eric. As exciting as it was having Eric pressed so close, Cian was anxious to touch Nell. Before her, he'd never had sex with a pregnant woman, and this was her first baby. It had been well over a month since Cian's previous visit, and her body had changed significantly. There was something beautiful and radiant about her—she loved being pregnant. Their whole family was affectionate, but Nell was even more high-touch, like Cian.

He felt Nell's warmth as she wrapped herself around him from behind. Skye was there too, but she only wanted Nell at the moment. Her physical interest in Cian was low, though not nonexistent. They broke apart to take things into the bedroom, closing the door even though there was no one else in the house.

The room was lit only by a lamp with a low-wattage bulb. There was a California king-size bed, which the three adults in the house often shared, plus a love seat and a plush chair. A door beside the walk-in closet led to a bathroom with a large, round tub. The other bathroom had an enormous shower with dual heads. Sometimes the tub or shower were part of their play, but not tonight. They were reconnecting after so much time apart.

As eager as they all were, they kept everything slow and sensual to draw out their night together. They'd been doing this for so long, it was comfortable and natural. Cian and his partners knew how to touch and how to communicate their needs, an art they'd perfected over years. Hands and mouths finding each other, bodies moving in rhythm, joy and closeness building. It was a complicated dance of many steps, and Cian buried himself in the pleasurable agony. He reached a point where he didn't think he could possibly take more, his hand gliding between Nell's legs alongside Skye's and his ass full with Eric's thick cock.

Cian came so hard he was sure he saw stars, and at almost the same time he felt Nell let go. Eric withdrew, and Cian adjusted his position to watch Nell finish him off with her hands while Skye rode her leg. They were so beautiful together. After, Nell curled up against Cian, with Skye at her back. He rubbed slow circles on her belly, loving the way his hand curved over the small, firm bump. He slid his hand back to cup her ass, massaging gently. They would need to give him a few minutes, but he wouldn't have any trouble going a second round with them, or alone with Nell if she needed it and the others didn't.

Skye kissed her neck from behind and rubbed her shoulders. Nell looked relaxed, bliss evident on her face. She had slipped her hand down and was lightly touching herself, a sight Cian found not only erotic but so intimate. She was unashamed of her body or of having her partners watch her.

Eric tapped Cian on the arm, and he turned to look. *Sleep here?* Eric asked.

Cian gave an affirmative. He would be able to stay in bed late and have breakfast with the others before heading back into the city for a gig at Grand Slam. He'd performed there a few times before, but only as part of fundraiser nights. The owners were big on giving back to the community, so they held such events about once a quarter. They'd asked if he would like to do a regular stint he could be paid for, and he'd agreed. Something about needing to fill a gap after one of the regular drag queens had to quit.

Nell stopped fingering herself and shifted so she could reach for Cian. He rolled away from Eric, aware of Skye slipping around to the other side of the bed. They often began and ended the night in one large pile. Their first round had been about connecting all together; this time they paired off. Eric seemed to sense Cian's need to touch Nell. The baby wasn't his, and he was only a sometimes-lover in their household. But being with her, his hands on her, reminded him he was still family.

He lay back on the bed, and Nell straddled him. She rested his hands on her thighs, and he massaged them, loving the soft feel of her skin under his fingers. Nell kissed him, long and deep. Beside him, Cian felt the motion of the bed as Eric slowly coupled with Skye. Without his hearing aids, Cian could only make out vague, muffled sounds, but he caught the urgency. He looked up into Nell's face when she pulled back, and she smiled. Licking his lips, he tugged on her legs, encouraging her to move up. He wanted so badly to taste her that he was shaking.

She braced herself, and Cian used his mouth on her until her chest heaved with the effort to control her breathing. Her head tipped back, and he knew she was close. He tapped her, and she sat back a little so she could see him better.

Finish this way? he asked. He was pretty sure he could get himself close just from watching her enjoy their intimacy.

She replied, *Ride you?*

When he consented, she slid back until she could sink down on him. He groaned, and at the same moment, Skye was so vocal next to him that he felt the vibrations of her begging Eric through her climax. Cian thrust up to meet Nell's hips on the way down, and when he felt the rocking from Eric speeding up, it sent Cian spiraling into another orgasm. It only took another minute and Nell's expert fingers before she, too, was over the edge.

Skye slipped out of bed and into the bathroom, returning with warm cloths and towels for all of them. Once they were clean, they settled down under the covers. Nell extracted the television remote from a drawer and put on a show they all liked. Cian nestled in between Nell and Eric, with Skye on Nell's other side. They might wake again in the night, switching their coupling so Eric could have his fill of Cian.

As he relaxed, Cian thought about what he had. As much as he loved all of them, he wasn't fully part of their nesting group. He'd put some distance there when he'd had other relationships, keeping things nonsexual to appease the people he was dating. The breakup with his last boyfriend had been painful and raw, and he'd turned to Eric, Skye, and Nell once again for comfort.

More than once, they'd offered their home to him on a permanent basis, and he couldn't say why he'd declined. It wasn't only that he didn't like the idea of moving so far from the city. He was restless there, empty in a way they couldn't fill. He wanted someone of his own, someone who would be with him every night and not only when it was convenient for everyone. He'd never thought much about children, but maybe he wanted those, too. It didn't bother Cian that the others had already done all those things without him. He wasn't in love with them the same way they were with each other. No, he wanted those things with his own family.

And yet, Cian didn't want to give this up, either. The friendship and love with Eric and Nell, and now Skye, had outlasted nearly everything else in his life since coming to the States. Would he ever be able to find someone who understood how much he still needed this family? And would his chosen family understand his need for something more? He saw the life he wanted as though in split screen, and he wished he could make the picture all one. His thoughts grew fuzzy around the edges, and he drifted off halfway between feeling loved and safe and feeling hollow inside.

Chapter Three

JAMIE SAT next to Brandon at a back table in Grand Slam, toying with the swizzle stick in his Diet Coke. On any other night, he would have appreciated the gesture of his favorite cousin taking him out to a queer bar. Brandon's almost-wife, Gemma, was bi, but Brandon was straight, though he was one of the most open-minded people Jamie knew. Tonight, Jamie wished he were anywhere else. He'd have said no, except Brandon didn't tell him what the entertainment was beforehand. Times like this, Jamie wished he drank, but he didn't ever touch it for a laundry list of reasons. He resorted to clinking the ice in his glass, knowing Brandon couldn't hear it and hoping Gemma wouldn't notice or care.

No such luck. Gemma rolled her eyes and poked Brandon in the arm. She gestured at Jamie. *What's wrong with him?* she signed. Her face looked simultaneously like she'd slurped lemon juice and smelled rotting garbage, she was that irritated with Jamie.

Brandon shrugged, turned to Jamie, and repeated the question, even though he knew perfectly well Jamie had already seen her ask. He gave them both the finger and a dark scowl, figuring the rude gesture was answer enough without having to explain why he was in a foul mood. Mostly, he was pissed off at Brandon for dragging him out to see this particular show. He didn't feel like telling Brandon how much his semi-famous friend annoyed him.

He didn't need to. Brandon glowered at him and turned back to Gemma. *He's mad because I brought him to watch Cian.*

Why? Gemma asked.

Ask him. I don't know.

Gemma leaned around Brandon and said out loud, "What the hell is your problem?"

She had the ear she could hear out of turned toward Jamie, so he could have spoken if he wanted to keep Brandon from the truth. Gemma would just tell him later, though. Resigned, Jamie decided to sign it to them both instead. He supposed he owed Brandon the explanation for why he had no interest in having anything to do with Cian ever again.

He's snotty. Jamie made his gestures come across as vulgar as possible when he explained that Cian was happy to barely cover his dick on stage while looking down on Jamie for taking it in the ass on camera.

It was partly true, if not all the details. Brandon had never seen Jamie's porn work himself and didn't know any more than that Jamie had done it. There were definite advantages to spending time with straight guys, although Jamie's web series had been a lot more than just cisgender gay men fucking. Jamie didn't want to tell Brandon the real reason he and Cian had argued or that it made him uncomfortable to think Cian may have been right. It was easier to tell people he didn't like Cian so he had the freedom to avoid contact.

Brandon shoved Jamie, frowning. *Crude. He doesn't think that.*

Jamie turned away from him to cover for feeling bad about lying by omission. The real story was that Cian had cornered Jamie at Brandon and Gemma's engagement party and tried to rope him into conversation about his past work. Given the fact that there was a limited audience for it, there was only one way Cian could have known anything about it. He'd had an awful lot to say about Jamie's character, something about why they hadn't hired an actual deaf actor for the part. Jamie wouldn't have minded discussing it somewhere other than in front of his friends, but Cian had sounded so arrogant, leaving no room for Jamie to explain anything. Cian didn't get to jerk off while watching Jamie and then judge him for his part in it later, as though somehow Jamie had put the notion in his head to watch the web series or as if casting direction was even his call in the first place.

The trouble was, Jamie had kind of liked that about him. As much as it made him bristle, he was pleased someone noticed anything beyond the size of Jamie's cock. Cian had opinions. His opinions had opinions. And goddamn it to hell, Jamie found it inappropriately hot. Everything with Sage had been about his opinions too, but those had been all about how dirty Jamie's work made *him* feel. Cian had not once shamed Jamie for the sex. Jamie had wanted so badly to push back at Cian, but there was a shitload of reasons why he couldn't, starting with the way he always tripped over his words in those situations and ending with Sage's jealousy any time Jamie talked to another man.

Is that why you brought me tonight? You want me to get over it? Jamie wasn't in a patient mood. Too many other things were weighing on him, between his misplaced feelings for Trevor and the texts from Sage. Griping about Cian was a good way to distract himself from pining away for someone he couldn't have or brooding over someone he never should've had.

No, Brandon answered. Jamie hoped he was being sincere, but Brandon looked guilty. *You're down lately. I wanted you to have fun. Cian's good at what he does.*

I'm fine, Jamie protested, making the gesture as casual and dismissive as he could.

Brandon put a hand on Jamie's arm and held his gaze for a long time before he let go to respond. *Not since Sage.*

He had Jamie there, though he was one of only two people Jamie would allow to get away with saying so. It had been an awful four and a half months, even after he'd talked himself out of calling Sage to apologize. He'd reminded himself he'd finally left on his own terms, not on Sage's. Many lonely weeks and an ill-advised crush on Trevor later, he still missed Sage. Not the person who lied to and manipulated and hurt him, but the man who understood him and kept him from numbing himself with food. Jamie missed having someone to do things with and someone in his bed on long, cold nights. He couldn't have explained it if he'd tried, and no one would have believed there was anything good in his relationship with Sage. They all hated him to the point of never learning his name.

I'm fine, Jamie repeated.

Brandon shook his head, but he didn't try to continue the discussion. Jamie sighed, giving in. He wouldn't have to talk to Cian, only watch him dance. Even Jamie could acknowledge Cian was mesmerizing on stage. He was powerful, but at the same time he possessed grace and poise. Jamie didn't know much about dance, but he understood how difficult it was for Cian and the other dancers to remain so well in sync, every step perfectly timed. Their backup band was incredible. Jamie had asked Mack about imitating some of their sound, but Mack wasn't interested in Irish folk-rock and had grumbled when Jamie made him listen to the CD Brandon had given him.

Brandon had drifted into conversation with Gemma, and Jamie stopped paying attention to them. He went back to stirring his drink until the entertainment started. They didn't have to wait long. The emcee announced Cian and his band, and next thing Jamie knew, the place was alive with the sounds of the drums, the flutes, and the electric strings. Without meaning to, Jamie let go of his dislike long enough to enjoy watching Cian move.

The dance and the costumes had an ethereal quality which evoked images of woods and the fair folk. The dancers all had on some kind of green makeup which caught the light and shimmered. Cian's midnight-black hair was slicked back, and he had a green mask covering the top half of his face. That was just about all he had covered, aside from a small, tight pair of green shorts. He wasn't tall and reedy like some dancers. He was shorter, muscular and broad rather than slim—almost stocky. He made faeries seem powerful and majestic rather than prim and delicate. In spite of himself, Jamie became absorbed in the rhythm, the music, and the storytelling. Whatever else he could say about Cian, he had charisma on stage.

At the end of their performance, the packed bar went wild. Cian was a crowd favorite, no doubt about it, and with good reason. Jamie caught Brandon and Gemma signing their applause, and he joined them. For a moment, Cian turned his attention to their table and signed his thanks to them. His gaze rested briefly on Jamie, who held his breath until the moment passed. Cian's face had remained neutral, and Jamie exhaled with relief.

Gemma, Brandon, and Jamie settled into a discussion about what the dance drama meant, and Jamie lost track of time. He supposed Brandon had been right and he'd needed the night out. Just as he was beginning to unwind, Brandon paused mid-gesture and looked up. He grinned, and Jamie followed his attention to the man standing beside their table. Jamie almost groaned. Brandon hadn't told him Cian was going to be stopping by. Finally having confirmation that Brandon was trying to set him up, Jamie elbowed him. Brandon ignored him and stood to give Cian a one-armed hug.

Cian slid into the seat beside Gemma, and she took his hand and squeezed it. They struck up a conversation, but Cian kept glancing over at Jamie, which made him sweat. Jamie couldn't tell what those looks meant. He wanted to leave, but it felt rude to do so when Cian had only been there a few minutes. It would be obvious Jamie didn't want to be around him. Not that sitting there with no idea what to say to him was any better.

He caught Brandon telling Cian something about Jamie's band, but he missed the rest of the exchange or why Brandon had explained. Jamie didn't care. He went to take a sip of his drink and realized he'd finished it already. On the verge of going to the bar for another one, Jamie paused at the hand on his arm. It was warm, and the grip was firm but not unpleasantly so.

"You don't have to go," Cian said, his soft, lilting accent making the words sound almost teasing.

His bright blue eyes twinkled, and Jamie caught a glimpse of Cian's hearing aids. They were custom designed to look like silver snakes, twisting up and over his ear. Jamie liked the way they looked on him, though he would never say so. He was determined to go on at least pretending to dislike Cian on principle. Jamie half wondered why Cian hadn't signed to him before realizing it might be a subtle dig. He frowned. Two could play at that game, and he wasn't giving in so easily.

He nodded at the bar and signed, *I'm getting another drink. You want something?*

Cian looked surprised, but he acknowledged Jamie. *Water, please.*

The exchange had been almost friendly, but Jamie knew it was all on the surface, at least on his part. He twisted away from Cian and made his way to the bar to order their drinks. While he waited, he watched the others from a distance. Cian was telling a story about a dance class, but from this far away and at an angle, Jamie missed some of it. They were comfortable with each other, laughing and signing like the old friends they all were. Brandon and Cian had gone to high school together, and they'd met Gemma sometime later. That was all Jamie knew about their friendship, and it was all he wanted to know. The less involved he was, the smaller the chance Cian would try to have another go at him about his web series.

It made him tense, watching them. Jamie didn't really believe

Cian would gossip about him while he was off getting their drinks, but he wouldn't put it past him either, not under the right circumstances. Brandon seemed determined to have them in the same place at the same time, and eventually, one of them was bound to let something slip. Then the whole story would come out, and everyone would be disappointed in Jamie. No matter Jamie's reasons, Cian was right to feel strongly about good representation. There would always be some measure of distrust between them.

Jack, the bartender on duty, handed Jamie the water and the Diet Coke, tracking Jamie's line of vision. He twitched an eyebrow, but he remained unusually silent. Jamie stayed where he was for a few more minutes, not wanting to go back to the table. Cian hadn't dropped in a word about his conversation with Jamie at the party, but Jamie wasn't going to let down his guard no matter how much time passed. He slid onto a stool and drank his Coke there instead of taking it back to the table, keeping his eyes on the others the whole time.

When he was done, he took Cian's water to him and set it down. "Here you go. I'm really sorry, but I'm not feeling great. I think I'll call it a night."

Gemma frowned at him because he hadn't signed it, and she was obviously puzzled—and probably annoyed. Brandon might have caught the gist, since he could lip-read acceptably if it was someone he knew well, but Gemma signed to him anyway. Brandon looked upset, but Gemma nodded at Jamie. They said goodnight to him, and Jamie escaped out into the night. On the walk to the subway, he tried to push off the uneasiness he felt every time he was around Cian.

Only it wasn't Cian's fault alone. Sage had already gotten his hooks in Jamie by the time he met Cian, making him feel more filthy than appearing in several seasons of a somewhat popular web porn series had ever done. Jamie had once been proud of his work, but Sage had seen to it that he'd lost all that confidence. Arguing with Cian about the value of what he'd done brought it all back and made him feel ashamed all over again. Everywhere Jamie went, there were reminders of all the years he'd wasted on Sage. He would never be able to forgive himself for them.

Cian watched Jamie leave. He'd seen him sitting at the bar, drinking whatever he'd ordered over there instead of bringing it back to the table. For the life of him, Cian couldn't figure out what Jamie's problem was. Not that Cian saw him often, but every time, Jamie seemed wary of him. It left Cian confused and torn between curiosity and frustration.

They'd seen each other in passing on occasion when there was a big event at Grand Slam, but the first time they'd spoken was at Brandon and Gemma's engagement party. Until then, he hadn't known they were related. Brandon had mentioned his cousin and that Jamie had lived with his family for a while, but Cian didn't know him or the circumstances. He'd already been away in New York by then.

Cian had finally figured out at the party why Jamie looked familiar: he'd starred for several seasons on Cian's favorite web porn series. It was really good, with a diverse cast and a lot of story to go with all the hot, explicit sex. Cian wasn't sure if he should've been embarrassed by how often he'd indulged and gotten off while watching. Jamie's arc had been playing a deaf character who ended up with a deaf boyfriend before he left the show. Sadly, Jamie had exited the show suddenly, and he hadn't been known for anything else. Cian vaguely wondered if Jamie had become one of those hard-core evangelicals like Cian's aunt after she left the Catholic Church. It would explain the teetotaling and the fear, although he didn't get the sense that Jamie's band was some kind of religious group. Brandon and Gemma weren't the church type either, so maybe that didn't fit after all.

It was too bad Jamie was so standoffish. He was a thousand shades of adorable, and no amount of pseudo-bad-boy-rockstar play-acting could hide it. While making his way to the table after performing, Cian had taken a few minutes to admire him. Jamie was tiny, probably barely five foot five. His brown hair was short and spiked. He had piercings all over, enough in visible areas that Cian wondered if he had some in less public places too. He didn't recall him having any in his videos, not that he wanted to admit how much of Jamie's body he'd seen. And those eyes—dark and sparkling, black-lined to give him a hint of being trouble. Even now, after Jamie's borderline unfriendly behavior, it made Cian's insides ripple to think about him.

Distracted, Cian missed the beginning of Brandon's question. He saw the rise and fall of Brandon's shoulders in an exaggerated huff when Cian didn't respond right away. Cian laughed and brushed it off to Brandon as being tired from the show. Brandon seemed to accept this and repeated the question.

We're sending wedding invitations soon. Are you bringing a date?

Brandon and Gemma had chosen not to have some big affair. They were getting married at Gemma's parents' house in Milford, outdoors if the weather cooperated and it wasn't too hot at the end of June. It wouldn't matter either way. Her parents owned a large piece of property and a sprawling one-story house they'd built themselves. Gemma's mother was an event planner, and her family was used to large gatherings. This wouldn't be big anyway, probably only a hundred guests or so. Mostly family, some friends. Brandon and Gemma only had so much patience for dealing with a crowd. This was more to appease her parents than anything else.

He evaded the question about a plus-one and adopted a casual air. *When are the invitations coming?*

Couple weeks, Gemma replied, but she gave him a stern look.

He knew what that meant. Gemma wasn't going to rest until she had a real answer. Cian sighed. He hadn't dated anyone seriously in a while, and he hadn't told Brandon or Gemma that he was involved with Eric, Skye, and Nell again. Like Skye, Gemma hadn't gone to school with them as Brandon had. She didn't know the history of any of them or what had happened when Cian left for college in New York. Cian had only lived in the US for a year when he met Eric, coming to stay with his American father after his mother pawned him off.

Still evading, he simply signed, *Good.* In theory, Cian could make himself part of Eric, Skye, and Nell's family for the day. They wouldn't mind. It would spare him having to coax someone else into joining him, at any rate. They might even invite him home for the night. He owed his friends that explanation, though.

I'll go with Eric, Skye, and Nell. We're together again.

The others didn't seem too surprised. They knew how badly his last serious relationship had gone, and his intimacy with his second family was part of why. He'd cut off having sex with them, but somehow, it was still an issue. There wasn't anything new or unique about that; not everyone understood. Apparently, something of Cian's mood showed because Brandon jumped in.

You're thinking too hard. Everything all right?

Cian ran a finger around the rim of his glass, trying to decide what and how much to tell them. He finally looked up at Brandon and Gemma, taking in their matching concerned expressions.

I don't know.

Cian didn't have a good way to express how even with their support, he still felt lonely every night he went home to his empty apartment. Nor did he know how to tell them about feeling torn in two every time they asked him to move in with them. He felt like he was letting everyone down by not taking that step. No amount of studying it from every angle had led to a clear answer.

What's going on? Gemma asked.

Swallowing back his emotions, Cian replied, *They asked me to move in. I said no again. They have the twins. Nell's pregnant.* He paused then repeated, *I don't know.* He couldn't really hide all this from them, nor could he deny how hard it had been lately. *I'm tired of feeling left out. I'm tired of not telling anyone about them. I'm tired of having to drive a long way when I want company. They don't want to move here. I don't want to move there.*

They stopped talking, and Cian watched some slinky singer getting set up on stage. If it wasn't working with Eric, Skye, and Nell, he could always end the relationship. He'd done it before, after all. But they were family, and his life didn't feel right without them. It made him feel selfish and angry with himself to want both what he had and something else.

Brandon tapped his shoulder to get his attention again. His expression was gentle. *Have you told them how you feel?*

No. Cian glowered at him, rattled by Brandon's care.

They have rights to know you feel this way, Gemma told him.

You think I don't know that? They never told me not to date. I don't know what I want. He stopped again, not willing to explain to them what was really on his mind—that if he started seeing someone else, it might be the end of their relationship.

Why not see what happens? Brandon asked. *I thought after last time we talked it was going this way.*

Cian scowled to make it clear he didn't want to discuss his lack of options. He wasn't interested in interviewing prospects only for them to be disappointed he wasn't exactly as single as they'd assumed he was.

Gemma shrugged. *We could set you up with someone.*

Suddenly Brandon asking him to stop by their table after the show made all the sense in the world: Jamie. It made him wonder if they knew about Jamie's porn series and guessed how much Cian liked it. He'd have been all right with the setup. Too bad Jamie didn't seem to have been pleased with it. The whole lead-in struck Cian as amusing, and he chuckled. *Why do I think you were already doing that?*

Brandon relaxed, laughing along. *It didn't go so well.*

Cian scoffed, but he was still smiling. *I don't think he likes me much.*

Do you know why?

Cian didn't, not exactly. He thought back to the party. Right away when they met, Jamie had put him at ease. He was every bit as cute and charming in person, possibly more. That's when Cian had been surprised to learn Jamie was hearing; the way he'd played his character was convincing enough Cian had believed him to be deaf like the other actor. He'd tried to discuss it with him, only Jamie had gone right into defensive mode as soon as Cian mentioned the show. He'd shut down and become tense, refusing to talk about it. At the time, Cian had thought Jamie was upset about being called out on playing a deaf character for the series. Tonight, and the way Jamie almost seemed afraid, made him rethink it. He wondered if Jamie had mixed feelings about having done the series.

Cian wouldn't be the one to speculate to Brandon and Gemma, though. He told the others, *I was pushy with my opinions at your engagement party.*

So surprising, Gemma responded, her sarcasm obvious in her body language. *I don't think that's it. He's been like this since his last boyfriend. He needs help getting over it.*

That set off alarm bells. Cian wondered what had happened. It didn't make him more interested. If anything, he thought Jamie should be allowed to have space to recover. *I don't want to be anyone's rebound.*

Brandon argued, *We know you two will get along. You're more alike than you think.* It was obvious there was a lot left unsaid, including some well-deserved accusations that Cian hadn't waited too long after his breakup before running back to Eric, Skye, and Nell.

Gemma filled in at least one of the blanks. *He watches you. You watch him.* Her pointed look made it clear she knew that meant more than on stage with his band.

Cian hated that they'd already zeroed in on how Jamie had captured his interest. To shut them up, he agreed. *Okay, fine. I'll try to be better around Jamie. No more dates unless I ask. Got it?*

They dropped it after that. The three of them carried on talking for a while as the bar emptied out of the patrons who had been there for the show and filled in with the late-night crowd. Eventually, they packed it in and went their separate ways. As he retraced his path to the train, Cian couldn't get Jamie out of his mind. Something about the whole situation nagged at him. He should stay away, stay out of it, mind his own. But he had a bad feeling there was more under the surface, vital information Brandon—or Jamie himself—was withholding from everyone.

Cian descended the steps to the train, shaking off the desire to find out more. On screen, Jamie'd had a lot of warmth and an almost sweet quality to him. After the engagement party, Cian had thought the gentleness hadn't translated into real life, but now he wasn't so sure. Brandon thought of Jamie like a brother, and there was no way he would pair them off unless he had good reason.

Thinking about Brandon brought up a new concern, one which Cian saved until he was seated as far from other people as possible on the train. Cian had foolishly agreed to talk to his partners about where they stood and about the possibility he might want to start dating someone seriously. Now he would have to explain it all to them, and he didn't know what they would say about it. He remained unsettled for the entire ride home, staring out the window into the blank darkness of the tunnel.

Chapter Four

Blowing on his fingers to warm them, Jamie shivered in the cool April evening. It had warmed up nicely during the day, but nights were still chilly. He waited patiently on the doorstep for someone to answer.

A moment later, Trevor appeared, baby Aidan in his arms. Before Jamie was even through the door, Aidan was wiggling his tiny fingers and reaching for him. Trevor laughed, and Jamie grinned as he plucked Aidan from his daddy's arms.

Jamie didn't even say hello to Trevor right away, too busy cooing at the baby. Aidan was chubby, with soft blond fuzz all over his head. He had hardly any hair, and what he did have was almost invisible. His eyes had already begun to darken, probably going to turn brown like his mama's. Jamie tickled under his chin, delighted as always when Aidan giggled happily at him. He would never get tired of it, and he didn't care if his friends all thought his love for babies—well, specifically Aidan—was weird.

Trevor, at least, didn't seem to find it all that strange. Of course, Trevor loved being a father, so that could have been why. In any case, he never made fun of Jamie for it. Come to think of it, the others didn't either. Nate was uncomfortable around babies in general, so he was probably happy to have Jamie as a shield whenever they visited. Jamie had no idea where Mack stood on the subject; he seemed indifferent.

Still holding Aidan, Jamie followed Trevor into the kitchen.

Andre and Marlie were both at the counter, chopping things. Andre tossed handfuls of peppers and onions into a large pot, where they sizzled as they hit the oil. He stirred while Marlie diced a tomato and drained cans of beans. The kitchen began to smell good.

Trevor pulled bowls from the cupboard. "Nate and Izzy will be here in about a half hour, and we're expecting Julian and Elise too. Mack didn't come with you?"

Jamie shook his head. "He ended up having to cover someone else's shift. He'll be here as soon as he's done."

Marlie laughed. "Leave it to Mack to show up just in time for food. Good thing it'll be a little while."

Andre's shoulders were tense, and he was quiet. It wasn't out of the ordinary for him to let the others do most of the talking, but he was largely silent. Jamie understood. It had been a difficult few months in multiple ways. Trevor stepped up behind him and put a hand on his back. Jamie almost sighed at the tender gesture, but he scolded himself for both his pang of envy and his promise to himself to stay clear of a relationship. It might look shiny on the outside, but what was on the inside wasn't worth it.

Aidan fussed a little, so Jamie took him back out to the living room. He grabbed a board book from a shelf and began reading to him. A moment later, a quiet chuckle made him look up to see Trevor in the doorway.

"You're a natural with him," Trevor remarked. "He adores you, you know."

Jamie grinned. "The feeling's mutual. I didn't know babies were so cool."

"They don't stay that little."

"I know." Jamie shrugged, jostling Aidan. The baby looked up at him then back at the book. "He's smart."

"How can you tell?" Trevor laughed as he bent to give Aidan a kiss. "He's only five months. I mean, yeah, I like to think my kid is brilliant, but it's a little early to say."

"He just is." Jamie didn't have a good reason other than that it sounded true.

They were interrupted by the doorbell, and Trevor went to answer it and usher in Nate and Izzy. Jamie tried not to feel jealous over the long hug Trevor gave Nate. Only a few months had gone by since both Nate and Izzy had received bad news about their health—

Nate's HIV and Izzy's multiple sclerosis. They were both doing well now, and their engagement a couple of weeks prior was proof. Trevor had been supportive, and it wasn't Jamie's place to get in the way of his friendship with Nate.

Izzy looked tired. He sat down next to Jamie and leaned back against the couch, stretching out his long legs. Nate followed Trevor out to the kitchen, and Jamie watched them go, absently bouncing Aidan on his knee. Izzy rolled his head to the side and looked at Jamie. He opened his mouth as though he wanted to say something, but he didn't.

Things were awkward any time the two of them were alone, somewhere between running into a former teacher at the grocery store and seeing your doctor on the T. Izzy had been the one on call the last time something happened with Sage. He and his coworker had been the ones to take Jamie to the emergency department, and the first time Jamie had ever had a conversation with him was from a hospital bed. Consequently, Jamie never had any idea what to say to him. For now, Jamie reluctantly returned his attention to the baby, who had grabbed the board book and was trying to eat it. Jamie pried it away from him, earning a cry of displeasure.

Once Jamie had replaced the book with something more drool-appropriate, he turned to Izzy, hoping to ward off intrusive questions by asking his own. "How are you guys doing?"

"Got a new job," Izzy said. "Val's not happy, but she understands." Val had been Izzy's partner when he worked as an EMT. "I can't risk having muscle spasms while transporting a patient, so I'm now doing a desk job at an outpatient clinic." He blew out a breath. "I don't completely hate it."

"But you don't like it."

"Not as much. I miss my coworkers. The hours are better, the pay isn't bad, and I don't have to worry that I'm going to have a medical crisis and hurt anyone. It's boring. I'm thinking about training for dispatch instead, and maybe instruction."

Singing drifted from the kitchen—Nate's full, deeper voice, joined by Trevor's higher one. Izzy smiled and closed his eyes. The twist of envy returned, directed at both Trevor and Nate for having found another person who filled in the gaps for them. Jamie wasn't sure he wanted what they had so much as wishing he hadn't wasted so many years trying to have it with the wrong person.

The doorbell rang, and Trevor called out to ask if Jamie or Izzy could get it. Jamie toted Aidan to the door and opened it for Julian and Elise. They didn't have their kids with them, to Jamie's disappointment. He'd been wanting to meet them and compare the baby to older children. While they were taking off their coats, Mack arrived. In short order, the food was out on the counter with the dishes, and everyone grabbed what they needed and settled down in the living room. Aidan was on the floor, playing with a few toys.

Jamie relaxed, the stab of frustration gone for the time being. He didn't need anything else. These people were his family. His eyes met Marlie's across the room, and she smiled. Something told him she understood his feelings about being an outsider. She turned her attention to Andre.

"I'm surprised Nia didn't come tonight," she remarked.

Andre snorted. "I didn't think it would be a good idea to introduce her to every single one of my white friends at the same time."

Jamie's eyebrows rose. It wasn't like Andre to say something like that, and Jamie wondered what was going on. It wasn't his business, but he was worried something had happened. Before he could make up his mind to ask, Trevor spoke up.

"Something with the daycare?"

Andre's shoulders slumped. "Yeah. Had to get the owner to step in. One of the caregivers wouldn't release Aidan to me today."

"What?" Marlie demanded. "I'm going to call them."

"No." Andre put up a hand. "It's fine. I took care of it, showed my ID and all. The owner had some words with the worker."

"It's not the first time, is it?" Nate asked.

Andre shook his head. "Far from, but it's something different every time. Checking the book to see if I'm listed. Asking for ID. Once, they called Marlie to ask if I was supposed to be there." He gave her an apologetic look.

Trevor frowned at them both. "Why didn't either of you say anything? Aidan's been at that place less than three months, and this has happened more than once?"

"Yeah, well, I'm used to it." Andre ran a hand over his hair. "It's gotten worse over time, and I don't know whether the problem is me or our family. They've also been putting pressure on me and Marlie both about how difficult it is to have him only part-time. I think they're working on trying to cover their racist asses, but I can't prove it. I didn't want to drag Nia into all this."

"Fuck." Trevor put an arm around him, but Andre still looked tense. "We'll figure something out. Who does Trinity take her kids to?" Trinity was Andre's older sister.

"An in-home daycare," Andre said. "I guess I could find out if the woman and her daughter can take another baby, but it's iffy."

After he fell silent, no one else spoke for a while, allowing the gravity of what Andre had told them to sink in. Jamie felt awful for them and wondered what they would do. With Trevor's recording and occasional travel schedule and with Andre and Marlie both working, they had to have someone to care for Aidan twice a week. He wished he knew someone he could recommend for them, but without children of his own, it wasn't a connection he had. He didn't know what he would do in their situation.

Aidan's soft fussing broke the silence, and Jamie automatically moved to take over from Marlie. Andre got there first, since he was sitting closer, and Jamie sat back down. Out of the corner of his eye, he saw both Izzy and Nate looking at him. They exchanged an amused glance, and Jamie scowled. It annoyed him that they found it funny. Izzy shrugged and changed the subject, talking to Julian about something.

Jamie sighed. Until having friends with kids, he'd never thought much about whether he wanted any. Aidan was the first baby he'd ever held, and he'd been smitten from day one. Sage would never have agreed to kids, and Jamie thought he'd have made a lousy parent anyway. Jamie's stomach churned, and he wished he could banish Sage from his memory. While he was trying to direct his attention back to the conversations around him, Marlie caught his eye and smiled. She nudged Andre, who looked over too.

"Your turn?" he asked Jamie.

"Yes, please." Jamie grinned and held out his arms.

Trevor laughed. "You sure earned your Cool Uncle badge."

The compliment made Jamie flush, and he ducked his head, unable to help the tingle in his gut over Trevor's warm attention. To cover for it, he concentrated on babbling at Aidan and keeping his mind occupied on anything but how much he craved Trevor's approval. A thought occurred to him.

"I—" he began, stopping when all heads turned toward him,

including Aidan's. "I could watch him."

Marlie and Andre exchanged a glance then both looked at Trevor. Jamie's whole head was hot. He felt exposed, embarrassed for having said anything and worried about what everyone else was thinking. The silence went on so long it became awkward.

Mack finally moved. He butt-scooched over to Jamie, plucked Aiden from his lap, and said to him, "You want Uncle Jamie to babysit you, huh?"

Aidan put out his pudgy hand and patted Mack's face before blowing a nice, juicy drool bubble right at his chin. Mack groaned, Aidan giggled, and the tension was finally broken. Mack lasted another fifteen seconds before he hurried to hand Aidan to Marlie so he could wipe his face.

Marlie bounced the baby in her lap and said, "Trevor? Andre? What do you think?"

Andre's brow creased. "I like the idea, but..." He cleared his throat. "Are you all comfortable paying one of our friends?"

"I'd do it for free," Jamie said, to which an entire room full of people all chorused, "No." Jamie flushed again.

"It's not that we don't appreciate it," Andre said. "But they're right. It's not fair on you to expect free childcare, no matter how much you love him."

"It's only twice a week," Jamie argued.

"Right," Marlie agreed. "But one of those days is my long one because of classes, and sometimes Trevor's out of town."

Mack nudged Jamie's leg with his foot. "We could use the extra, Jay." He didn't look at Nate when he said it, but Jamie knew it would take some of the burden off him. Nate was starting a new job soon, but it would be good to have a cushion in the meantime. His medical care was unreasonably expensive, and Jamie didn't like to burden him more than he could manage.

"Yeah," Jamie said.

"Then it's settled," Trevor told him, and he smiled in a way that made Jamie's face heat up all over again.

"Good." Marlie passed the baby to Izzy then stood. "Time for dessert to celebrate."

She went to take Aidan back, but Jamie was on his feet in a flash, scooping Aidan from Izzy's arms. He was eager to prove his fitness for the job. Marlie looked like she might say something, but then her face softened and she put her arm around Jamie.

"Thank you," she murmured. "You've done more than you know."

For the millionth time that evening, Jamie had a rush of embarrassment. He didn't think he'd done all that much, but it obviously meant a great deal to Marlie. He looked over at Trevor, and his flush turned into a jolt of shame at how much he wanted it to be Trevor thanking him right then.

A tiny hand brushing against his lip brought Jamie back into the moment. He rescued his piercing from exploring baby fingers, distracting both himself and Aidan with tummy tickles. Trevor's stamp of approval or not, Jamie was about to have as much time with Aidan as he wanted, and that was all that mattered just then.

Chapter Five

CIAN CHANGED quickly out of his dance clothes and packed them away with his shoes into his duffel. As he was zipping it, the lights flicked, and he looked up. He grinned at the studio owner, a lanky woman in her late fifties. Cian waved then put in his hearing aids.

"Hey, Marta," he said. "How's it going?"

Marta's smile was stiff. "Not too bad." Slowly, she signed, *How are you?*

Cian appreciated that Marta always tried, and she mostly got it right, even if her syntax was often a little odd and formal. They'd enjoyed a good working relationship for the past few years, with Marta renting out space in her studio for Cian. It worked well, since they shared some students. They were just about to hold their combined recital, and Cian was wrapping up the last couple weeks of classes.

"I'm fine. Looking forward to the recital?"

"Yes and no." Marta's posture relaxed in a defeated way. "I have some bad news."

"Do I need to sit down for this?"

Marta shook her head. "I don't know. Listen, I've truly enjoyed working with you, and I wanted you to know that."

Cian frowned. "You sound like you're firing me."

The laugh Marta delivered was more nervous than amused. "You don't really work for me."

"Yeah, I know. But the way you said it..." Cian had a feeling he knew what was coming, but it was easier to dismiss it with a bit of humor.

Marta's whole body moved with her deep inhalation. She folded her slender fingers together in front of herself. "I'm closing the studio."

"What?" Cian had thought she was expanding and possibly asking him to help find another location. He hadn't expected her to close entirely.

"This is the second year in a row that I've barely broken even. The rent is going up on this space, and I can't afford it, even if I offer more classes and even with your portion. I've got some family issues going on, with my father's Alzheimer's and my brother moving back home to take care of him. Cluelessly, I might add. This seems like as good a time as any to wrap things up before I go into debt over it."

"I don't know what to say. I'm sorry it's come to this."

Marta nodded, and her eyes welled up. "I've run this place for twenty-five years, and this was my studio as a child."

Cian gave her a firm hug. "This has to be really hard for you. What are you going to do next?"

"It is, and I'm not sure. I'm moving back to Springfield, and I might look to teach a few classes there once I'm on my feet again."

Springfield. That was where Cian's partners lived. It was tempting to suggest he and Marta pair up again, look for something out that way to rent out. He'd be closer to them, more involved. They'd been asking, and he'd hedged. Now he had an opportunity if he could secure a day job out that way.

Except for the small detail that he didn't want to give up his regular performances, and he didn't want to leave his students. There weren't many noncompetitive studios, and his was certainly the only one specifically geared toward deaf and disabled students. Cadence would be devastated if Cian left. It was a terrible dilemma, not made any easier by the fact that he couldn't afford the rent without Marta.

"I really am sorry," he told Marta again.

"Me too." She clasped Cian's hand. "What about you? I know I'm leaving you in the lurch here."

"I'll be all right. You just worry about your own stuff." He didn't want to burden her with how troubled it all made him. "What about the summer programs?"

Marta shook her head. "I'll be busy packing up and clearing out.

We have until August thirty-first, so if you still want the space to run classes, you're welcome to it. Just be sure you clean everything up at the end."

"All right."

Cian wasn't sure if he would do classes under those circumstances, and certainly not if Marta was leaving before the lease was up. He'd always run a couple of *Sean Nós* and country set classes, and his musician friends rotated through coming in and performing traditional songs. The summer classes were pay-as-you-come, which meant he could still do a few. Knowing the studio was closing, however, put him less in the mood to do so. He didn't know if his heart was in it.

"Oh, Cian." Marta sighed as she pulled him into another hug. She let go and said, "I'm sorry. I wish it could be different."

"No, I understand." He did, but that didn't mean he had to like it.

"I'll keep you posted. I've just finished the letter to our families, and I can send it to you to modify as you need. We'll make it official at the end of the recital." Her smile was sad, a little wistful. "We'll go out with a celebration. What do you always call it?"

"Céilí," Cian replied. "Or—" He signed, *Party*.

Marta's expression brightened, and she copied his motions a little awkwardly. Cian adjusted the way her fingers shaped the *P*.

Party, she repeated.

Cian gripped her hand. "I enjoyed working with you too."

Marta let go and stepped out of Cian's room. Once he was alone, he looked around at the dance posters and the framed class photos from the last few years. He would miss this place. In less than three months, he had to make a decision about what to do next. Surely there was space somewhere else, but could he afford it? Everything these days was so expensive, and he didn't want to ask families to pay more for the lessons.

Still turning the studio situation over in his mind, Cian gathered his things and flipped the light switch. As hard as it would be, he needed to bring it up with his family over dinner. Maybe his father would have a suggestion. His stomach tightened. Cadence. He would have to break his sister's heart by telling her what was going on. There was never a good time for that kind of conversation.

###

The drive to visit Cian's father and his family wasn't enough time to plan out everything he needed to say, but at least it gave him a chance to relax first. He loved spending time with them. He was glad to have their love and support, especially when he was the bearer of bad news.

Cian had gone to live with his father and stepmother when he was fourteen. His mother hadn't dealt well with Cian's illness nor the loss of his hearing. She still didn't, and the subject of his various partners never came up at all if he could help it the rare times he had to communicate with her. He doubted very much that she would be anywhere near as accepting as Dad and Annette.

When he'd arrived in the States, angry at everyone—especially Mam—he'd expected a cold welcome. He was pretty sure Mam had as well, since his trip overseas was meant as a punishment to get him back in line. Maybe it was meant as a punishment for Dad too. Dad had been a thirty-four-year-old newlywed, suddenly parenting a teenager he hadn't known existed until a month before Cian showed up.

Cian wouldn't have blamed Dad or Annette for being resentful, but neither of them had ever expressed that in the least. Instead, Annette in particular took charge. Rather than demanding, as Mam had, that Cian use hearing aids, she allowed him to make the choice for himself. She was the one who knew who to talk to so he could receive everything he needed at school, and she was the one who listened to him when he finally unleashed all the pain and frustration underneath his adolescent rage. She was the one who urged him to pour all that energy into dancing again, and she was the one who went with him when he decided he wanted the hearing aids after all. Not once did she judge or belittle his decisions. Both Dad and Annette knew about Eric, Skye, and Nell, and they'd surprised him with how open-minded they were, if a little confused.

Dinner with Cian's family, as usual, was full of enthusiastic conversation. For a number of reasons, family meals always involved a mix of spoken conversation and ASL, much like most areas of Cian's life. All three of his younger half-siblings were full of news about their days. Finding it hard to keep up, Cian let it wash over and around him, trying to work out a way to explain what had happened with the studio. Cadence especially deserved to know now, rather than finding out in a form letter with all the other families.

As a way of stalling, he reached across the table for the potatoes, which Cadence delivered into his hands before carrying on with her chattering. She was liberally mixing sign and speaking out loud, which amused him. In any language, she had more to say than anyone else Cian knew.

He caught a familiar name and paused with his fork halfway to his mouth. Setting it down on his plate, he said, "Lisanne from your dance class?" He hoped this might be a good lead-in to the necessary discussion.

Cadence nodded. "She goes to my school. I can't stand her."

That was unexpected. Cian would need to address that before springing the bad news on them. "Why didn't you tell me? Is something going on?"

Shrugging, Cadence looked suddenly uncomfortable. "It's nothing. I shouldn't have said it, okay? Forget it."

Cian looked at their father, who tipped his head in a *you got me* gesture. He clearly had no more idea than Cian did about what was wrong between the girls. Determined to get to the bottom of it, Cian hushed the others and pressed Cadence for more information.

"I missed what you were saying, sorry. Can you repeat it?"

Cadence frowned. "She thinks we ought to be doing the feiseanna like some of the other girls at school do, that's all. It bugged me."

"Why?"

"It's just snotty, like she thinks we're not real dancers if we're not always competing. She used to do all that stuff before her parents took her out of the other dance school. And she thinks it's because..." She stopped, her cheeks turning red.

Cian signed, *Because of me?*

Cadence shook her head vigorously. *No,* she signed back. *Not you. Then what?*

Me, Cadence signed. *I told you, forget it.*

No. Cian let his posture speak for him; he wasn't going to drop it so easily. If something was happening, he had to know. Otherwise, the last push before the recital could be strained for more than one reason.

She sighed and reached for a biscuit, changed her mind, and dropped her hand into her lap. Cian waited for her to explain, and the others all remained silent as well.

She calls me names.

Cian's head snapped up. Angrily, he signed, *In my class?*

At school. She shaped a Y with her fingers and made a motion. *Whale. She signs it so teachers won't know.*

Do you want me to— He stopped at the force of Cadence's *no.*

Out loud, Cadence said, "She thinks you won't compete because you know I'm too fat to make us look good."

Cian chewed his bite aggressively. He didn't compete because it was intense and he didn't like the idea of media hounding his deaf and disabled students and making them into inspirations for the general public. Dance was meant to be about their history and culture, not a spectacle for creating a media following. It had nothing to do with Cadence or any other specific dancer. Sure, some of them might have enjoyed all the work that would go into competing, but he wanted them to have fun and move their bodies. He knew what it took to be a professional, and it was why he stuck to teaching and performing only the local gigs he wanted to. He remembered the agonizing days of traveling and performing and how much it took to stay at the top. It was a lot more fun to dance in a queer bar than it would be to tour internationally and face everything that went with that level of fame and dedication.

"You know that's not true, right?"

"Of course I do!" Cadence snapped. She rolled her eyes and relaxed her shoulders. "I don't care what names she calls me. I'm okay with me, and she can stick it up her—" She glanced at their father's raised eyebrows. "—nose. Anyway, I'm just mad that she's talking about *you.*"

Despite being irritable and worried and disappointed about everything, Cian chuckled. Leave it to Cadence to be more concerned about him than about herself. She was a tough cookie, and Cian admired her for it. He'd been nothing like that at her age. To be fair, he'd also spent a month in the hospital with meningitis and lost most of his hearing by the time he was thirteen. He sobered quickly, realizing he still had to break the bad news to her.

"You're about to be even more mad."

"Why?"

"The studio we rent from is closing."

Cadence's mouth hung open for a moment. "That's—but—how could they do that?"

"Money," Cian told her. "Miss Marta is moving because of her family. Rent's too high, and I can't cover it myself. Even if I took on more classes, I couldn't do it."

"See?" Cadence said. "We never even got to do anything cool, and now you're quitting on us."

"I'm not quitting. The studio is closing. Are you disappointed we don't do anything but our one recital?"

Cadence was now glaring at her potatoes so hard Cian was shocked they didn't burst into flame. When she looked up at him, she trained the same intensity on him. "Maybe. I've never done anything like what you used to do, so maybe I'd hate it. I guess that's what made me so mad at Lisanne. Thinking she's kind of right. Why don't we? I sometimes feel like you're trying to hide us or like you think we can't."

Her words rattled Cian. He had it in his mind that he was doing the right thing, sheltering his students from being turned into something abled people would enjoy gawking at. But what if Cadence was right? He covered his self-doubt with anger and thumped his hand on the table. It made the dishes rattle, and the little ones jumped.

"You know perfectly well why we don't. I've told you all this before," he snapped. "It's *our people*, Cadence. *Our* dance, *our* music. This is where we come from. I'll not have that taken away so you or any of my other students can be made into some kind of—of—inspiration porn!"

As his voice rose, the others at the table went still. Caleigh, the youngest sibling, stared at Cian as they asked, "Daddy, what's 'in-sip-ration porn'?"

Dad shot Cian an annoyed glance and said, "He just means people might get some wrong ideas about what it means to be disabled is all."

Cadence shrank back, her gaze still focused on Cian but more wary now. "I know what you've said."

Cian took a deep, shaking breath and tried to calm down. "We're not going to compete. I know what it's like, and I know what teachers sometimes have to do to get their students to that level. It's cruel, and I cannot do that to you. And I certainly don't want you all to be the feel-good story of the year."

The look on Cadence's face plainly said she didn't believe him, but she backed off. "Can we at least do something?"

Feeling more steady, Cian relented. "I can look for some different places for us to dance, okay? Maybe over the summer." He swallowed, thinking about what else he'd be doing over the break. He had no idea where they might perform, but surely someone knew of something. He could always ask his friend Jomari, who not only played fiddle with Cian's dance company but also performed in other venues. "Is that fair compromise?"

Cadence turned sunny again. "Yeah! I think I'd like that."

It was settled, then. Cian turned it over in his mind. If he played it right, he might have a chance to save his studio and keep his classes, provided he could locate a new place to rent. Otherwise, he would have to tell Cadence and the other kids they were out of luck. Unless someone had a better idea, he had nowhere to take them when the lease was up.

Chapter Six

JAMIE'S FIRST day on the job with Aidan was one of Marlie's light days. It hadn't been too hard. Aidan was an easygoing baby, and he'd napped twice, which meant Jamie had some time to go over Mack's notes for Friday's gig. When Aidan was awake, Jamie kept him occupied without much trouble. He suspected it would be more difficult once Aidan was on the move, but he wasn't there yet. If things went well after a few days, Jamie might get permission to take him out to the park now that the weather was warmer. There was a nice one just a couple of blocks from the house.

When Marlie returned home from work, Jamie was sitting on the floor facing Aidan, who was contained in the bouncy seat suspended from the doorway. Every motion Jamie made with his hands, Aidan imitated it, much to Jamie's delight. He was a quick learner. Jamie heard quiet laughter behind him and twisted around.

Marlie set her bag by the door and came over to them. Aidan raised his little hands to her, and she lifted him out of the seat. Jamie stood and faced the two of them.

"What's so funny?" he asked.

"That was really cute. Are you teaching him baby sign?" she asked.

"Uh...what's baby sign?" Jamie had never heard of such a thing.

"It's supposed to help them communicate more easily before they can talk," she explained. "It's probably not true, but there are dozens of websites and videos on it."

Jamie snorted. "That's ridiculous. No, I'm not teaching him baby sign."

"Agreed, but lots of people buy into it. So, what were you doing, then?"

Jamie laughed. "It's ASL. You know, actual sign language."

"I know what ASL is. Your cousin—he's deaf, right?"

"Yes. I lived with his family for a couple of years." Jamie's happiness faded a little. He didn't want Marlie to ask a bunch of questions about it, so he quickly added, "Aidan's so smart. I thought it would be fun to teach him now so he can be bilingual. I can teach you too, if you want."

Marlie perched on the couch with Aidan squirming in her lap. "I've never been great at languages."

Jamie shrugged. "It's not quite the same as learning a foreign language in school. I picked it up really fast."

The truth was, Jamie had never been good at languages either. He often struggled to get the right words out when he talked. Growing up with a mild speech delay, he was always self-conscious when he spoke. The beating he'd gotten from his mother's boyfriend, the months he'd spent on the streets, and illness left him incapable of expressing what he was thinking without tripping over every sentence. Once he moved in with Brandon's family, they had opened his world by communicating with him in sign language.

"Maybe," Marlie said, breaking Jamie out of his thoughts. She giggled. "Or maybe Aidan will teach me someday."

Aidan fussed, so she set him down on the floor. It didn't help; he started to cry in earnest. Jamie moved to pick him up but stopped, unsure what to do now that Marlie was home. He'd never been alone with her and the baby, and he didn't want to overstep what she would consider polite. She scooped Aidan up and stood, rocking him.

"Did you need me to stay for a bit so you can get some stuff done?" Jamie asked.

"You don't have work?"

"Not tonight." He looked at the clock on the wall. "I have to be over at a friend's house by six because he's letting me use his basement to practice. I'm good for another hour or so, though."

Marlie nodded, but her shoulders slumped. "I hate how tired I am all the time, and I hate asking you to do more than you've agreed to. Are you sure?"

"Positive." Jamie was about to reach out for Aidan, but the baby let out another wail and clung to Marlie.

"Let me nurse him first, and then he'll be more mellow for you." She sat down in the recliner. "Um...will this bother you?"

Jamie shrugged. He'd never seen anyone breastfeeding before, aside from an occasional blanket-covered patron in a restaurant. "No, but I can go in the other room if you want."

Before Marlie could answer, he stepped into the kitchen and got to work taking care of the dishes for her. He wasn't sure when the others were expected home, but it wasn't as though Jamie had a lot to do while he waited. In the other room, Aidan's cries stopped, and everything was still and peaceful. It made Jamie wonder what it would be like to have a family, a house, children. He didn't really want any of his own, but he liked the idea of his friends bringing theirs over.

It was too much to hope for. He didn't see himself ever working his way out of a crappy shared apartment and a crappy underpaying job. But at least in this moment, he could pretend he was part of this picture-perfect life, even if it would all fade the second he stepped out the door.

After helping Marlie with Aidan, Jamie set off for his friend's house, one of his mother's exes. Over the years, Jamie had stayed in touch on and off with a few of his mother's former boyfriends, and Douglas was one of the good ones. He was now married and raising kids in Milford, not too far from Brandon's soon-to-be in-laws. Jamie had a flicker of envy for what Douglas's kids had. Their life was different from the one he'd had as a child, and Douglas, as nice as he was, ended up being different too. Jamie didn't begrudge him, but he couldn't help wondering what it would be like to spend a day in Douglas's shoes.

Tonight, Jamie had use of drums and a room in which to practice. Douglas had loaned space in his basement to mess around on his son's kit. He cherished these rare times. Lovingly, he pulled his sticks out of his bag. They'd been with him for as long as he could remember, a gift from another one of his mother's boyfriends. Maybe number three or four; he couldn't recall which. They'd lived with him for almost a whole school year when Jamie was nine. When he and Jamie's mother broke up, they were back to looking for a place to stay.

The sticks had the markers of being well-seasoned, and they felt right in Jamie's hands. He practiced a number of different fills for the songs they had. Mack needed to find his magic and write some new things. People seemed all right with their few original songs and a lot of covers of nineties music, but Jamie would have liked something fresh to play.

It felt good to have an uninterrupted stretch of time to work out his rhythm muscles. There weren't many good places for Jamie to practice in between rehearsals with the band. He couldn't do it in their apartment, of course, except a little with his sticks and a drum pad. Anything more complicated had to wait until he was able to take his equipment somewhere or find someone with a set he could borrow. It was more or less all right. The Creepy Crullers weren't so good they were in high demand, and Jamie didn't have a deep investment in the band. None of them did. Most of the time, it felt more like a hobby than anything they were actively trying to improve.

When he was done, he packed up his sticks and thanked his friend. He drove back to the empty apartment and tried not to wish he could go visit Trevor even though he'd briefly seen him before leaving earlier. He probably could have, but it would've been weird. Alone in his room, Jamie put his drumsticks away. Restless and bored, he flopped onto the couch and mindlessly flipped channels on the television.

His stomach growled, and Jamie impatiently told it to shut up. He was going to do better this time, get control over everything. He wouldn't give in to the hollow, needy feeling. Hunger wasn't his only current mood. Thinking about Trevor stirred both his libido and his guilt. Jamie had promised himself to stop those thoughts now that he was working for them. Didn't mean he had to like it or that he couldn't wish it were different, but he needed to get his runaway crush under control.

He contemplated both a shower and simply lying on his bed and taking care of himself. The shower sounded too tiring, and no matter how hard he tried, he couldn't get rid of Sage's voice in his head telling him not to touch. Sage had been a master of clever manipulation. He would deny Jamie for days, sometimes weeks, and then pounce on him. Every time, he used Jamie's desperation to get relief as proof he was right to impose those conditions.

Jamie's stomach hurt the way it did every time he thought about Sage. He was always caught between the way Sage had made him at times feel loved, worthy, special and the times Sage made him feel lower than dirt. He couldn't put it into words. When he tried, it sounded ridiculous, the foolish ways he reconciled Sage's Jekyll and Hyde routine. Loving and sensual one minute, telling Jamie how gorgeous and talented he was. Angry and demanding the next, expecting Jamie to be ready, willing, and able at every minute. He'd never liked Jamie's work on the web series, which was why Jamie quit after only a few years. Sage had made him feel guilty and ashamed of enjoying his job.

The truth was, Jamie missed the work. He'd liked his costars, people of all genders and sexualities. They'd felt more like family than anyone in Jamie's life aside from Brandon. The company was small, but they catered to a crowd interested in specific tastes. There was a lot of plot to it, and the directors allowed them wide flexibility in shaping their recurring characters. Jamie's work was probably borderline; into his twenties, he'd continued to play a "teen" because he didn't look old enough to be anything else. It had been a lot of fun working with his regular partner, including the occasional not-for-hearing-ears jokes. If not for Sage, Jamie wondered whether he would still be with them.

Thinking about Sage was definitely a mood-killer, so Jamie turned his attention to the television instead. He switched channels again, but nothing caught his eye until he landed on a movie. The lead actor reminded Jamie of Cian, with dark hair and brilliant blue eyes. He had a similar build, and his accent was a stronger version of Cian's.

Jamie groaned. He did not need to have Cian on his mind any more than he needed to think about Sage or Trevor. It made no difference that Cian was gorgeous. He knew it, and he used it to his advantage in his dances. Jamie grudgingly admitted he'd like to know if Cian was as intense in bed as on stage, but that was the wrong line of thinking.

Deep down, Jamie didn't really believe Cian was awful. He simply had bad timing. If he hadn't been at that party, if he wasn't someone Brandon knew more than casually, if Sage hadn't been there too and mad as hell, if Jamie had been single, Jamie might even have entertained Cian's questions. But anything with Cian would've led to more complications than Jamie was prepared to deal with. Jamie had known at the time that Sage would've gone off the rails at Jamie meeting a fan. If he'd decided to make a scene, Cian—and everyone else at that party—would've known the whole story by the end of the night.

Enough wallowing. Jamie couldn't sit around doing nothing all night, and he couldn't call Trevor. The next best thing was to find some fun to take his mind off things. He debated whether he should stay closer to home, but then he remembered it was Drag Night at Grand Slam. Izzy didn't perform regularly anymore, but there were plenty of others. He stood, shoved his phone in his pocket, and headed out the door.

The music thrummed in Cian's chest. He closed his eyes and felt the rhythm, counting and visualizing his steps. He and the other dancers in his troupe were working on a new set with their musicians, and this was the stage he loved. There was something exciting about the blank slate of crafting a new dance.

He pictured it all. Their latest had been the set with the faerie theme. This time, he wanted to create a historical feel but with a distinctly American slant. Instead of using exclusively traditional and modern Irish music, he'd decided to mix in bluegrass. There was a composer who had put out some new music which blended the styles well, and Cian had snapped it up as soon as it was available for purchase. The musicians could listen and imitate the sound. He'd asked two of the other dancers to come up with costume ideas and sketch them so the group could decide what they liked.

For now, he was working on their steps. His hope was to bring some of the others to the forefront this time around. They all looked to him because this had been his baby when they started, but Cian didn't want them to think of themselves as "Cian's backup dancers." He'd intended their troupe as a co-op, and now he was making good on that promise.

He motioned to the band to play the song again, and he worked for the next hour on nailing down the first bit of choreography. They still had a number of shows performing as the faeries, but he wanted fresh material as soon as possible. Having a monthly performance at Grand Slam was a little higher pressure in that regard than taking whatever landed in their laps.

When he was through, he wiped down with a towel. There was nowhere in this ancient theater to get cleaned up, even on three floors. This was the auditorium where the South Boston Community Orchestra rehearsed, though it was used by other groups as well. Half of Cian's band members played in the orchestra, which was how they were allowed to use the stage to practice. Some opera company used the building as well, and there were apparently after school theater workshops on the third floor.

Cian grabbed his bag, said good night to the others, and left the auditorium. A few of them followed him out, and the rest stayed for their regular rehearsal with the orchestra. Cian sat in his car for a few minutes, letting the cool air from the fan blow over him. It had been a good practice, and he was excited to see where he could take this dance.

Back at home, he scrubbed quickly and dried off. He lay naked on his bed, grateful for the air-conditioning unit on an unusually warm night. As wiped out as he was after rehearsal, his mind was keyed up. He had too many thoughts to properly sort through them: the new choreography, the upcoming recital, the dance studio closing, summer programs, and Brandon and Gemma's wedding.

He groaned at the last one. He hadn't given much attention to dating again so Brandon and Gemma would stop feeling sorry for him. He wished now that he hadn't told them anything about his conflicted thoughts about Eric, Nell, and Skye. Brandon and Gemma obviously now thought he was using them as a convenient escape. There was something nagging him about the way the two of them had conspired to get him together with Brandon's cousin. If it had been anyone else, Cian would've had much harsher words for them. As it was, it annoyed him how much they thought he and Jamie would like each other.

How did that make any sense? As far as Cian could tell, aside from Jamie being fluent in ASL, the only thing they had in common was Cian's appreciation for Jamie's work. And if Cian was honest, that translated mostly to his appreciation for Jamie's gorgeous big dick. None of which Brandon knew. All right, they'd lived together, so Brandon possibly knew about Jamie's anatomy. He likely also knew what Jamie had been doing with said anatomy, though he certainly didn't know how much Cian liked it. And none of that was anything to base a relationship on.

Now Cian was annoyed in addition to having untamed thoughts. He rose from the bed and pulled things out of his closet. He was walking distance from Grand Slam. Surely there was something interesting going on over there. He thought it might be Drag Night, which was always fun.

Cian hurried to yank a shirt over his head and snag his keys from the dish by the door. If he walked fast, he'd make it before the first act was over.

Cian stepped inside just as Brunhilda the Great, the emcee, finished introducing someone called Sister Charity Bang-Bang. She didn't quite look like any of the nuns Cian had ever known. He might have enjoyed attending his parish school if there had been a bit more crossover.

He slid onto a bar stool, paying no attention to anything except Sister Charity and her swaying hips. It was much quieter over here, away from the stage. The gentle tap on his shoulder brought him out of his trance. Denver, the bar manager, smiled and asked what she could get for him.

"Rum and Coke, please."

He watched her for a moment, but then his gaze traveled past her to Jack, her second-in-command for the night. Only one stool separated Cian from the man Jack was talking to, and when Cian saw who it was, he froze, watching them converse. Slowly, he leaned closer; he could hear them if he concentrated.

"Just a Diet Coke," Jamie said.

"You want it with a flavor shot?"

"What do you have?"

Jack grinned. "Anything you want. I can do chocolate, vanilla, lime...I wouldn't recommend the banana, though." He grimaced, and Jamie laughed.

"Tried that one yourself, huh? Thanks for the heads-up. I'll have the lime."

Still not drinking alcohol, Cian noted. It wasn't a big thing, but he supposed it struck him as unexpected for some reason. It didn't seem like part of Jamie's overall persona. Then again, Jamie couldn't really hide the shine of sweet innocence even underneath all those piercings and black clothes.

When Jack glanced at him, Cian realized he was staring, and he flushed. He couldn't help it; Jamie was entirely worth staring at, maybe even worth the risk that he'd be annoyed about it since everything Cian did seemed to irritate him. Cian looked away, but not soon enough. Jamie turned slightly and followed Jack's line of vision.

He groaned. *You again.* He'd signed it, and that—plus the hint of a wry smile—made Cian pause.

Yes, me. Public place, and I happen to like Sister Charity. Jamie didn't need to know that Cian hadn't come to see her.

Jamie swiveled around to face the stage. He watched Sister Charity for a few minutes then shrugged and turned back to Cian. *Yeah, she's not bad. I miss TaTa.*

TaTa? Cian asked before remembering who she was. *Beard? She was good.*

She's my roommate's fiancé. I don't know what name to call her. I know her when she's in street clothes. She's really nice, and she makes him happy.

Oh, your roommate's a man. I thought TaTa was straight. Cian cringed. He shouldn't have been stereotyping, but TaTa sort of had a vibe.

Jamie laughed. *She would hate me for saying, but she's a little straight-acting when she's not in character.*

Cian joined his laughter, still chiding himself for making assumptions. The fond look on Jamie's face made his assessment seem softer, like they must have the sort of relationship where TaTa wouldn't really be angry with him. It made Cian appreciate Jamie for his easy acceptance.

They paused their conversation because Sister Charity had finished, and the room exploded with applause. Cian joined in, signing his and noticing Jamie doing the same out of the corner of his eye. Interesting. He knew Jamie was hearing, but he didn't think simply having a deaf cousin would be enough for it to be so natural to him. Cian wondered what he would find if he could peel back all Jamie's layers.

As soon as the next act started, Cian took a risk. He turned to Jamie, tapped him, and signed, *Would you like to join me so we can watch the rest in more comfortable seats?* He indicated the tables farther into the room.

The change was nearly instant, a wall of tension springing up between them. The only way to describe the look in Jamie's eyes was pure fear. Cian couldn't imagine what he'd said wrong to put Jamie in such a state. As quickly as it had come, the expression passed over his face and Jamie turned cool.

I'm sorry. I can't tonight, he signed. *I should get back home.* He left some money on the bar and slipped off the stool. He hesitated with his back to Cian before he turned around again. *It was nice talking to you.*

And then he was gone, making his way to the door and leaving Cian staring after him. Every time they met, Cian felt wrong-footed, and it was frustrating. He didn't care about Brandon's weird itch to see them together. All he cared about was what made Jamie behave like a cornered rabbit whenever they were in the same room. There was something more to it, but it was like trying to put together a thousand-piece jigsaw puzzle. Unless Jamie felt like giving him a clue, Cian would never know what made him so nervous.

The hand on his shoulder made him rotate back to face the bar. Denver indicated Cian's drink and said, "Can I get you another?"

"No, thanks. Just a regular Coke this time." He looked toward the door, but Jamie was long gone by then.

Denver touched his hand. "Jamie's had it hard," she said. "If you really like him, give him some time." Her smile was soft. "I think you'd be good for him, but you didn't hear me say it."

She set his Coke on the bar, and Cian picked it up to take a sip. He considered what she'd said. Maybe there was something to Brandon and Gemma's constant urging. He'd assumed Jamie simply didn't like him, but from the sounds of it, the situation wasn't so simple. Frowning, Cian swirled the ice in his glass. He wouldn't be the one to make the first move. From now on, he was leaving it up to Jamie.

Chapter Seven

Jamie had been seeking out various spaces to practice, but he was running out of options. It was one of the frustrations of the band not having a consistent place to play. That by itself was a likely culprit for some of the problems they'd had. None of the four of them owned a home, and all of them had day jobs and other things which kept them busy.

After spending the day with Aidan, Jamie was prepared to leave once Trevor came home so he could call around for some practice space. He hadn't meant to rush out the minute Trevor walked in, but if he expected someone to help him out, he had to take care of it. He grabbed his things and shoved his feet into his shoes.

"What's the rush?" Trevor asked, not unkindly.

Jamie bent down to tie his laces. "I need to get home so I can find a place to practice."

"Oh," Trevor replied. He looked confused. "Don't you guys have a studio or something?"

"I wish. I go to random friends' houses or wherever else I can."

"Oh," Trevor said again. "Well, uh, you could...you know...come with me over to the church in a bit."

Trevor, like most of their friends, had a series of odd jobs. Less than a year ago, he'd lost his job as a church music director. One of those mouthy, asshole bloggers got hold of the story that his worship song was about a blowie, not about Jesus. Jamie had always thought a lot of worship songs could be interpreted that way, but Trevor insisted not. Regardless, he'd been out of full-time work since then.

His various part-time jobs gave him more flexibility than Andre or Marlie, so he hadn't pressed for something permanent. He sometimes played piano with his friend, gospel singer Irina Clay-Jones, but only when she wanted his particular style. Otherwise, he filled in as an accompanist at the middle school. His new gig was playing piano at the church he now attended with Andre and Marlie.

"You don't think anyone would mind if I played there?"

"Nah. Besides, you'd be with me. I could just tell them I needed a practice buddy, and no one would care. It won't be that interesting. I need to go over the music for Sunday."

"Sure, okay." Jamie shrugged.

"We can't leave until Andre's home. You want to just stay here and hang out? Or did you need to go home first?" It was hard to read Trevor's tone. Did he want Jamie to stay, or was he being polite?

"I..." Jamie played with the piercing in his lip, trying to discern if there was some hidden meaning in the offer. If it had been Sage, there would've been, and he'd have expected Jamie to guess it correctly. Like the time Sage walked out on Jamie during their anniversary dinner for not choosing the right movie to see afterward. Or when Sage had "asked" if Jamie wanted to go to some party with a lot of Sage's friends. Jamie had been meant to know there was only one answer. Nate had stepped in that time, making Jamie simultaneously angry and grateful.

"Jay?" Trevor was peering at him with a slight frown. "You okay? I lost you for a sec there."

"Yeah. Um, I'm good." But no closer to knowing what he should tell Trevor.

Still frowning, Trevor tilted his head toward the couch. "C'mon. Sit down for a bit."

Jamie breathed a sigh of relief. Trevor wanted him to stay, or at least didn't mind. Spared from figuring it out on his own, Jamie followed Trevor back into the living room.

"I'll have to get my sticks before we go. Is that okay?"

"Yeah. Why wouldn't it be?" Trevor plunked Aidan down beside the couch and gave him a rubber toy that looked more like something for a dog. Aidan promptly put it in his mouth, and Jamie caught the flash of his two tiny bottom teeth. "Was he all right today? He might be teething again."

"He was fine. Maybe a little grumpy, but nothing big."

"Good." Trevor was quiet for a moment then said, "What about you?"

"I'm neither grumpy nor teething," Jamie assured him.

Trevor laughed. "I'm sure you're not." Another pause. "What was all that back there? You looked kind of like...I don't know, maybe you thought I was just being polite or something."

Jamie didn't answer right away. He kept his eyes on Aidan, but he could see Trevor out of the corner of his eye. He couldn't have summed up for Trevor everything that was wrong.

Picking up on it, Trevor said softly, "Hey."

"Hm?" Jamie finally made eye contact.

"It's none of my business, but I know it's been a little rough this past winter. I'm not so good with the whole advice thing, but if what you need is just to watch some mindless garbage on TV and not have to cook dinner, I can do that."

The tension in Jamie's gut loosened. "That sounds pretty good."

Trevor located a ridiculously cheesy movie about a lesbian wedding which Jamie found charming if a bit clichéd. They heated some leftovers from the fridge, which Jamie only picked at even though Trevor kept his attention on his own dinner and didn't comment even once. After dinner, Aidan fell asleep in Jamie's arms. Jamie kept half an eye on the movie, enough to make it seem like he was fully present. In reality, he was watching Trevor.

He couldn't have said what it was that drew him in. Sure, he found Trevor attractive. Jamie liked big guys; he couldn't recall a time when he hadn't. That wasn't it, though, not entirely. It was something in the way Trevor seemed so relaxed these days. He was undemanding. Jamie didn't feel a need to so much as have a conversation, let alone justify anything in his life.

Jamie thought back to when Trevor was struggling with his growing relationship with Andre, trying to keep it under wraps because of his church job and his friendship with Nate. Jamie had said he knew they all hated Sage, which Trevor denied. He'd been wrong. Mack called Sage every name in the book except his own, but he wouldn't outright say he despised Sage, even though Jamie knew he did. Nate had made the mistake of openly telling Jamie he couldn't stand Sage, which put a rift in their relationship. Trevor, on the other hand, never said a word.

Everyone thought Jamie was confessing his deepest secrets to Trevor or some bullshit, but the only thing he ever did was spend a lot of nights curled up on Trevor's couch while he watched some game or another. His way of taking care of Jamie never included anything else. This was the one place Jamie knew he could count on the safety of silence.

The film was almost over when Andre turned up. Trevor stood and stretched. He walked to the door and greeted Andre with a kiss. Jamie averted his eyes, but he could still sense them, murmuring quietly in the entryway. He wished he had someone to greet him like that.

Louder, Trevor said, "I'm bringing Jamie with me over to the church to practice a bit. He needed a place to play, so I offered."

Andre peered around Trevor and nodded to Jamie. "That's a great idea. Tonight's a good time because there won't be too many people there, if anyone."

After placing Aidan into Andre's arms, Trevor turned to Jamie. "You ready?"

"Anytime."

While Jamie slid his feet back into his sneakers, Trevor kissed Andre goodbye. It was painfully sweet, the kind of kiss Jamie had always wished Sage would give him. The kind that promised to be back soon and that he was glad to have someone to come home to. Sage's goodbyes were nothing like that. Sometimes he'd nag Jamie about something. Other times he'd kiss Jamie in a way he knew to mean Sage expected sex later, no matter how worn out Jamie was from work. And sometimes Sage delivered a nasty parting shot because Jamie had walked away from him for the hundredth time.

He kept his eyes carefully on his shoelaces until Trevor and Andre were done. Trevor put a warm hand on his shoulder, and Jamie stood. With a last cheerful goodbye to Andre, Trevor was out the door, Jamie trailing behind him.

They stopped at Jamie's apartment for his sticks then headed to Trevor's church. The drive was quiet but not awkwardly so. It was nice to have a few minutes of peace after a day of baby babble and the previous few minutes of bustle to get going. Jamie tried not to stare at Trevor, but his eyes kept drifting. When Trevor caught him at it, he only gave Jamie a half smile. He didn't seem bothered.

Jamie couldn't help it. It took everything in him to turn his thoughts away from what it would be like to touch him. Trevor was solidly off-limits and shouldn't have been in Jamie's thoughts. It wasn't healthy, and he knew it. What kind of person was he, obsessing over a friend like that? No better than Sage, that's what. Sage had chased Jamie for two solid years before Jamie caved and agreed to go out with him.

"Going out" was a stretch. What Jamie agreed to was rushed, uncomfortable sex on Sage's parents' boat. He couldn't even now remember what the appeal was other than the threat of being caught. Afterward, though, was one of the only times Sage made him feel truly loved. Maybe it was all faked, but Sage had cried. Said he hadn't known sex could be like that. Now Jamie wasn't sure if he'd been making the whole thing up to guarantee Jamie wouldn't leave.

It took Trevor shaking his shoulder a bit for Jamie to realize he'd dozed off with his head resting against the window. Trevor chuckled in a way that at first made Jamie embarrassed. Then he realized it was understanding.

"Gotta admit, I'm jealous," he said. "I don't think I've had a decent nap in ages. Babies take it out of you. I sure hope this parenting thing gets easier at some point. You'd think it would be easier with three adults plus a caregiver, but...nope."

Jamie laughed softly then yawned, which made them both laugh harder. "I love your kid, but yeah, it's a lot of work."

They got out of the car and went inside. Trevor flipped on the lights. It was chilly, even though the weather had warmed up. Trevor messed with the heating system controls.

"I wouldn't bother if I was alone, but I figure you'll want some heat."

"It's fine," Jamie assured him. He would warm up soon enough from playing. "Where are the drums?"

Trevor led him into the front of the church where a space had been cleared for the piano, drums, and a handful of music stands. There were three stand microphones lined up by the wall. Jamie went over to the drums and ran his hand along the rim of the snare. It was a nice kit. Maybe not as nice as his, but nicer than what he'd been playing on.

He sat on the stool and pulled his sticks out of his bag, which he set on the floor behind him. He paused, watching Trevor disappear into another part of the church. Jamie tapped a few experimental beats to get a feel for this kit before setting in to practice in earnest.

For a long while, Jamie lost himself in going over the notes Mack had given him and experimenting with fills for the new songs. He tested out a new brush he'd gotten a couple of weeks ago, liking the way it felt in his hand. It was a while before Trevor returned, some sheet music in hand. Jamie stopped and looked up.

"I was practicing in the choir room, but I thought I'd come see how you're doing. Everything working out okay?"

"Yeah. I think I got through all Mack's stuff. I was going to mess around with some of my own, but I don't need to if you're ready to go."

"No, go ahead. I want to test out this song in here, but I'm not in a hurry. You can finish up first."

"It's fine," Jamie insisted. "You do your thing."

Trevor shrugged, but then he grinned. "You want to hear it?"

Jamie wrinkled his nose a little. "A church song? Uh...what is it?"

"Something I've been working on." His cheeks had gone red.

"It's not about"—Jamie leaned closer and whispered loudly—"another blow job?"

"Oh, God. No. No, it is not. Seriously, I don't even sing that one anymore. Some local band gave me a crap-ton of money to be allowed to record it, which I took, and I'm done with that thing forever."

"Hm. Too bad." Jamie winked, but then he backed off, horrified at himself. "I...uh...sorry..."

Trevor snorted. "Nah, 's okay. Anyway, I think this one is way better."

"Well, let's hear it, then."

Trevor sat down at the piano. For a moment, his fingers hovered over the keys, and then he began to play. The melody was soft and gentle at first, gradually building. Jamie closed his eyes and listened. The first verse was about being lost and finding his way, afraid to let go and be loved. The words haunted Jamie.

Trevor had a nice voice. Not as broad and polished as Nate's, but decent nonetheless. He was a tenor, like Izzy, with warm, mellow tones. When he reached the chorus, Jamie picked up the beat and joined in. He used a brush and kept a steady rhythm, feeling it when Trevor slowed down slightly to match his pace. Jamie felt the song—the words, the tune—in every heartbeat. There was no bridge, just a last repeat of the chorus ending on a low, achingly sweet note.

The vibrations hung in the air for a few seconds before fading out. Trevor turned to Jamie. "Wow," he said. "You made it sound good."

"You were speeding up a bit, so I thought I'd give you something to hang on to."

Trevor's laugh was quiet and a little breathy. "Andre and I both tend to do it when we play together. We have to work hard not to." He tilted his head and studied Jamie. "You should play with us sometime."

Jamie shivered. He'd tried with Sage, years ago. It was Jamie's fault Sage gave up playing keyboard, a fact which he intended to take to his grave now they were through for good. They didn't fit together at all, and the result was their first messy, painful breakup and Sage ditching their entire friend group even after they got back together. But this was Trevor, and he'd already proved they could work together. Jamie was torn.

"I don't know..."

"Andre's friend Julian joins us now and again. He plays trombone. We sure could use a drummer."

"I'm not a jazz musician." Jamie swallowed. Anything to hide how much he wanted to play with Trevor again.

"Aw, come on. You'd do fine. Listen."

Trevor began playing something vaguely familiar, an old-style tune. He kept it up then nodded to Jamie to indicate he should play too. Jamie followed the song for another moment before picking up his sticks. He let himself fall into it, the winding patterns and syncopated rhythms. It was different from a rock beat, and at first he had a little trouble keeping up. But soon he was following Trevor through the melody and giving him an anchor. Trevor was right; he did tend to speed up. Jamie held him steady, though, all the way to the end and the last few tinkling notes.

Sliding off the piano bench, Trevor grinned at Jamie. "See? Told you."

Jamie couldn't help smiling back. "Okay, okay."

"You don't have to, you know. But I'd love if you played with us." He put his hand on Jamie's arm.

The contact made Jamie shiver, and he looked up into Trevor's eyes. The longing hit him full force. Here was someone who didn't expect anything of him, didn't chastise him or judge him. Someone who let him sit quietly when he needed to and didn't push him to talk. Someone Jamie didn't feel a need to pressure for conversation either. They'd shared their music in a way he didn't quite do with Mack, something more intimate. It felt both right and so, so wrong at the same time.

"We should go," Jamie blurted. "I mean—I need to get home."

The joy on Trevor's face dimmed a little. "Sure. Of course. Let me get my stuff."

He let go, and Jamie stepped away to get his bag. His stomach ached from knowing he'd just hurt Trevor's feelings. It was an unfortunate necessity. Jamie had to get them both out of there before he did something stupid. Trevor didn't need the stress of Jamie's crush on him. It had to remain firmly buried. He swallowed. There was only one sure way to do that, but he crossed and uncrossed his fingers that the desire to numb himself with food might pass by the time Trevor dropped him off at home.

The apartment was empty when Jamie arrived home. He tossed his bag onto his bed and flopped onto the couch. He didn't much feel like doing anything, still feeling the energy from his practice session and playing with Trevor. His phone vibrated in his pocket and he pulled it out.

The text from Mack read, **Staying at Amelia's.**

OK, Jamie sent back.

Practice this weekend. Got some new stuff.

Yeah, yeah. Jamie sent a thumbs-up and was about to put his phone away when it buzzed again. He rolled his eyes. What else could Mack possibly want? It wasn't as though anything important was going on. Jamie glanced at it and nearly vomited.

Fucking Sage.

He didn't want to read it. Whatever message Sage had for him, he'd said it all a long time ago. There was nothing new to communicate. Except his eye was drawn to the message even as he made to delete it.

Just wanted to make sure you're getting my texts.

As he swiped with a shaking finger, a new text arrived. **Miss you.**

This time, Jamie opened it. He hesitated, knowing if he began typing Sage would be able to see it. He wanted so badly to tell him to fuck off. Before he could make a decision, Sage sent a new text.

**We fit so right, didn't we? It's making me hot thinking about

your gorgeous bod.

There was a pause, during which Jamie sat frozen with the phone in his hand, watching the dots indicating Sage was still typing. He sent two more texts in a row.

You have no idea how much I want you right now...not to mention how I want you...and where I want you.

Remember when we used to do this?

Jamie did remember. When things were good, he'd loved getting Sage's random sexy texts. When things were bad...

I miss your mouth on me. I miss mine on you.

Know what I'm doing right now? Bet you can guess.

I know you're reading these. Want me to tell you what I'm thinking?

I'm imagining it's your hand touching me.

So hot.

Picturing your lips around my dick. My hands in your hair.

You're begging me to suck you too.

Fuck. So close.

You're getting turned on now, aren't you?

Damn it all, yes, Jamie was. He had no trouble recalling every detail of doing exactly what Sage was describing. It wasn't the increasingly explicit descriptions that had Jamie fighting arousal. It was the memories of every time they made up. He still hadn't sent a single return text, not even to tell Sage to stop. The unresolved tension earlier with Trevor already had him on edge, and he couldn't look away.

Go ahead. Think about me while you touch yourself.

Imagine it's me inside you. Just like we used to.

Jamie's breathing was labored, and he was somewhere halfway between sobbing and wanting to obey Sage's directions. He gripped his phone tighter.

So good, baby.

That's it...

Gonna cum. Wish I could see your face.

When I tell you to fuck off and die, you lying, cheating scum.

With a hoarse cry, Jamie hurled his phone. He was lucky he had shitty aim and it landed on the plush chair instead of hitting the television or the window. He curled into a ball on the couch and grasped his hair in his hands, shaking so hard he had to shove up against the cushions to stop from falling to the floor.

The phone vibrated several more times, but Jamie made no move to get up. How, in a single day, had everything gone so horribly wrong? Sage was supposed to be in the past. Trevor was only a friend. The world felt upside down and backwards.

Slowly, Jamie's shaking subsided, replaced by agonizing, brutal need. Not for the relief Sage had denied him nor for resolution to whatever was going on with Trevor. No, Jamie wanted something else. He had to make all of it stop the only way he knew how—with food.

If he gave it too much thought, he might be able to talk himself out of it. So he didn't think; he moved. There was no one home now. No one to watch him race into his bedroom and slam the door. No one to see him yank out the bin from under his bed. No one to stop him from digging through it for whatever might make his mind blank enough for sleep.

He put on music this time. Out of desperation, he grabbed the first thing he could find—the CD of Trevor's old church band. It was probably a bad idea to listen to Trevor's voice while he was cramming food into his mouth, but he didn't care. It was something. The first strains of Trevor's blow job song began while Jamie tossed three music supply catalogs onto the floor.

Jamie never made a production out of what he ate or in what order. There was no arranging and selecting. From start to finish, it was whatever he'd acquired and stored in the bin. Tonight's prize was Ritz crackers and jelly beans, a store-brand version of the ones that came in weird flavors. Who the hell knew what he'd been thinking when he bought them? It didn't matter.

The only important thing was making sure he gauged the amount right. He wanted enough to push past the first pinch of too much, but not enough to feel heavy and nauseated. Enough to make him black out. He'd thought once that only happened with mind-altering substances, but he could achieve a semiconscious state this way. The perfect balance of pain and anesthesia.

In the background, the music changed from Trevor's one-time signature song to something about a heartbeat. The drums in that one were unrelenting, mimicking the pounding of blood. Jamie had always thought the song's mood and rhythm were far more sexual than worshipful. It did nothing to kill the arousal Sage had caused earlier.

Even while he ate, Jamie stripped down to his underwear. He

flipped open one of the catalogs and focused on the photos to distract himself. If he thought at all about what he was doing, he would be consumed by rage and shame. Using a picture of a high-end kit as a focal point, Jamie shoved a hand into his underwear.

It was weird and yet not, working himself with one hand while using the other to pull crackers from the package. He let the sensory overload drag him in—the throb of the song, the feel of his palm on his cock, the salt on his tongue. There was nothing but this moment; the world outside faded and disappeared until Jamie had sated his cravings and fallen asleep on the empty packages and the sticky, ruined catalog.

CHAPTER EIGHT

MACK HAD taken the van for the afternoon. It was a good thing Jamie had finally bought his own car so he could go visit his mother in Woonsocket. Jamie knew she would be at church in the morning, so he waited until lunchtime. He hadn't come across a church he wanted to attend. The closest he'd gotten was going to Aidan's baptism a couple of months back. They'd done it at Andre's church, and it was...nice. Jamie wouldn't say it had a profound impact on his spiritual life or anything, but there hadn't been anything upsetting. The minister there seemed fully aware of the relationship among Aidan's parents, although Jamie couldn't discern how many other people thought Andre was Aidan's godfather or Marlie was his godmother, pairing the people they presumed to be Aidan's "real" parents.

Jamie tried not to judge his mother's church attendance. She was a born-again, and she maintained that it helped her stay clean, so he didn't question it. He didn't have any memories of her when she'd been using, so he had no idea what did or didn't help her. If church meant so much to her, it wasn't his place to tell her his feelings on the matter. Besides, he was sure she knew. He wouldn't be welcome in the church she attended, no matter how much they embraced and accepted her. She had left behind her "sin," after all, but he had not.

He pulled into the crumbling parking lot behind her building. A group of preteen boys were there, laughing and shoving each other. One of them had a bag full of bang-snaps, and they were tossing them at each other's feet and shouting. A woman with a toddler in a stroller passed by and glared at them before going back to her loud conversation on her cell phone and pushing the stroller with her free hand.

Jamie pressed the buzzer, and his mother let him up. He ascended to her fourth-floor apartment and opened the door. Inside, it smelled like a combination of cooking food, her cat's litter box, and stale cigarettes. For Jamie, those were all familiar, comforting in the same way as his mother's embrace when she put her arms around him.

Like Jamie, Mama was short. She was a little rounder than he was, with lean legs and long, dark hair. He smelled her shampoo when he rested his cheek against her head. He held on for a while, wanting to implant the feeling of her hug to save for later. He didn't see her nearly often enough, the problem of living too far away, working odd hours, and playing with the Creepy Crullers. Mama never scolded him for it, though. She took what she could get, and he called her every week.

When she let go, she reached into her pocket and pulled out a brand-new smartphone. "Look!" she said. "I can keep up with your band now."

"It's nice, Mama. Where'd you get it?"

"Bruce."

Ah, her new boyfriend. Jamie had met him once. He wasn't much older than Jamie. Mama had found him through some of her friends, and he seemed decent enough. Jamie didn't comment on why he was already buying her expensive gifts.

"I'm glad he's being good to you," was all he said.

"He is. I think he's going to move in here soon."

Jamie looked around the apartment, wondering where he would stay. It was a two-bedroom which she shared with her half sister and niece. They had the bedrooms, and Mama had a futon in the living room. The place—at least what Jamie could see of it—was freakishly tidy. He supposed it came from their years of having to keep everything together in case they had to move again. They'd never had a whole lot to keep track of.

The others didn't seem to be home, which suited Jamie. He wasn't fond of them, or at least not fond of the ways they seemed to take advantage of his mother's relative innocence. He used that term loosely; Mama wasn't entirely unaware of the way the world worked.

She simply liked believing the best of people, especially from her church.

Her half sister and niece were both of the opinion Jamie needed a lot of prayer. They would never come right out and say it, but they'd invited him on more than one occasion to a group at their church for "people dealing with sexual sin." Mama was fully accepting and supportive, but this branch of her family was not. It was a good thing neither they nor Mama had any idea what he'd done for a living before the band had regular paid gigs. They were sure it was Mack and the "rock lifestyle" leading him astray, and Jamie didn't correct them.

Mama stepped to the side into the tiny kitchen and pulled a pan of stuffed shells out of the oven. Jamie's mouth watered, and he fidgeted, trying to hide his reaction from Mama. He looked through her cupboards for a couple of plates and glasses. She had more dishes than they'd had when he was a kid, but it was still sparse. He put them on the counter next to the pan. Mama served some to both of them, and they took the food to the living room. There wasn't a table even though the corner was supposed to serve as a dining room.

"Make sure you save some for the others," Mama warned. "This is for everyone."

"I will." Jamie's stomach clenched at the way she'd implied he might eat that much. It wasn't a big pan, but even so, it was more than enough for four or maybe five people to share. He knew better than to take more than was allotted to him.

Jamie blew on a bite, making sure to cut and arrange the food so it looked like he had a full plate. An old habit, born out of reassuring Mama he had plenty no matter how hungry he was. The skill had come in handy over the years. Mama probably hadn't been fooled; what mother ever is? But Jamie knew she appreciated it all the same.

"So, what's new with you?" she asked. Her tone was casual, but she was asking about more than the weather.

There was a long list of topics Jamie would rather not cover: Sage, Brandon's wedding, whether or not he was seeing anyone new, his day job, running into Cian again at the bar the other night. He stalled by way of taking another bite, scorching his mouth because he hadn't blown on it. Hastily, he reached for his water glass. When his tongue had cooled, he answered Mama with the only thing he thought might be safe.

"My friends have a baby," he said, enjoying the way her eyes lit up.

"Oh? How old?"

"Um." Jamie calculated in his head. "About five months. He's the happiest kid ever. I wish you could see him. He's so blond he's nearly bald, but his eyes are dark. Oh, and he's so chubby! When you hold him, he just cuddles right up. I think he loves everyone. They're paying me to watch him a couple days a week now."

As he talked, Mama's eyebrows rose higher and higher. Jamie's cheeks burned, knowing he was admitting to how much he loved Aidan even though he wasn't one of the baby's parents. Mama laughed softly.

"He sounds sweet." There was a wistful note in her voice.

Jamie swallowed another bite of food to avoid saying something foolish, like asking Mama if she ever wished she'd had more. Long before his father disappeared, before they'd lost everything and spent years trying to survive, he remembered his parents telling him he was going to be a big brother. He must have been five or six then. Looking back, he guessed his mother must have miscarried, but at the time, they'd only told him they'd been mistaken. Nothing was ever said about it again. His child self had wondered if everything would have been okay if they'd had the baby, but his adult self knew better. His parents' problems were inevitable, much like his own.

After lunch and an afternoon spent focused on anything but the things he needed to protect Mama from, Jamie left. He had to resist another old habit, creating a story and a trail to cover for where he'd been all day if Sage was upset. He reminded himself he didn't need to do that anymore. He could drive home and go back to their probably empty apartment.

Or he could come up with a better idea. It wasn't late, and he didn't need to make excuses anymore. He pulled out his phone and hit Trevor's number before he could change his mind.

"Hey, Trev? It's Jamie. You busy?"

"No," Trevor replied on the other end of the line. "Just me, Marlie, and the baby. You want to come over?"

"I'd love to."

###

Jamie declined Marlie's offer for him to stay for dinner, but he did accept another tin of her homemade kale chips. As far as he knew, he was the only one who ate them besides her. He didn't love them, but they weren't terrible. For Trevor's sake, he took them, and he didn't tell her the other guys wouldn't eat them.

By the time he got home, he wished he'd had dinner with them. Mack was home, and Nate had Izzy over. It was obvious they'd eaten already, which meant Jamie would need to figure it out on his own. He wasn't upset, exactly. They couldn't have known he would want them to wait. It was only that he didn't want to make something while they were all sitting around in the other room. It made him feel self-conscious, like he was on display and would have to choose carefully what he ate.

"There's leftovers in the fridge," Nate called. "Izzy brought us food."

"Uh...okay," Jamie said. He hesitated then added, "I ate at Trevor's a while ago." What they didn't know wouldn't hurt them.

Except now Jamie was hungry, and the only thing on hand was the tin of kale chips. And the new things he'd stashed under his bed, but he wouldn't touch those right now. He sat down at the kitchen table and popped the top off the kale chips. It wouldn't matter if he ate the whole thing. No one would comment on it, aside from Mack turning up his nose at them. They wouldn't ask if he was sure he needed them or pinch his sides until he bruised and warn him about developing love handles.

He flinched at the memory even as he bit into a kale chip. If he did eat them all, it would surely make him sick. Maybe he deserved it. His wandering thoughts left him vacillating between hunger pains and tears. He crunched slowly, fighting both.

Mack stood up, stretched, and came into the kitchen to deposit his Coke can in the recycling. "How the hell can you stand those?"

Jamie shrugged, swallowing both his bite and the angry lump in his throat. "Marlie means well."

Muttering something about her being overzealous and a health nut, Mack went into his room. He emerged with a bag and bid the others good night, heading out to Amelia's. Jamie's insides squirmed. He hadn't realized Nate and Izzy wanted the place to themselves. They usually went to Izzy's because he lived alone. Jamie didn't want to be their third wheel. Half of him hoped they would leave; the other half hoped they wouldn't. He didn't know if he wanted to be alone right then.

"We're just gonna watch a movie," Nate said. "My new job starts tomorrow, so I didn't want to be out late. You wanna join us?"

"Um...oh. I—" Jamie's fingers tightened on his kale chip, and it broke in half. "What are you watching?"

Nate pulled it up on the screen and read off the title and description. It sounded horrifically boring, but it was better than hiding in his room and giving in to things he knew he shouldn't be doing. He ate the chip and put the lid on the tin. Maybe after Izzy left and Nate went to bed, he could scrounge dinner then. He joined them in the living room.

Before they could start the movie, Nate's phone buzzed. He looked at it then stood up and answered as he walked into his room. He turned and mouthed *work* before closing the door. That left the other two sitting awkwardly at opposite ends of the couch.

Jamie hadn't spent much time alone with Izzy before. He still felt shy around him. Collectively, he and Nate were nearly giants in comparison with Jamie's small frame. That wasn't what made talking to Izzy feel uncomfortable. Nor was it the age difference. Izzy was in his mid-thirties, nearly ten years older than Jamie. It was more the lingering embarrassment over what Izzy knew from when Jamie broke things off with Sage for the last time. He'd seen the evidence of what Sage had done to him, and he knew at least some things Jamie preferred to keep to himself.

He struggled for a topic of conversation. He didn't want to talk about how weird things had become for him regarding Trevor or his mother's latest boyfriend drama or the bin hidden under his bed or the half dozen messages from Sage he'd ignored in the last week alone. Izzy was one of those people who had two settings: too little conversation and too much. Jamie recalled Izzy was an athlete—a runner. He thought about asking him if he liked any sports, but since Jamie couldn't even name one player, he figured it would turn boring pretty quickly.

Izzy looked over at him, and Jamie braced himself. But all Izzy said was, "How are you doing these days?"

Jamie shrugged. "I'm fine." Something in him snapped, and he let out a little of his frustration. "Unless you want a real answer to that question, maybe you shouldn't ask."

Izzy's eyebrows ascended almost to his hairline. "You can give me a real answer if you want."

With a heavy sigh, Jamie tried to dial his inner turmoil back a notch. "The truth?" When Izzy nodded, Jamie said, "Everything is one big, soggy mess. It's like I can't get it together since Sage. God. He really fucked with me."

"I'm sorry it's been so rough." Izzy paused, but when Jamie said nothing, he nodded. "You don't have to tell me any more if you'd rather not."

"I'd rather not," Jamie agreed.

Maybe he didn't want to tell Izzy, but he wanted to explode everything from his years of being held emotionally captive by Sage's insecurities. Sage had sucked the life out of him, but Jamie missed him every day. He didn't miss Sage telling him he'd never look hot enough if he didn't keep his weight down. He didn't miss Sage groping him and breathing on his neck, ordering him to be available for Sage's whims. He didn't miss Sage jealously hoarding Jamie's time yet parading him around like statement jewelry. But he did miss the constant small touches, the sexy whispers, and the way every fight ended with intense sex. He missed having one person who knew his secrets and helped him hold things together. He missed knowing he had someone to go to so he wouldn't be stuck sitting on the couch with his lovebird friends.

None of that was anything Jamie could say to Izzy without it being an overshare. He curled his legs up and scrunched on the end of the couch, intending to make sure he took up as little space as possible when Nate returned. Izzy eyed him sideways, his lips parted, and Jamie sighed.

"What."

"It's just..." Izzy clamped his lips shut.

"No, go ahead. I know there's something you want to ask."

"Did you really eat at Trevor's?" Izzy blurted.

Jamie hadn't been expecting that. He'd assumed Izzy had something more to say about Sage. Thrown off guard, he almost gave in and told Izzy the truth. "Yes," he snapped. At Izzy's wide-eyed shock, he backed down. "No."

Izzy frowned. "Are you eating at all?"

Oh. Jamie breathed a sigh of relief. At least he could dispel that idea without giving away everything. "It's not what you think," he said. "I get enough to eat." He held his breath, waiting to see how Izzy would respond.

"Do you?" Izzy grimaced. "I mean, Nate said—never mind. It's none of my business. Sorry."

"I get enough to eat," Jamie repeated. "I sometimes can't—" He stopped, seeing Nate emerge from the bedroom. For the moment, he was spared having to explain to Izzy that his problem was not knowing when to stop and that it was better not to start at all.

Jamie put a hand to his stomach, thinking about the way he needed to feel the stretch, the ache. It made all the other pain so much easier to bear if he could concentrate on it. He turned back to the television, his mouth clamped firmly shut.

Izzy got the hint. He said to Nate, "Everything all right?"

"Yeah, of course. Del is fussing over me like he's my mommy. I swear to God, he's more excited about this job than I am." Nate clapped a hand over his mouth then lowered it slowly. "Shit. Oh, God—argh! Sorry!"

Chuckling, Izzy held out a hand to Nate and pulled him onto the couch between himself and Jamie. "I think it bothers you more than it does me, babe."

"Sorry," Nate said again. "I'm not used to filtering my...blasphemy?"

Izzy kissed Nate. "Stop worrying about it."

"Okay, okay." He laughed. "Wait. When I convert to Judaism, can I still use Jesus Christ as a swear?"

With a groan that turned into a laugh, Izzy pulled Nate closer. "No."

"Why not?" Nate demanded, shoving on him a little, with no effect on Izzy's arms around him.

"Ex-Catholic guilt." This time, Jamie caught the flash of tongue when Izzy kissed Nate.

Jamie choked on the rude noise threatening to erupt from his chest. Sitting with the two of them making goo-goo eyes at each other was not Jamie's idea of a good time. He was going to need to do something because there was no way he would make it through the whole evening without hurling. He stood.

"I'm, uh, kind of tired. I think I'll...just...turn in."

Nate gave him a puzzled frown. "At this hour?"

Jamie shrugged. "Or maybe I'll go listen to the songs Mack wants me to learn. Yeah, I should probably do that anyway."

"Okay."

It didn't seem to faze Nate, who returned his attention to Izzy and hit play on the movie without another word to Jamie. Izzy glanced back at him, but Jamie shook his head. He slipped into the bedroom just as he caught the motion of Nate dragging Izzy into another kiss.

Jamie heard the volume increase on the movie, no doubt to drown out the other sounds the two of them were making. There was no end to Jamie's annoyance over his roommates and their living room sex. So much for the rule about warning the others when they wanted privacy. Everyone now seemed perfectly comfortable to go at it whenever and wherever they wanted. Knowing Nate and Izzy were distracted in more ways than one, Jamie pulled the bin of food out from under the bed. Guilt bubbled up because he'd already replaced what he'd taken out over the past few weeks. He used to be able to go much longer in between, but that was back when he had Sage to keep him in check.

He hesitated then reached into the bin. As long as he had enough control tonight not to make himself actually sick, he could indulge. What no one else knew wouldn't hurt them. In the morning, he would skip breakfast and start all over again being good.

CHAPTER NINE

JAMIE NEEDED to get out of his own head. He'd talked to Mama again on the phone while Aidan was napping, and that always left him missing both her and Sage. She'd never met Sage, and Jamie hated the reasons why. He hadn't spent much time with Sage's family either, but he'd at least been to their house. Jamie had trouble deciding which he was more ashamed of—that he hadn't wanted Sage to see how Mama lived or that he knew Sage would have things to say about it that Jamie didn't want to hear.

It took several rounds of should-I-or-shouldn't-I before Jamie finally talked himself out of doing anything stupid. He certainly wasn't going to steal food from his friends, and even living in the same town, he wouldn't bring the baby back to the apartment. He had to be clear-headed to take care of Aidan. Fortunately, Aidan woke up, which gave Jamie something to do other than wallow.

It was Jamie's long day with Aidan, since Marlie had class. Trevor had some work as an accompanist at the middle school, and afterward, he was supposed to be in the studio. Jamie wasn't sure whether he would show up first or Andre would. He glanced at the time and realized it was nearly five thirty. One of them would be home soon.

Sometime after that, Jamie heard the front door. Aidan wriggled, and Jamie figured out why half a second later. He had just picked up Aidan and retrieved a diaper from the shelf when Trevor walked into the living room. Aidan reached out his hands, and Jamie laughed as he handed Aidan off. Trevor peered over his head at Jamie, wrinkling his nose at the smell.

"Yeah, I was just about to change him when you showed up," Jamie said.

"I'll do it," Trevor answered, holding out his hand for the supplies.

"Nah, I got it. You just got here."

"You really don't have to."

"I want to." Jamie held the diaper out of Trevor's reach.

"You...want to?" Trevor blinked. "I'm his dad, and even I don't think I'd use the word 'want,' other than that I 'want' him to stop reeking."

Jamie laughed. "I just mean I like doing things for him."

Trevor shrugged one shoulder and handed Aidan back. Jamie laid the changing pad on the floor and set the other things down. He began taking care of business. As soon as he opened the diaper, he covered Aidan's teeny unit with the fresh one so he wouldn't take aim at Jamie's face. He'd learned that lesson the hard way on day one.

Chuckling, Trevor said, "Good call. Marlie and I both know better, and he's gotten both of us. Andre thinks it's hilarious, but only because he's never had it happen to him." He stood. "I'll get us some drinks while you do that. Just water? Or you want a Coke?"

Jamie called after him, "Water's fine!" before returning his attention to Aidan.

A couple minutes later, Trevor was back with the drinks. By then, Jamie had Aidan clean and dry, and he was rocking him. Trevor stood in the doorway, watching.

"You're good with him." He sounded surprised or puzzled.

"He's cute."

That was as much as Jamie could say. He didn't know himself why Aidan fascinated him, but he felt protective and almost overwhelmed when he had the baby in his arms. He'd never given any thought at all to fatherhood, not the way Trevor and Andre both said they had since childhood. Until Aidan, Jamie had found babies largely confusing and strange. The idea of having to raise a kid was intimidating. Jamie thought maybe he'd stick to babysitting. That had all the fun plus the advantage of giving the little one back at the end.

And yet, here he was, unable to explain what Aidan meant to him. It was more than caring for him twice a week. Jamie loved him, even though he couldn't have explained it to anyone. Mack would've penned some deep, poetic lyrics about it, he was sure. Words weren't that easy for Jamie. He stumbled over them all the time and struggled not to jumble them up. Maybe that was why he liked being around Aidan. The baby didn't expect him to say all the right things in the right order.

"You want to stay for dinner? Andre's out with Nia tonight, and Marlie's in class until late."

"Okay." Jamie swallowed any anxiety he had about it. This was Trevor, and surely he could manage one meal, no matter how hard that had been for him lately.

Trevor fixed them a simple supper, and they ate quietly while Aidan played with a cup on the floor. He moved between that and sitting in Jamie's or Trevor's lap, and Jamie thought this must be how family dinners usually went. He envied them this coziness, even when Trevor said dinner wasn't always so peaceful.

Afterward, Jamie helped Trevor with the dishes, and then they sat down in the living room. Trevor flipped on the television and turned the volume down on whatever game he was watching. It was nice, being the two of them like this. Once again, Jamie thought about what life would be like if he had something this settled to come home to. He'd never pictured it with Sage, although he couldn't have said why. Maybe eight years and countless breakups and makeups made it hard to envision the future.

"Aidan needs a bottle," Trevor said, interrupting Jamie's thoughts. "You want to give it to him? It's okay if not. You're off the clock now."

"I don't mind."

Aidan let out a giant yawn as Trevor went back to the kitchen. Jamie settled into the rocking chair with Aidan, and Trevor returned with the bottle. In no time, Aidan had finished it and drifted off to sleep. It felt almost miraculous, holding him while he snuggled in close.

Trevor lifted him out of Jamie's arms. Aidan opened his eyes briefly, but as soon as Trevor swayed him, he was back asleep. Trevor carried him up the stairs, returning only a couple of minutes later. He flipped on the baby monitor on the coffee table and settled himself there.

He patted the couch. "Come on over."

Jamie joined him. They stretched their legs out, and Trevor rested his arm across the back of the couch. He had his gaze fixed on the game. Jamie settled in. A boring night of baseball beat a boring night home alone any time, so Jamie didn't complain or ask Trevor to turn to something else. Jamie didn't care much for sports himself, but he didn't mind much if a game was on. When all four of them had lived together, there was something in the background most of the time, as he was the only one who didn't have at least one team he followed.

He might not have been interested in baseball for its own sake, but when a particular player was at bat, Jamie sat up a little. He'd seen an interview with him on some sports channel—or maybe it was a post-game spot. The man was sinfully attractive, and Jamie developed a sudden focus on the game. He almost groaned when the guy adjusted his cup. It should definitely not have been sexy, but Jamie's body didn't seem to care about the rules. He shifted, bumping Trevor's knee with his own.

The warm press of their legs made Jamie shiver a little, and Trevor looked over at the motion, his eyebrows raised. Jamie's neck prickled with heat as he adjusted himself. Trevor shrugged and angled so they were touching hip to knee.

"He's fucking sexy," Trevor remarked, not taking his eyes from the screen.

"Yeah."

Fingers brushed against his leg. Jamie swallowed. There was no way it was accidental. His heart thudded, and he was hyperaware of every motion. Trevor placed his hand on Jamie's thigh, and Jamie parted his lips as his breath came in shallow pants. He'd wanted Trevor for ages, but he'd seen him as off-limits. What Trevor was doing to him now made his pulse pound and his nerves glow.

Trevor moved again, turning so he could lay back against the pillows at one end of the couch. He brought Jamie with him so Jamie was tucked into his side. Lifting his hand, he ran his fingers down Jamie's cheek. The light touches were a combination of arousing and relaxing, and Jamie sighed as his eyes drifted closed.

He woke with a start but quickly realized he'd only been asleep for a few minutes. Trevor stirred as well, and the room came back into focus. The sounds of the game were low in the background. Trevor stretched, displacing Jamie so he rolled up against the back of the couch. He was still half-lying on Trevor; it was pleasant, tucked up warm and safe against his side. Trevor's arm slid around Jamie's shoulders, and Jamie hiked himself up so his eyes were level with Trevor's.

"Hey," Trevor said. "Sorry...think I fell asleep."

"It's okay. Me too."

They were so close, and Jamie wanted to do it—lean forward and kiss Trevor. The way Trevor was looking at him was inviting, especially the way he poked out his tongue to moisten his lips. Jamie warred with himself. Trevor was with Marlie and Andre, and this would be cheating. Not only that, they were paying him to be there. On the other hand, it was Trevor's job to say no. Without another thought, Jamie pressed against him and kissed him.

It was like lighting a fuse. Heat spread out from where their lips were joined, sending sparks down Jamie's spine. He opened his mouth, half groaning and half hoping Trevor would use his tongue. Jamie got his wish, delighting in the urgent moan Trevor delivered along with it. The fiery kisses seemed to have a direct circuit to Jamie's dick, which had already begun to swell. He rolled his hips, pleased to get a response from Trevor matching his own. In short order they were rocking against each other in rhythm with their hungry kisses. Jamie wasn't sure how much more he could take. He didn't want to do this fully clothed, though, writhing on the narrow couch. He reached for the button on Trevor's jeans, hoping to hint at what he needed.

Trevor ripped his mouth away and held Jamie's wrist. "Stop."

Jamie sat up, gulping air and waiting for his pulse to slow. He slid off Trevor and leaned against the other end of the couch. He should have known better. Trevor was right not to want to break the trust he had with his partners. Jamie only hoped he wasn't too angry.

Full of remorse, Jamie said, "I'm sorry. This is wrong in so many ways." His cheeks flushed. He'd never meant to intrude on Trevor's relationships.

"It's not that." Trevor wriggled into a sitting position as well. "Andre and Marlie and I are all adults, and we talk about stuff. We've all made choices about who we see or sleep with aside from each other. I've been out with a couple of other people. That's not the issue here."

Jamie chewed his lip. "Is it because we're friends? Like you and

Nate?" He thought about Nate and Trevor's once-strained relationship and about Mack's rule that he didn't date friends other than Amelia.

Trevor shook his head. "Nate's off-limits for a lot of reasons, but there isn't a no-friends rule. I'm not cut out to get with random strangers, a lesson I learned in some really awkward ways." He sighed. "I'm more worried about you and what this means because of Aidan."

Right. The same concern Jamie had, really. Jamie didn't think this amounted to paying him for sex, but it wasn't in his job description, either. If things went south, he could be out of a job and a friendship.

"Would the others be okay with it?" he asked.

For a few minutes, Trevor neither moved nor spoke. At last Trevor nodded and got up from the couch. He padded into the bedroom. Jamie heard him on the phone, only catching bits of his conversation before he shut the door and muffled the sounds. Eventually, he reemerged with a strip of condoms and some lube.

"Wasn't sure what we needed." Trevor set them on the coffee table.

"So...we're doing this?" Jamie asked.

"Yeah. Look, you should know I called Andre and texted Marlie. They had the same concerns I did, but they're both all right with it if you and I are. The only real rules are safety and that we don't fuck in either bed—that's sacred space for now. The couple times I've done this, I've gone to the other person's house."

Jamie shrugged. It wasn't as comfortable, but couch sex could be plenty hot. Mostly what he wanted was to see Trevor's body naked, and the rest didn't matter as much. He stood up and stripped off his shirt.

"No problem."

Trevor undressed as well and draped a towel over the couch. He sat back down, his hand on himself and his eyes on Jamie as he finished taking off his clothes. Jamie thought back to doing this with Sage, and his hand trembled as he flicked open the button on his jeans. He drew the zipper down slowly, not daring to look away from Trevor. Jamie made tiny, slow circles with his hips, a subtle thrusting as he palmed the front of his jeans. Trevor licked his lips and moved his hand slowly, and Jamie warred between being turned on that Trevor was enjoying it and anxious about making it good. He paused then fell into familiar territory, making a show of touching his body all over then sliding his hand into his open fly. He allowed himself to partially dissociate, the way he'd learned to do with Sage.

"Hey," Trevor said. "You don't have to do that for me."

Broken out of his trance, Jamie nodded and finished undressing with less ceremony. He stepped over to the couch and stood there. Trevor reached up and rested his hands on Jamie's hips for a moment before drawing him down into his lap. Jamie straddled him, his cock resting against Trevor's belly and Trevor's pressed against Jamie's ass cheek.

"You're pretty big," Trevor remarked. "I wasn't expecting that." He reached out with one finger and ran it gently over Jamie's erection, fondling the piercing at the end almost reverently.

Jamie didn't want to find it funny; he usually didn't like comments on his size. But something in the way Trevor was admiring him seemed almost analytical, and it amused Jamie. He chuckled.

"What?" Trevor asked.

"I don't know. You're playing with my dick like you're trying to read my fortune or something."

Trevor snorted out a laugh, but then he turned serious again. "I like the way everyone's cock is different. It's...interesting, I guess. Sexy."

Jamie liked the sound of that. Trevor's words and his far-too-light touch sent another ripple of excitement through him. He leaned in and pressed his lips to Trevor's. They kissed for a long time, Trevor's hands stroking Jamie's back in gentle up and down motions. Jamie used his hands to explore Trevor's gorgeous, curvy body. It felt so good Jamie wanted to cry. He hated his own, the way he was both too thin and not thin enough. Trevor had so much confidence in his own skin. He never seemed to have the fears that he wasn't fit or muscular enough the way so many men did. Jamie's hand gripped the flesh around Trevor's tight brown nipple, and they both groaned. He was so turned on it was almost painful.

Jamie sat back enough to gaze down, staring at his cock nestled against the rolls around Trevor's belly. He wanted them, wanted to devour them with his fingers and lips. He'd never thought much before about what appealed to him—he hadn't had much opportunity—but he knew physically Trevor did it for him. Jamie put his palms against Trevor's stomach. The soft feel sent a long shiver up his spine, and he moaned loudly.

Trevor's quiet laughter brought him back to earth. He opened his eyes. "What's so funny?"

"You and Andre both really have a thing for my belly fat," Trevor answered. His eyes twinkled. "The way you reacted just now was kind of funny, but damn if it's not so fucking hot."

Jamie tried to laugh, but it came out slightly forced because he was on the verge of another aroused moan as he couldn't resist thrusting against Trevor. "Oh, yeah."

All he could think about was getting Trevor gloved up and inside him so he could ride Trevor's dick with his own continuing to rub against Trevor's glorious stomach the way it was now. A bit of precome oozed out, and he shivered when Trevor used his thumb to swipe it away. Jamie rocked his hips faster, feeling like he was flying and never wanted it to end. His skin tingled everywhere, the sensation concentrating between his legs.

"You're so close already," Trevor said, sounding surprised. He put his hands on Jamie's thighs, trying to hold him still.

It was too much anyway, and Jamie couldn't stop. He pushed his hips forward, straining against Trevor's grasp. His breath caught, and a full-body tremor shook him. "*Shit*," he breathed as he came so hard it was dizzying.

And then he was shivering. He hadn't meant to come fast like that. All he could think about was how humiliated he was, how he hadn't even properly gotten Trevor close first. He'd reacted like a teenager having his first hand job. He shook and tried to pull away from Trevor, feeling sick at how desperate he must have seemed. Trevor would be angry—might lash out, the way Sage sometimes had. Part of Jamie knew Trevor wouldn't hurt him, but he couldn't stop the panic gripping him. Ignoring the mess on his own belly and Trevor's, he curled into a ball at the end of the couch.

"Hey." Trevor's voice was soft. "Can I touch you?"

"No!"

"Okay. I'll stay here. Jay, it's all right. I'm not upset."

"Don't hurt me!"

Jamie hadn't meant to say it. He wasn't going to tell Trevor what Sage did to him. The room was suddenly plunged into semi-dark silence; Trevor must have turned the television off. Jamie still couldn't look at him.

"I'm not going to hurt you, but we need to talk about this. You're upset, and I'd like to know what I can do."

"Nothing. Leave me the fuck alone."

The couch moved, and Jamie heard Trevor's footsteps retreating. He curled further in on himself, clutching his rolling stomach. The empty feeling consumed him, and he wanted it to stop. The urge hit him forcefully with the desire to fill the hole with a more familiar, manageable pain.

A few minutes later, he heard a soft thunk of Trevor setting something on the coffee table. The couch moved again as Trevor sat back down. Jamie was naked on another man's couch, freaking out about the sex he'd just managed to ruin, and yet Trevor still wasn't being an ass about it. Jamie breathed slowly, trying to come back to himself. Over and over he repeated to himself that Trevor wasn't Sage and that he was safe here. Trevor didn't say a word, simply sitting quietly and waiting for Jamie's anxiousness to recede. When his pounding heart finally slowed down, Jamie dared shift enough to look at Trevor.

"I'm sorry," he muttered. He reached for the glass of water Trevor had left for him on the table and took a long, slow drink.

"You okay?" Trevor asked. "You legit just had a serious panic attack or something."

"I—it's—I'm fine." Another sip of water and a deep breath. "That was...not so great for you. I really do feel bad."

"It happens," Trevor said. "Should've seen me the first time Marlie blew me. God. You know what the worst thing to do is? Come on a woman's face when she hasn't invited it. I was so embarrassed." He chuckled.

Curious, Jamie sat up a little. "What did she do?" He had some experience with the purposeful variety of face jizz, though not with a woman, and he didn't like it much. That may have been because Sage never really cared if Jamie enjoyed it or not.

"I apologized about a hundred times, and she kept saying it was okay. She got that I hadn't been playing porn star with her, that I was just overeager."

Jamie flinched at Trevor's casual "porn star" phrase. There was no way he could have guessed it would bother Jamie or he wouldn't have said it.

"I'm sorry anyway."

"I'm not mad." Trevor slid closer. "Can I come over there now?"

Jamie nodded, and Trevor moved to his side. He hadn't put his clothes back on either, and when his arms went around Jamie, the skin-to-skin contact sent new ripples of desire through him. Despite his shame, he still wanted Trevor badly.

They stayed like that, Trevor's fingers massaging Jamie's shoulder. In their current position, he felt it when Trevor's dick began to swell with renewed interest, and it provoked his own reaction. He adjusted so he was angled with one leg draped over Trevor's, giving Trevor access to touch him if he wanted to. Trevor leaned down and kissed him.

"We don't have to do this."

"I want to," Jamie replied. "I want us both to feel good this time."

"We'll go a bit slower." He touched Jamie's PA with his fingertip. "Do you think I could—?"

"What?" Jamie asked.

"I kind of want to...lick it. Does—does that feel good?" He went red. "I mean, I've never been with anyone who had one."

"Yeah," Jamie acknowledged. "It feels good. Might take some getting used to for you." He hadn't had it long. Only since calling it quits with Sage. No way would his ex have let him. He could picture it even now, Sage finding yet another reason not to give him head. He'd never liked to as it was, or so he claimed.

"Okay." Trevor played with it with his fingers. "We can take our time."

Jamie wanted to tell him he didn't think they could, he was already on his way to worked up, but his mouth became occupied before he had a chance. This time, he intended to make sure Trevor was satisfied too. They took it easy, and it was obvious from Trevor's cautious movements that he wanted to draw things out. He maneuvered Jamie so he was up on his knees, with Trevor slouching between his thighs. Trevor didn't try to give him a full blow job, instead exploring Jamie's piercing with his thumb and the tip of his tongue. The teasing touches made Jamie shiver with pleasure, heightened by the adoration rolling off Trevor.

They shifted again, back to a position good for using their hands on each other. Jamie finally relaxed. He eased down to rest on Trevor's thighs, unable to hold back a pleasure-soaked sigh. It felt exactly right to Jamie, the way he fit against Trevor's body. He'd missed this give-and-take. It was the one thing Sage had always known how to do right, when he wanted to.

Shutting out all other thoughts, Jamie focused only on moving just so to bring them both right to the brink. A little push and they'd both come. Jamie took Trevor's mouth in a sloppy kiss and let go. Under him, Trevor pulsed and shook with release. It was a rush, more even than the orgasm itself. Jamie clung to Trevor until they'd both calmed down.

He slid off gracefully then grabbed the extra towel Trevor had brought out. Jamie worshipped Trevor's body with it, loving the way Trevor rested his head back and relaxed into it. Jamie quickly tidied himself as well and then curled up next to Trevor. His mind and body were both loose, free of the tension he'd brought with him earlier.

Jamie closed his eyes, thinking it would only be for a few minutes. The next thing he registered was Trevor waking him because it was time to go home.

CHAPTER TEN

AFTER A Friday night performance, Cian spent the rest of the holiday weekend with Eric, Nell, and Skye. The recital had gone off smoothly the weekend before, and now Cian was trying to enjoy the calm after the storm. On Saturday afternoon, they'd gone to Forest Park with the twins, who were now well-fed, tanked up on bedtime stories, and tucked under their blankets fast asleep. The adults stretched out in the living room to share the bottle of wine Cian had brought.

He only half paid attention to the conversation around him. His focus was off. Sunday, he'd scheduled a get-together with his students and their families to go over what came next. He still hadn't made up his mind, and he went back and forth on it nearly every day. Marta hadn't suggested pairing up once she'd established a new studio, but she also didn't know Cian had family—his partners—in Springfield. As far as she was aware, she and Cian were ending their business relationship permanently.

Eric noticed and nudged him to get his attention. *What's wrong with you tonight?*

Tired. Cian hadn't told them anything, and he wasn't sure he was ready. Certainly not when it involved such a big decision.

Talk to us, Nell urged.

Cian sighed. He might as well get it over with. He explained to them about the studio closing and looking for a new place and Marta's move to Springfield. It didn't escape him that the others exchanged a look when he mentioned that part.

What do you want to do? Skye asked. Everything about her was open, inviting. Cian had always thought she seemed mildly uncomfortable around him, but now he saw the warmth in her expression.

He examined his plate, feigning fascination with a small chip in the edge of the dish. He still didn't know, and he couldn't figure out why he was so hesitant to tell them what was really in his heart. He loved them so much, but what they had with each other wasn't what he wanted. He felt so selfish even thinking about it. They were a nesting group, and he loved coming to see them. But he wanted that for himself, too. His own nest, but still connected to them. It sounded awful in his head, as though he was rejecting them.

I don't know, he admitted. *I don't want to leave the city. Maybe I'm missing a chance to do something new here.*

Change is hard, Skye told him. She took his hand in hers and brought it to her lips. *We're here for you no matter what you choose.*

Cian sniffled. He hadn't realized how hard it would be to say goodbye to a place he'd come to love so much. Maybe that was as much the problem as his internal conflict about his chosen family. Everywhere he looked, he was surrounded by more love and affection than he knew what to do with. Losing any part of that hurt deeply. It brought him back to a time when he was a lonely, angry fourteen-year-old, moving to a strange country on his own. He'd always assumed he would have a family by now, and for whatever reason, this felt like a blow to his hopes.

Skye stood, and Cian looked up at her, then to Nell and Eric. They both nodded. Cian rose to his feet, and Skye kissed him. He let her touch soothe him, slow and soft and comforting. They'd never shared this kind of intimacy, and Cian was overcome with the tenderness of her touch. They broke apart, and Skye touched his cheek.

Go on, Eric instructed. *You both need to connect. We'll join you later, after dishes are done.*

Skye led Cian to the adults' bedroom. Cian closed the door, shutting out the rest of the world and leaving his troubles on the other side for the time being while he let Skye minister to him.

###

The students had the run of Cian's studio. There were no more classes now that the recital was over, and Marta had already cleared out a lot of her things during the week. Although Cian had sent a letter to the parents, and there was an announcement at the recital as well, he wanted to discuss the options with all the families at once. There was no better way to do so than an end-of-year pizza party.

While the children ran from room to room, messed with the CD player, and left paper plates in the waiting area between classrooms, the adults milled around making polite conversation. Cian checked in with the twins on their progress for the school talent show, which was coming up in a week or two. He'd promised he would go see them, since he didn't have to perform that weekend.

When everyone had settled down at last, Cian called them into the largest room. He'd set up some chairs for anyone who wouldn't be comfortable on the floor. Most of the students grouped themselves in small clusters toward the front, facing the floor-to-ceiling mirrors.

Cian waited for them to quiet down. He'd asked Skye to come with him so he could avoid having to attempt sign and speech simultaneously. He also hadn't wanted to put pressure on his father or Cadence to interpret for him in either direction. Now, he beckoned Skye and she stepped up beside him.

"This is Skye," he told the group. "She's going to help me out talking to you."

She conveyed what he'd said, and Cian was pleased to see they all greeted her silently. He spent a few minutes praising their skill at the recital and thanking them for the support over the previous three years. Then came the hard part. He glanced at Skye, and she nodded.

"First the bad news," he told them. "I don't know what I'm going to do for next year. I don't want to lose what we have. You've all come such a long way together, and I hope to see what we can do in the future." He took a deep breath. "But with the studio closing, I don't have a home right now. Some of you were Miss Marta's students, and I know you're losing her too. I hope to have a place by September, but there's a chance I'll have to take next year off."

There was a collective *awww* around the room. Cian hated letting them down, but in the previous month, he hadn't found a workable solution. It didn't help that he was still torn on whether or not he should move out to Springfield after all. He didn't know what was stopping him. It wasn't as though his performing schedule was so grueling he couldn't have made it back into Boston two weekends a month.

He held up a hand again to quiet the group. "On the bright side, we're going to do something fun this summer. I'm having my usual classes, but at the end, we're going to perform again. Some of you have been hoping we'll do something more public than our recital. A friend of mine is checking to see if where he performs might be available, and we'll have a real show on a big stage—not in a high school auditorium."

That produced a much happier reaction, and Cian relaxed. He still had a little over three months to figure out what he was going to do afterward, but at least he could give them something to look forward to.

Once they'd settled down again, he said, "If most of you come over the summer, we'll practice your recital dances and perform those again for a different audience. We're also going to do a dance-drama that everyone can be part of, even if you only come for a few classes. First, we'll need to pick a theme."

One of the boys blurted out, "Leprechauns!" and giggled.

Cian rolled his eyes, but he laughed. "Why is that the only thing anyone ever associates with the Irish? Well, that and Saint Patrick. C'mon, get creative!"

Cadence said, "How about history? Like something about how our families came here."

"Not a bad idea," Cian said, thinking about his troupe's new show and wondering if he could create some crossover. "Any others?"

They spent the next ten minutes or so throwing out ideas. At the end, Cian wrapped up the meeting and dismissed the families to clean up and go home. Once they were gone, he set to work on picking up the last of the trash and sweeping the floors.

Skye was waiting for him in the doorway after he put the broom back in the utility closet. He grabbed his bag, and she looped her arm through his on the way out. On the sidewalk outside the building, Cian stopped and turned around. The studio was the second floor, with a Papa Gino's and a Dunkin' Donuts below it. The set of stairs and the entrance was around the back. He wondered now if the restaurant patrons could hear all the stomping of the hard shoes or the taps in Marta's classes. He'd never given much thought to it before. No one had ever complained, so he assumed it must be well-insulated.

Where would he go in the fall? He'd come into this agreement with Marta accidentally, by way of a mutual friend. Cian wasn't well-connected in the dance world anymore and hadn't been since he left the competitive circuit. Even his first performance with his troupe had been born from a random idea at a holiday party for work.

He turned to Skye. Maybe it was better this way. He could close up shop, find a new job, and move. This could be a chance to start over, to be near his partners, to become fully integrated in their lives. So why did he still feel so uncomfortable with it?

You're thinking too hard, Skye told him. *Come on. Let's go home.*

Home. Cian swallowed and agreed, even while thinking "home" didn't feel like the right word to describe the house Skye shared with their other partners. Perhaps he needed to try harder. He took Skye's hand, and they walked to the parking garage without exchanging another word.

What a way to celebrate the holiday weekend. Jamie and Trevor were tangled together on the couch, Trevor moaning loudly as he mouthed his way down Jamie's chest. Jamie loved the sounds Trevor made during sex. It only occurred to him once or twice to wonder if he was as noisy with Andre or Marlie, or if they kept things quieter because there were so many of them—and a baby—in the house.

Trevor took Jamie between his lips, and Jamie let loose with a swear. As yet he hadn't tried to talk to Trevor about where they were going, but he hoped one hell of a blow job and whatever else Trevor was in the mood for might help loosen them both. He would be a lot more successful if he weren't in danger of coming from watching and feeling Trevor suck him. This was what he loved, the way Trevor put everything else out of his mind with one burning touch. There wasn't any pressure to think or talk or do a single thing other than go with it.

It only took a little more until Jamie gripped the couch cushion with one hand and Trevor's hair with the other as he came. Trevor pulled off and tugged himself rapidly until he finished. He collapsed onto Jamie, who loved the feel of his thick body so much it sent another pleasurable tremor through him. As much as Jamie loved having his hands all over Trevor, enjoyed having their mouths on each other, he wanted this even more. He relished feeling Trevor's weight on top of him, being fucked in this position, his whole body covered by Trevor's.

They lay there panting. Jamie ran a hand over Trevor's sweaty skin. He would never get tired of fondling his curves. A flash memory of Sage pinching Jamie's waist passed through his mind, and he flinched. He grunted as his now overstimulated dick throbbed painfully with the motion. Trevor opened his eyes and put a hand on Jamie's arm. He ran it up and down gently.

"You all right?"

"A little sensitive."

"Shit, sorry." Trevor adjusted, relieving some of the pressure.

Jamie was about to get up to bring them water from the fridge before round two. He was startled by the sound of the front door opening. There was no time to make themselves decent before Marlie walked into the room. She looked at them, rolled her eyes, and stood there with her hands on her hips.

"Get dressed," Marlie snapped. "Andre's on his way home."

"What?" Trevor pushed on Jamie until he climbed off. "Why is Andre coming home? I thought he was on a date with Nia."

"He was. He tried calling you, but obviously you didn't hear your phone. So he called me and asked me to check in on you."

"I—" Trevor started.

"Oh, hell no. You do not get to make any excuses whatsoever." Marlie stalked across the floor and swept up Jamie's clothes, throwing them in his lap. "Get dressed," she repeated.

"Can I at least clean up?" Jamie asked, shrinking back from Marlie's cold stare. Trevor had said she was okay with this, but it certainly didn't seem that way now.

She pointed to the bathroom. "I suggest you stay out of Andre's way when he gets home."

Trevor looked sideways at Jamie. "Probably a good idea to do what she says. Maybe you should go."

Jamie was annoyed by Trevor's sudden cool tone. He knew what they were doing wasn't the same kind of relationship Trevor had with the others, but he'd at least thought it meant more than brushing him off when one of them came home.

Trevor gathered his clothes and tossed them into a hamper outside the bathroom. Jamie heard the water running, and a few minutes later Trevor emerged in a bathrobe. He called to Jamie the bathroom was free, and Jamie ducked inside with his clothes. As he closed the door, he heard Andre's voice in the entryway followed by footsteps and a brief glimpse of him as he joined Trevor in the bedroom. Jamie noticed they left the door ajar, so he kept the bathroom door open a crack. It was rude, but he wanted to know what was so important he was being asked to leave.

"...come home to find you like this. Hell, you still smell like him."

"I thought you were okay with us seeing each other."

That confirmed what Jamie had believed too. He strained his ears to hear Andre's answer.

"I was. I am. I don't know!" Andre made a low, angry noise. "I'm not pissed off because you were with him, but I'm not sure it's a good idea."

There was silence and some shuffling, then Trevor said, "I know. It probably isn't. We were supposed to talk about it later, but Marlie came home." There was another pause. "If you're not upset about Jamie, then what is it?"

"It's Grams. She—" There was a muffled sound. "She's in the hospital, Trev. It's bad. We need to get up there tonight."

"Oh, God."

Jamie shut the door and flung his clothes back on, his heart shattering. He didn't know Joyce well, but if it hadn't been for her, he might be dead. The news banished all worries over what was going on between himself and Trevor. He stepped out into the hallway.

From inside the bedroom, he heard the distinct sounds of their intimacy. Not physical but emotional—the way Andre's words were shot through with pain and tears and the way Trevor made soft, soothing sounds. They were a couple, bonded and sharing their heartbreak in a way that didn't welcome anyone else in. They didn't seem to be aware of Jamie's presence in the hallway or even that he was still in the house at all. He swallowed a sigh. It made sense, the two of them needing each other now. He crept past, hoping to slip out the door without anyone noticing.

No such luck. Marlie cornered him and without a word dragged him into the kitchen. Jamie glanced back, giving himself a minute to wonder if Marlie could hear the others and if it bothered her that she was excluded too. She didn't seem upset. Not with them, anyway. If looks could kill, the one she was giving Jamie would have crucified him.

She leaned against the counter, arms crossed. "Explain, please."

"Uh…"

"How often has this been going on?"

"It's only been a few times since the night Trevor called you, I swear. We were supposed to talk about it tonight." Not only his cheeks but Jamie's whole head was hot.

"Good." Marlie's posture relaxed. "I'm sorry for being so harsh with you. We both told him he had to talk to you before it went any farther. Not for his sake but for yours. Trevor has a bad habit of picking the worst times to make decisions, and he tends to think with the wrong body parts. And he was about to do it again, from the sounds of it." She huffed and ticked items off on her fingers. "Orgasm, afterglow, Trevor springs shit on you. Yes?"

Despite the situation, Jamie almost laughed. It certainly sounded like Trevor. Realization hit, though, and he understood what Marlie meant.

"I didn't know he wanted to break things off."

"At least he talked to us about it, but I am sorry for you." Marlie rubbed her temples. "A damn conversation. That's all any of us ever ask, but he doesn't know how to do it. He never means to hurt anyone, and somehow, he thinks his way is going to soften the blow. He needs to get his shit together before our son is old enough to understand what goes on in this house."

"Is that why you're mad?" Jamie fidgeted, finally letting his gaze connect with Marlie's. "Because I'm the one taking care of Aidan?"

She bit her lip. "No. I'm sorry for taking it out on you back there. It's just that there's no owner's manual for this, you know? I've thought a hundred times about what the hell we're doing and whether I want to keep going. Then I remember that at least this way, I'm not dealing with Trevor all by myself, and neither is Andre. No matter what else, I honest to God do love him."

Jamie didn't know what to say. He'd never been in a relationship like the one Marlie was in with Trevor. He wasn't opposed to it, but Sage never would've agreed. In his mind, it was better to break up over and over or cheat on Jamie and then come back with empty promises. Or blame Jamie's imperfections, depending on his mood.

"I don't think I could give you any advice," Jamie said.

"I don't expect you to. It's ours to work through. I've talked a lot to Nia about it. She hasn't been in a monogamous relationship since high school, and she doesn't ever want to be. But I don't think it's fair for her to have to play relationship coach for Trevor and me just because we're new to all this." Marlie's sigh was resigned. "Just once, I'd like to have a conversation with her that doesn't revolve around the men."

"So...you're not mad at me?"

"Oh, Jay. No. I wouldn't even be mad at Trevor if he'd really wanted you to be part of our family, and neither would Andre. We all adore you. But Trevor was stupid about it." She stepped closer and put her hand on Jamie's shoulder. "I think he really does love you, you know. He needs each of us for different reasons. Under other circumstances..." She trailed off on a sigh and pulled Jamie in to wrap her arms around him. "I'm sorry you ended up in the middle of our problems."

Jamie sniffled into her shoulder, but he didn't cry. He and Trevor had never worked out what they were doing or what they were about, and that wasn't exclusively on Trevor. If Jamie had known what he needed or wanted, he could've told Trevor. Maybe he never would've come to him in the first place.

He pulled back. "I'm really sorry about Andre's grandmother. I overheard."

"Me too." It was Marlie's turn to choke up. "I don't know what's going to happen now. She hasn't been doing well for a while, and we were already in process of closing the clinic. I doubt she'll recover from this enough to keep going—if she recovers at all. We'll need to clear out everything and close down sooner than planned, but at least we're doing it without a lot of debt, thanks to last fall's fundraiser." She kissed Jamie's cheek. "We'll call you and the other guys, okay? For now, go home and get some rest. Can you tell Mack? I'm sure Trev will call Nate."

Jamie thought she might be wrong about that, but he nodded. "Yeah. If he's not home, I'll tell him first thing tomorrow."

"Thank you." Marlie passed by him and ascended the stairs.

After she'd disappeared into her darkened bedroom, Jamie turned around and walked out of the kitchen. He didn't hear anything more from Trevor and Andre's room, and neither of them had emerged. As he pulled his keys out of his pocket, Jamie hoped Mack wasn't home when he got there. After everything that had happened, all he wanted was to be alone to numb his confusing mix of emotions. It had been happening all too often these days, and he couldn't seem to get a handle on it.

In the morning, he promised himself as he slid into the driver's seat. *I'll start over in the morning.*

CHAPTER ELEVEN

THE CREEPY Crullers' next gig was in Pawtucket. Mack jokingly called Rhode Island the queer capital of New England and claimed there were almost more gay bars than residents. Judging from the app on Jamie's phone, he wasn't wrong. Their band was playing at a bar on a strip of road that had at least four others, all within walking distance of each other.

While they were unpacking everything from Mack's van, Jamie's mind wandered to Trevor. They'd "watched the game" only a few times after the first one before Trevor broke it off. Or Marlie did, really. Jamie wasn't sure. Was it a breakup if there was never a clearly defined relationship? They were still friends, as far as Jamie was aware, even if it was probably going to be awkward when they saw each other. And he was still caring for Aidan, which was about the only bright spot left in the whole thing.

He'd considered telling Mack what happened, but it wasn't like there was anything Mack could do. There was no point in sharing something that had begun and ended before they'd even figured out what it was they were doing. Mack would probably have considered it none of his business anyway. It wasn't as though he and Jamie ever had long conversations about their relationships. Mack had kept his comments about Sage minimal, limiting it to a once per week reminder that Sage was a dickhead. Which Jamie already knew, but the pull of being with Sage had always been overpowering until he'd gone too far.

Jamie had been thinking about sharing his other secret with Trevor before they ended their whatever it was. Not the one about Sage; Trevor knew about him. And not the one about his few years on the web series, which wasn't much of a secret. Trevor probably wouldn't judge him—he never had about Sage—but Jamie didn't want to answer a lot of questions. No, he thought about sharing what he kept under his bed. Not even Mack knew he still did it, and Nate simply referred to Jamie as having "weird food issues." It stung a bit, but Nate wasn't always tactful at the best of times. Jamie couldn't imagine what he'd say if he knew the truth.

Except now he and Trevor weren't anything extra to each other, and everything was still so raw from Andre's grandmother being in the hospital. She'd been discharged to a rehabilitation facility, but as much as everyone tiptoed around it, they were all aware it was a matter of time. She wasn't doing as well as they'd hoped. Jamie thought it might be better not to talk to Trevor about anything but Aidan for a while until everything settled down. They all needed their space, and the best thing Jamie could do was be there in case any of them needed something.

Thinking it over now distracted him from what he was supposed to be doing with the equipment, and he nearly dropped one of the speakers. Mack huffed at him on the way past. Jamie focused his attention and brought it inside.

When they returned to the van, Mack stopped him. "What's up with you?"

"Nothing." Jamie turned away from him, but Mack put a hand on his shoulder.

"It's not nothing. You've been acting like your head's in outer space all day. You gonna be on top of shit tonight?"

Jamie scoffed. "Like it matters," he muttered.

Mack turned angry. "Hey. I don't know what your problem is, but maybe you could get over it before we play. Unless you have something else to say to me?"

"What, like about how we've been at this for y-years and-and are only now g-good enough to play at a few places where someone h-happens to...happens to...happens..." Jamie made a frustrated noise. He was losing his cool and tripping over his words. He had to calm down. He signed it, but he knew Mack wouldn't understand him. Jamie tried again. "Where someone h-happens to remember m-my dick?"

Mack looked like Jamie had hit him. He stumbled back a couple of paces. "Are you saying you don't want to do this anymore?"

Did he? Jamie hadn't thought about it much, but he supposed maybe he didn't. He'd always loved playing—it was what got him through the loneliness of being constantly on the move. It was how he made it through the last couple years of high school when Brandon's parents wouldn't let him drop out. It was how he survived after leaving the web series and through all the years of Sage being in and out of his life.

Now, faced with Mack's anger, he wasn't sure anymore. It didn't seem important the way it once had. Like everything else lately, it had lost its shine. Ever since things had ended with Trevor, he'd lost the beat. He couldn't seem to bring himself out of this low.

"I d-don't...I don't..." he said. "I don't know."

Mack frowned and looked Jamie over. "I haven't seen you this bad since—wait. That asshole isn't back, is he? I swear to all that's holy, Jamie, if he shows up at our apartment, I am going to do something we'll all regret."

"No." Jamie let out a shaky breath. What Mack didn't know about Sage's voicemails wouldn't hurt him. Neither would keeping him in the dark about Trevor. He chose his words carefully and spoke more slowly so he could get it out. "It's not Sage. I'm...I'm just a little down, okay? It's n-nothing."

"Is it about Andre's grandmother?"

"Maybe." Jamie felt guilty using her as an excuse, but it might get Mack off the scent for a while.

"Are you eating enough?" Mack said it quietly, leaning in so only Jamie would hear him.

"Yeah." Jamie wasn't going to admit he was probably not eating the right things, but at least it was something. He'd gone back to not being able to have dinner with the others, and obviously Mack had noticed.

"I have water in the van. At least get that in you before the show, okay? I'm worried about you."

"I swear, I'm fine." And he was, for now. His pulse had finally slowed.

Mack nodded and squeezed Jamie's shoulder. After a pause, he said, "Maybe you need to get laid?"

"Jesus. That's your answer for everything, isn't it?" Jamie finally cracked a smile.

"Hell, yeah. Seriously, though. You want me to talk to Amelia? She knows people. I'm a realist. I know a new guy won't solve your problems. But maybe just some fun, huh?"

"I can get dates on my own." At Mack's incredulous look, Jamie said, "Fine, whatever. Ask her."

"Good. You ready for this?"

"Any time."

Jamie headed back to the van, and Mack went inside. As he pulled parts of the drum kit out, Jamie thought about the conversation. Mack was right that it wouldn't solve anything. Jamie didn't need to meet someone who was going to use him or string him along or be confused. Mack wasn't entirely wrong, though. Jamie had to get out of his repetitive thoughts. Anything had to be better than feeling miserable over either Sage or Trevor. He could try, at least. Anyone Amelia had in mind had to be better than his unsuccessful attempts over the last several months.

Now wasn't the time to deal with it. Jamie turned his attention back to unloading the van. Tonight, he would show Mack that his head was still in the game. Brandon had texted to say he was going to be there to watch Gemma, and Andre and Nia were supposed to show up as well. Apparently, Nia was a longtime fan. For their sake, Jamie could set aside his worries.

Brooding was hardly the best mood for Cian's thirtieth birthday. For no good reason, he felt like he was now past wanting to sit in a crowded bar to watch a terrible cover band play. Truthfully, he didn't know whether they were bad or not. He didn't enjoy keeping his hearing aids in for this sort of thing. They might have been amazing for all he knew, but he was only going to hear them in a vague, filtered sort of way.

Cian sipped his drink and kept his eyes on the stage. He should be annoyed with Brandon for bringing him out to see this specific band—what had he been thinking? Cian was aware it was partly about supporting Gemma, since she was playing keyboard, but that wasn't the whole story. Brandon could've done that on his own or brought a different friend. It wasn't as though they'd needed to go out right on Cian's birthday or anything. Brandon had chosen to bring Cian here for a reason, in the same way Cian suspected he'd brought Jamie to watch him dance for a reason. Brandon wanted two of the people closest to him to get along, but Cian didn't see it happening any time soon.

He watched the band set up, experimenting with their equipment. Jamie was talking to the band's front man—Mack, Cian thought—about something. He was animated and had a tendency to talk with his hands even when he wasn't signing. The biggest problem Cian saw with Jamie was how he was so damn hot. He didn't seem to want anything to do with Cian in person, but he certainly was fun to watch from a distance.

Tonight, Jamie had on ripped, faded jeans and a loose black A-shirt with a silver design on the front. They were close enough to the stage that Cian could tell he'd painted his nails a silvery-black, and he'd applied eyeliner around his gorgeous dark eyes. His myriad piercings caught the light and glinted as he moved. His lips, perfectly pink and plump, glistened with something. Not gloss; probably just some kind of lip balm. Cian's breath caught; staring at Jamie had awakened more than mere appreciation for the eye candy. He wanted to know what was underneath his stage persona.

Up on the stage, Jamie looked flustered. He made a motion, but Mack didn't seem to understand. It only made Jamie more agitated. Cian frowned, wondering what they were talking about. He looked more closely and saw that Jamie was signing, but Mack apparently didn't know enough to catch what Jamie needed. Cian wondered why Jamie didn't just tell him.

When Cian caught the phrase *where someone happens to remember my dick*, he jolted. It made him blush even though it wasn't directed at him—as far as he knew, Jamie was still blissfully unaware of his presence. Still, it made him curious. Jamie seemed to have managed to resume speaking, and he and Mack were less heated now. Cian turned to Brandon, who was frowning.

What in the world was that all about, do you think? Brandon asked.

No idea. Although Cian had caught the remark about Jamie's web series, the rest of the context was lost on him. It probably wasn't about him directly, but the possibility rankled. For good measure, he added, *Why would I care?*

Brandon scowled. *I know you two have some weird thing between you, but you need to stop.*

Cian sighed. Thirty was probably too damn old to hang on to

these things. There wasn't some big rivalry or anything, as though he and Jamie were mortal enemies. They didn't even dislike each other. It was more like Jamie kept avoiding him, slipping away before they could get to mutual tolerance, let alone friendship level. God knew, Cian had tried. He'd also tried leaving Jamie the hell alone, which didn't seem to have worked any better.

There's nothing wrong.

I hope not, Brandon replied, but it was evident in his expression that he didn't quite believe Cian. *You think I'm setting you up. I'm not. I was the first time. Not now. You're both going to be at our wedding. You have to get along. Don't make things difficult.* He wasn't showing anger, but Cian noted the set of his jaw. Brandon was making himself clear.

Okay, okay. Cian didn't have any problem with that at all, as long as Jamie didn't.

The band had finished setting up, and someone from the bar introduced them. Cian settled in, relaxed and feeling more calm than he had before. They began their set, and to Cian's surprise, there was an interpreter. He hadn't realized they'd added that element. Brandon nudged him and grinned. Cian felt the beat and fell into the rhythm. Gemma was good fun on stage, and she and the bassist, Cassie, played off each other well. His gaze strayed from the interpreter to Mack's antics to Jamie, and he stopped dead; he couldn't look away.

Jamie was beautiful like that, caught up in the music and focused solely on his part in the complex interplay between himself and the rest of the band. Mack stopped singing and moved aside so everyone could see Jamie while he soloed, giving Cian a much better view. He had never watched Jamie play before, but it was one of the most intense things Cian had ever seen. All his motions were graceful, like a dance. The only way Cian could describe it was that Jamie's drumsticks were an extension of his soul.

Cian's insides vibrated in time with the beat, with the pure, sensual bliss and agony of it. Watching Jamie was physically and emotionally satisfying, as though somehow he was providing an outlet for all the things that couldn't be spoken. Words would never be enough for the depth of feeling Jamie poured into his solo, evident in his body language. Cian had no idea how a drummer could accomplish such a thing, but somehow, Jamie had managed it.

Mack resumed the vocals, and they brought the song to a conclusion. Cian felt the energy of the crowd around him going wild for them, and he realized he was breathing hard and fast as though he'd been the one playing. He was also turned on, but not so much it was unpleasant. Sure, he found Jamie attractive, but something in him was drawn to the performance Jamie had just given.

Cian looked up at the stage again, and his eyes met Jamie's. For a moment, they stared, and then Jamie looked away. Cian's ears went hot. He turned his attention back to his drink, and Brandon nudged him.

Having fun?

Sure, yeah, Cian answered, trying to appear casual under Brandon's scrutiny. *They look like they're enjoying themselves up there.*

They must have done really well, Brandon signed. *I never saw this excited a crowd.* He laughed. *Jamie says people think they sound awful.* He made a disgusted face and laughed again. *Are they?*

I don't know. Don't have my hearing aids. They have good energy.

Brandon acknowledged him. *Gemma said they have some new songs.*

Grateful that Gemma was now a distraction from his complicated feelings about Jamie, Cian signed, *Was interpreter her idea?*

Brandon looked at him like he'd grown another head. *Haven't you seen them before? They always have one.*

No, Cian hadn't realized. He wanted to say more about it, but the Creepy Crullers had started a new song. They left off their conversation to watch. Cian's birthday wasn't turning out so bad after all.

When the Creepy Crullers finished their second song, Gemma beckoned to Mack. She said something into his ear, and Mack nodded. He looked over his shoulder at Jamie, gave a tiny shrug, and turned back to the mic.

"Our next song is dedicated to a friend of Gemma's." He waved a hand in her direction. "Sounds like he's celebrating three decades on this planet tonight."

While their interpreter signed what Mack had just said, Jamie frowned and craned his neck to see around his bandmates. Of course. He should've known. Jamie had spotted Cian sitting with Brandon at a table near the stage, but he hadn't given it much thought. Now he watched as Cian slid down in his seat, hands folded on top of his head, looking like he wished he were anywhere else right then.

Mack continued, "This is one of our new songs. It's a little about love and a little about luck. We hope you enjoy it, and happy birthday, Cian!"

As soon as the interpreter had finished signing all that, Jamie caught Cian's eye again. Without thinking, he signed, *You okay?*

Cian looked startled for a moment, but then he relaxed. *Yes. Embarrassed.* He buried his face in his hands, but then he looked up and smiled. *Good luck.*

It was Jamie's turn for surprise, but he didn't have time to consider it before Mack motioned impatiently at him. Recovering, Jamie gave them the beat and shifted all his attention to playing. The new song was one of their best yet, Jamie thought. It had a throwback folk punk feel to it, and Mack's lyrics were brilliant. He sang with humor about all the wrong ways to find love, and then one day stumbling on it by accident. It was by far Jamie's favorite, and it put him back into his love for playing.

At the end, the crowd went wild. They were, on average, an older mix than Jamie was used to, and chances were good that many of them were familiar with the style Mack emulated for the song. Jamie had never seen anyone enjoy their band this much. He couldn't help the rush of elation, the high of playing a good set for a receptive audience.

Mack looked back at him again, and Jamie grinned. It looked like it was going to be a great night after all. He was about to throw himself wholeheartedly into the rest of the set when his gaze met Cian's for the third time that night. There was something in his expression that pulled Jamie in, and he couldn't look away. Warmth, appreciation, and a touch of gentle humor. Cian was expressive and open in a way that both confused and intrigued Jamie.

In front of Jamie's face, Mack snapped his fingers. "Pay attention!" he hissed.

Jamie shook himself, and the break in his concentration was enough to bring back all the gnawing guilt he'd lived with since leaving Sage. He shouldn't be thinking at all about someone like Cian; it would only end the same way as everything else. Mack's lyrics were a little off, he thought. Jamie had already looked in every wrong place to pack the gaping wound in his soul, and none of them were funny. There wasn't any luck to be had for someone like him, not even in the arms of a friend. He would always end up hurt—or worse, destined for the same kind of life his mother had.

He would never let that happen. Time to throw himself fully into the music. Judging by the response of the crowd, they were headed down the right path. That might have been a first for Jamie, and he wasn't going to throw it away. Tomorrow, he would finally delete Sage's number from his phone. Then he would make damn sure Trevor knew whatever sort-of thing they had wasn't just over because Marlie called the shots. After that, no more. He was done, and he would tell Mack and Amelia and anyone else to stay off his back about it. He wouldn't live from boyfriend to boyfriend, always hoping the next one would save him from himself. He could do that on his own just fine.

Mack pointed to him, and Jamie poured all his energy into the rhythm. Tomorrow, he could start over. Again.

CHAPTER TWELVE

SO MUCH for everyone leaving Jamie alone; he had a date. He should've told Mack no at any stage of the process. He'd meant to after the gig in Pawtucket. Only he'd forgotten to say something the next morning, and then he'd gotten sidetracked because Sage had called a bunch more times and sent him a goddamn email. Correction—three emails. In a row.

The first thing Jamie had done, which was how he forgot to say something to Mack in the first place, was to change his phone number. He'd managed to call or text everyone with the new one. Then, with his gut churning and heart pounding, he'd deleted Sage's contact information from everywhere. Blocked him on social media, not that Sage had tried to get to him that way—yet. All except for the band's email. Jamie was lucky he'd checked the business address before Mack did or Jamie would've gotten an earful. Well, as much of one as Mack ever gave, anyway.

He'd sent it to spam and emptied that folder, but now he would have to keep on top of it so Mack wouldn't know. Afterward, Jamie's resolve not to touch what was left under his bed crumbled. There wasn't much there. Jamie spent the rest of that morning pacing and trying to talk himself out of replacing it. He'd been so good since Pawtucket.

During the long months after Sage, and before Trevor, he'd needed something—anything—to put Sage out of his mind. For two months after they broke up, even with the piercing Sage had said was a deal-breaker, Jamie had almost called him dozens of times. He'd wanted warm arms and a body pressed up against his and the feel of another man's mouth on him. There were endless, restless nights of sitting with the phone in his hand, shaking all over, willing himself not to call. They all ended the same way, with Jamie filling the hole by eating the foods he'd stashed under his bed and then sobbing from pain and embarrassment. The stomachache was easier to manage than the loneliness and hurt over Sage.

Jamie had tried other ways of taking his mind off Sage, including dipping his toes back into the dating pool. He'd decided before Trevor, and affirmed it afterward, that his luck had run out—or maybe never started—when it came to finding someone else. That had frustrated Jamie. He was easy to please and didn't have much of a type; he pretty much just liked men. He'd known he liked boys from the time he was nine and discovered Mama's boyfriend-of-the-moment had an extensive collection of books. They were photographs of sex positions, which Jamie hadn't quite put together, but he knew he was fascinated by the men in them. He'd liked looking at the pictures until Mama caught him at it and made sure those books were somewhere he couldn't find after that. As humiliated as he'd been, it didn't stop him three years later from letting a neighbor boy put a hand down his swim trunks at Boyfriend Number Four's—or was it Five's?—apartment complex.

Over the many years he and Sage had been on-and-off, he'd done his share of dating in between. He'd had a couple memorable hook-ups he'd thought were fantastic and might lead to more. He wouldn't have minded seeing either of those guys again. But the first one ghosted him, and the second sent him a text saying they "wanted different things." Jamie didn't see how that could possibly be true, given how they'd never discussed what they wanted aside from *oh, yeah, right there* or *make me come*. It hadn't mattered much anyway; when it hadn't worked out, he'd been back with Sage within days each time.

After a different breakup with Sage, and following Mr. We-Want-Different-Things, Jamie met up with a gorgeous, sweet femme in the same coffee shop where Nate worked, and from the first minute Jamie could tell the guy wanted someone more like Mack. Jamie never tried to butch himself up, but it was obvious that's what the man had been looking for when he saw on Jamie's profile he was in a rock band. It had been a nice first, and last, date, but at least Jamie had a new friend out of the deal.

There was also the guy who immediately jumped to "I'd like to piss on you" and the one who'd gotten drunk, tried to grope Jamie, and then puked out the open door of the Lyft ride Jamie had called for him. Or the one who had called six times the day after their date even though Jamie had told him he wasn't interested before parting. Or the nervous-as-hell boy—all of fifteen—who had really only wanted someone to talk to. Jamie had referred him to the Lighthouse, but he gave the kid his number if he needed someone who understood.

The worst was probably from a few months back, his final attempt before Trevor. The man had taken him to a high-end restaurant. Then he'd spent half their date on the phone with some kind of investors, after which he'd treated the possibility of having sex like he was closing a deal on Wall Street. The final straw, not that Jamie had needed one by that point, was when the man called his husband to tell him he was "working late on a big project, but I'll tell you all the juicy details later," followed by a predatory wink. Jamie had slammed some money on the table for his part of dinner and dashed out the door without looking back. The asshat sent him a dick pic— probably not even his own—ten minutes later, captioned with, "Are you sure?" Yes. Yes, he was one hundred percent sure, and he told the guy as much before making sure he couldn't contact Jamie again.

So at the Creepy Crullers' last gig, he'd vowed not to repeat his old patterns after a breakup. Only now he had this date he'd let Amelia score. He'd tried to beg off, but Mack seemed convinced he should go. Jamie could let the man down politely; he never had to see him again after tonight. It would get him out of the house, at least. Maybe he would have a nice time and get his mind off his other worries. It was only one evening. He sounded all right, anyway. Interestingly, he was deaf and wanted someone who knew ASL. Mack said Amelia told him the man was warm, sexy, open-minded, and looking for a relationship that might include other partners. Someone like that would understand when Jamie said he'd only gone because of his friends.

While he was getting ready, Jamie's mind strayed to Sage yet again. Angry at himself for letting those thoughts in, he refocused his attention. Unfortunately, none of the other things that popped into his head were any more appropriate. Trevor, his mother and how serious things seemed to be getting with Bruce, what he was going to eat for dinner, seeing Cian at the bar in Pawtucket. The last one made him want to throw something. He and Cian kept running into each other. That wasn't completely random, since he was Brandon's friend, but Jamie didn't have to like the situation.

Jamie forced himself to think about the man he was meeting instead. He didn't even know the guy's name. Mack wasn't great with those details. He'd said something like Keith or Kevin, but he wasn't sure. With the exception of Investment Guy, Jamie tried not to meet dates in restaurants. It always meant navigating around how to eat socially. Jamie had developed a few tricks for places he knew well or when he was out with friends. If he had to go somewhere new, it helped if their menu was online and he could make a choice ahead of time. Now he had a date he'd never met in a restaurant he'd never been to, without the cushion of an online menu. His stomach was in knots thinking about it.

An hour later, he stood outside a nice little Italian place, about to meet Amelia's "friend of a friend." After hedging until he was five minutes late, Jamie opened the door. Surely he could find something acceptable to eat. He didn't know anything about his date, but maybe Jamie would get lucky and he'd be a little older, like Izzy. Those guys sometimes liked playing gentleman and ordering for two. It didn't solve the problem of actually eating the food, but at least he wouldn't have to deal with the sweating, shaking anxiety of picking a dish.

At the hostess station inside the restaurant, Jamie explained to the woman he was looking for someone and what the situation was. It took a few minutes for him to finally learn from her that his date had already arrived. She led him through the room and right to a table in the back. When the man seated there looked up, Jamie's first reaction was probably not the most friendly. In fairness, he was nervous and stressed, and this was not at all what he'd been expecting.

At a loss for anything to say to Cian—not Keith or Kevin—Jamie just stood there for about fifteen awkward seconds. At last he found his voice. "You!" he exclaimed.

A friend of a friend. That's who Cian was supposed to meet. Jomari had said his name was Jay or Jason. Not someone Jomari knew personally. Someone in the orchestra with Jomari knew him.

Turning thirty had shifted something in Cian's brain. The desire to make his own nest, just like Nell and Skye and Eric, loomed large. He knew what his lovers would say, that he belonged with them. They'd left that door open a hundred and one times already. But they were a family unit, had been since before he came back to Boston. He couldn't say what was blocking him from accepting other than that something in him told him he would always feel like a guest in their home. The physical distance between them was enough by itself to create a barrier.

Cian had gotten Brandon and Gemma off his back about the wedding—he didn't need a date for that, and he'd told them as much. But he wanted to try again to meet an open-minded man or woman interested in something long-term. He knew from experience that was a lot harder than it sounded in his head. He supposed that was his decision made, then, on whether he was moving out of the city.

First, he'd had to talk to Nell, Skye, and Eric. One emotional conversation about it later, he had their full blessing. Then he had to seek ways to connect with people who might be all right with dating a polyamorous, bisexual man. So far, Cian had tried speed dating, a website, and an app. Now he was resorting to blind dates because the rest had been one frustration after another. He could have simply found someone at Grand Slam to go home with, figure out if they were compatible, but he didn't care for the idea. His internal conflict over dating at all had reached combustion point.

He didn't regret allowing his fiddler, Jomari, to set him up. Jomari's other job as an orchestral violinist had him in contact with plenty of the types of people Cian generally liked. Supposedly this friend-of-a-friend was also a musician. He had not too long ago ended a relationship, which should have been a red flag for Cian. However, he trusted Jomari's judgment, even if he didn't know the go-between.

He'd asked Jomari if he knew someone deaf. It wasn't as though dating someone hearing was a deal-breaker, but having to teach them how to communicate was not on Cian's list of priorities. After his last two dates, he'd decided he should put "fluent in ASL" at the top of his list. Jomari had assured him that though his date was hearing, he was indeed quite capable of signing. Cian wondered if he was an interpreter, like Skye. Jomari had also said the man was attractive and open to poly relationships, which was certainly a plus.

The hostess seated him, and when the server came by, he asked only for water. He told her he was waiting for his date. The person was late, and Cian was already annoyed. Whoever it was needed to be really terrific to make up for the lack of punctuality.

Cian had a good vantage point to see people coming in. Not a minute later, the door opened and a short, slim man walked in. Cian nearly groaned. He hoped his date showed up soon to distract him from having to sit in the same restaurant with Jamie. Every time they met, Cian's interest in him grew, right along with Jamie's wariness. He was definitely off-limits, but it did not help that he was so attractive.

Tonight, Jamie looked good. Not ordinary, out-for-a-night-with-friends good. No, he looked positively edible. Slim-fit black Henley with the buttons undone and a pair of blue jeans with a wide white belt. Cian saw Jamie's gold necklace peeking out of the shirt. He had on a pair of black-and-white checked shoes, and he'd tamed his spiky hair. And of course, all those piercings that always made Cian long to know exactly where else and how many he had.

Cian was nearly drooling, and it pissed him off. He was there to meet his date, not dwell on his friend's hot cousin who was probably the last person on earth he should've been thinking about anyway. Jamie clearly wasn't into him. How could one person have so much power over him? Jamie made Cian's blood hot, whether out of annoyance or lust didn't matter. Cian had to admit he liked it. He only wished Jamie would show some of that fire himself. He was always so withdrawn, it made Cian want to do something to ignite him. He wanted to see more of that raw passion Jamie'd had the night he played in Pawtucket.

Jamie spoke to the hostess, and Cian kept his eyes on them. He should've been looking out for his date, but he was too busy watching Jamie's quick, graceful motion. He'd have been a good dancer. It was probably what helped him be successful on-screen. He never looked like he was simply *fucking*. There was a fluidness and an underlying air of total devotion to his partners. What he'd done really had been art. Cian wanted to smack himself for thinking about what Jamie looked like during an artificially constructed sex scene.

While pondering it, Cian had been distracted long enough to miss when Jamie disappeared from the host's station. The next thing he knew, the hostess tapped him lightly on the shoulder. He looked up to respond to her and found himself staring right into Jamie's dark eyes. They looked at each other, speechless, for so long that the hostess patted Jamie on the arm and walked away.

"You!" Jamie said. No pretense, no hiding—just what sounded like unadulterated loathing.

I could say same, Cian signed. He already knew Jamie could sign, so he didn't feel bad at all about not speaking. What did upset him was that this was beyond the cool indifference Jamie had expressed before. Cian couldn't imagine what he'd done to deserve the full force of Jamie's ire.

Jamie's face twisted into a deep scowl. "I can't believe this." He didn't seem to be talking to Cian at that point, so Cian turned away even though Jamie continued speaking. Even with his hearing aids in, Cian usually only caught about three-quarters of what people said unless the room was quiet and he focused on them. That made it a lot easier to ignore Jamie.

That was it. Cian was not ever asking for his friends' help again. He could only assume Jomari had never met Jamie or he would not have agreed to let whatever friend they had in common arrange this. Or maybe he had and this was his way of playing some kind of joke. Cian might not talk to Jomari for a week after this little stunt.

Cian finally looked back up at Jamie, who was no longer saying anything. *I'm not interested.*

"That makes two of us." Jamie crossed his arms.

"Why are you still here, then?" Cian demanded out loud. "I was sitting at this table first. Get your own or go away, hopefully to some other restaurant."

Jamie glared at him. "Who says I want to—want to st-stay, anyway?" His cheeks reddened.

Cian frowned at him and signed a not-so-polite suggestion to leave, along with slipping in a bit of snark about Jamie being hearing. Jamie's face went from scowling to shock to enraged in under five seconds. He responded by signing back a string of rude things. Cian was about to respond in kind, but then two things struck him. First, Jamie knew a hell of a lot of really good insults. Second, Cian realized Jamie wasn't talking about him. He was ranting about their mutual friends and their lack of respect. Now that, Cian could get behind. Jamie's distress made more sense now.

They're shipping us, he said.

Jamie paused, mid-name-calling. *What?*

Our friends, Cian answered. *They're shipping us. Pairing us up. Like fan fiction?*

Jamie played with the piercing in his lip, and Cian wanted to tell him to stop it. God, it was sexy. After a minute, Jamie signed, *They're assholes. I'm sorry. I can't do this. It won't work.* For an instant, he looked regretful, as though he really meant it when he said he was sorry. Then he turned around and walked away.

Cian sat back in his chair, staring after him. So there *was* a bit of fire in him, but it had burned out as quickly as it had come. He wouldn't even sit at the table and pretend to have a nice dinner before saying it wouldn't work. Why not? He thought back to what Jomari had said about him, and that made it all the more unbearable. Jamie was indeed attractive, and it wasn't surprising he was open-minded, given his work on the web series. So what was it about Cian that made him shut down so fast?

It wasn't too late. There wasn't any reason not to make the best of their night. Cian rushed to leave money on the table for the drink he'd had while he waited. As soon as he'd paid, he stood and hurried after Jamie, hoping to catch him and ask him to stay. He wasn't fast enough. By the time he reached the door, he'd lost track of Jamie.

Frustrated, Cian stood there for a few minutes next to a pair of men who had come in and were waiting at the host's station. Out of the corner of his eye, Cian caught one of them signing *blind date* and saw the other introduce himself as Keith. Apparently, they were in a similar boat to Cian, and they had his sympathy. He hoped it worked out better for them than it had for him.

CHAPTER THIRTEEN

JAMIE STORMED to the front of the restaurant. He shoved his way past two men, overhearing one of them say he was meeting a blind date and introducing himself to the host as Jayden. The other responded that he was too. Maybe they were meeting each other. Good for them. Jamie was almost too distracted to be mildly interested that their conversation switched to ASL. He dismissed it; he didn't really care who they were or what they were up to or whether they thought he was rude for pushing his way through.

He could've stayed. Maybe he should have, just to see what would happen. Now he was angry, but he didn't know who to be more upset with, himself or his friends. It had been wrong to agree to this date. It wasn't going to get his mind off Sage or Trevor, and they weren't necessarily the problem anyway. The real threat, as far as Jamie was concerned, was that Cian was someone he could be with. Not the nameless, faceless date he was supposed to have had and rejected.

Everything Mack had said Amelia told him before the date were all good reasons why it should've been right. And therein was the problem. Cian was too perfect. The same way Sage had been too perfect and Trevor was too perfect. Jamie was always going to end up heartbroken. It was easier to accept a dozen dates with men he didn't want to love than one date with someone he did. This was going to be a date with a man he could let down gently. Running out on Cian was a perfectly reasonable thing to do because the alternative was more than Jamie was ready for.

He sat in his car, taking slow, deep breaths. Amelia couldn't possibly have known her friend was setting him up with Cian, right? She had no idea Jamie's feelings about Cian were a horrible mix between desperately trying to avoid him and wanting to get him naked and see what kinds of moves he had off stage. Maybe that made Jamie a terrible person; he didn't know.

He could blame Mack, who should've vetted the date Amelia picked. Mack was full of pearls of wisdom, but he was utterly clueless about matters of the heart. Not that Jamie was a hopeless romantic, but he couldn't think of anything less likely to work out than setting him up with a man who had the power to expose all the things he kept carefully tucked away about himself. He'd already nearly done it once with his accusations about Jamie's work on the web series. The only thing worse would've been setting him up with a man who was in it for a fact-checking mission on the actual size of Jamie's cock. Or maybe not, come to think of it. That still might've been better.

There was no one to blame, but Jamie was still upset. He gripped the steering wheel. He needed something. This strip of road had several fast food places and a Walmart with a grocery center—advantages to having a date in a slightly less built-up area. Any of those would do. No one would question it, and if they did, he could say he was getting dinner for friends or hosting a party.

He pulled into the parking lot of the Walmart. Fast food wasn't one of the things he ever ate compulsively, but the store would have anything he wanted. He emerged from his car, shaking from the combination of rage, anxiety, and a low-level shame from knowing what he was doing.

Jamie knew exactly what he wanted. It was the same thing he always bought—the kinds of foods the rich kids had in their lunches when he was growing up. He'd been lucky if he got butter on his bread. He'd always had to bring his own lunch because half the time, they weren't legal residents of the school district and couldn't get free lunch. On really good days, he brought a slice of American cheese because they'd gotten a donation. Now and again, they had stuff from the food cupboard, but a lot of the time, Jamie didn't have more than a few crackers. The other kids got granola bars and little bags of chips and Jell-O in cups, with their sandwiches full of bologna or Swiss cheese or real peanut butter and jelly.

His favorite were the Goldfish crackers. Once, when he was about nine, a girl had brought a whole bag and offered them to everyone at her table. Jamie had taken a handful, and the girl scolded him for having too many. He'd shoved them all in his mouth at once so he wouldn't have to give them back.

That's what he went for first this time. He'd only taken a basket. If he took a cart, he might try to bring home more than he could safely stash under his bed. He threw two cartons into his basket. As he headed for the next aisle, he stopped dead in his tracks. His heart raced.

There, entering an aisle two before the one Jamie wanted, were Izzy and Nate. He'd forgotten that Izzy worked in this part of the city now. They were laughing, playfully nudging each other as Nate steered the cart. Their happiness made Jamie irritable. They were probably picking up a few things before going to Izzy's apartment. Together. To do all the happy-couple things Jamie wanted to do. Meanwhile, he was still reeling from the shock of being set up with Cian.

Jamie ducked into an aisle to avoid running into them. He tried to fake an interest in the powdered coffee creamers just in case they headed down his aisle. The sheer volume of single-serving coffee pods was fascinating enough to keep his attention while he waited. He caught the sound of laughter and held his breath.

"Oh, hey, Jamie!" That was Nate.

Jamie let out his breath and turned slowly, his hands now so clammy his grip slipped on the handle of the basket. "Hey, guys. What's up?"

"Just getting some stuff for dinner. Whatcha got?" Nate peered into Jamie's basket. "Oh, my G—gosh. Goldfish crackers! I haven't had those since, like, middle school."

"And you're not having them now," Izzy said, chuckling.

"Why not?"

"They're not kosher."

The two of them were so wrapped up in their discussion about whether or not Nate should still be allowed to eat the crackers that Jamie considered slipping away and hiding until they left. He was stopped by Nate being nosy, as usual.

"I thought you had a date," he said.

"We decided it wasn't going to work out." That was as polite as Jamie felt he could be under the circumstances.

The desire to numb his anger and embarrassment had begun to fade with his friends there, though it was still at a low level in the background. Nate was intrusive but oblivious. Izzy, on the other hand, was looking at Jamie's basket, his brows drawn together in a slight frown. Jamie could tell he was putting two and two together, but so far, he hadn't managed the right answer. It was only a matter of time before he arrived, likely at the wrong conclusion. He would get pretty close, though. Jamie caught his eye and shook his head. Izzy gave him a curt nod in return.

"We should go," Izzy said to Nate. "I'm really hungry." He made an exaggerated wink, which caused Jamie to finally laugh and Nate to grin lecherously.

"Sounds good. Later, Jamie."

They took off up the aisle, and Jamie breathed easier. He looked at the crackers in his basket. They would be enough for tonight, if he still needed them when he got home. The upset from earlier was leveling off already. Maybe he could will himself not to do this again, to simply go home and watch a movie instead. He could put the crackers back and leave. The trouble was, deep down, he was fully aware that even if he stopped himself this one time, it was only delaying the inevitable. He would do it again another night, sometime when he didn't have his friends nearby. Hell, he'd even done it with them in the apartment when he was sure they wouldn't know.

He left the crackers in the basket. A safety net, that was all. He didn't really need them for now, but at least they would be there if he changed his mind. He carried them to the front of the store, pretending this was the last time but knowing it wasn't.

An hour after leaving the restaurant, Cian arrived back at home in a foul mood. He spent some time angrily washing the few dishes he'd left in the sink, but it wasn't doing anything to calm him down. He wasn't angry with Jamie at all—disappointed, maybe, but not mad. His wrath was directed at his friends for setting them up in the first place.

Brandon had said only that Cian and Jamie should get along for the sake of the wedding. Of course, that was partly because he thought there was some kind of rivalry between them. Cian had been decent enough not to tell Brandon that they were more awkward than enemies. This thing where they all thought they'd be perfect together had to stop.

Cian plunked down on his couch to send a text to Jomari. There was no way Jomari could've known, but Cian was pissed off at him anyway. Jomari should've at least had the name right. Cian had a lousy night and no dinner, and he was impulsive. He fired off the text without pausing to think if it was a good idea.

What the hell were you thinking? Next time, make sure you know who my date is.

A few minutes later, Jomari replied. **No idea what you're talking about. What happened?**

Cian huffed and texted, **Turned out to be a guy I knew through Brandon. He doesn't like me and walked out.**

The wait was longer this time, and Cian fidgeted. At last his phone vibrated, and he picked it up.

I just messaged my friend. She says you no-showed for the date, but the guy had a real nice time with someone named Keith.

Cian blinked. That made no sense. Who was Keith? And of course he'd showed up for the date. He'd sat in the restaurant, waited, and then had a near-argument with Jamie.

He texted back, **I was there. Jamie was late, and when he saw it was me, he wouldn't stay.**

Jamie? Jamie who?

This was getting ridiculous. **Jamie, Brandon's hot cousin.**

The wait was so long this time Cian thought Jomari had forgotten about him. Cian was about to find something else to do to get his mind off the evening when Jomari finally responded.

You were supposed to be on a date with Jayden, not Jamie. What. The. Fuck.

Jayden…Keith…Cian groaned and slid down on the couch. He ran a hand over his face. The two men who arrived as Cian was trying to catch up to Jamie and beg him not to leave. He'd seen their conversation, but being distracted meant he hadn't processed it. He reread the texts, his neck flaming when he saw that he'd called Jamie "hot." It was true, but he hadn't meant to tell Jomari that.

An incoming text pulled his attention back to the phone. **You still there?**

Yeah. Humiliated, but here.

Okay, well, I'm gonna see if I can figure out what the hell happened.

I'd like to know too, Cian replied. He added, **Tell Jayden I'm sorry.** There probably wasn't much chance of a do-over, not if Jayden and Keith had hit it off. The least Cian could do was apologize.

Sure. I'm texting Amelia again now, the one who knows Jay. She should be able to sort it out.

Good.

Cian set his phone back on the coffee table. That figured. So Jamie had been supposed to meet this Keith Whoever, only somehow he'd gotten mixed up and thought Cian was his date. No, that wasn't quite it. Cian frowned. Ah, the host. She'd brought Jamie to Cian's table and assumed they were supposed to be together.

He wondered what he'd missed out on. All the good things he'd been looking for were apparently true of Jayden, not Jamie. And now, because of his own stupid assumptions and his lack of self-control, he'd lost that. He'd wanted so much for it to be Jamie when he looked up and saw him there. It was foolish. He barely knew Jamie. Instead of thinking logically about it, he'd made an assumption.

Jomari texted him again. **Amelia says there was a mix-up. My friend and hers were supposed to meet you two, but it got swapped. They're not mad.** He sent a series of laughing faces. **I think she interrupted them when she texted.**

Oh, my God. Cian laughed. Well, at least his date had gotten something out of the deal.

I can set you up with someone else if you want. I got connections.

I know you do, Cian answered. **Maybe after Brandon's wedding.**

You're on. Sleep well, and sorry about the date.

No worries. Goodnight.

Cian put his phone down. Good thing the other guys weren't upset, or Cian might have felt worse. He wondered how Jamie was doing and then reprimanded himself for it. Jamie was fine, as long as Cian stayed away from him.

With a heavy sigh, Cian dragged himself through the motions of getting ready for bed. He had enough other things on his mind to keep from dwelling on any might-have-beens about what had happened earlier. This was more proof he needed to look organically for whatever type of relationship he thought he needed. Or maybe it was the last sign that he'd been wrong and he was meant to move after all. Sleeping on it couldn't hurt. He would make a decision after the wedding in two weeks' time.

Jamie finally arrived home, tired and cranky and still fighting the urge to lock himself in his room with his Goldfish crackers. He didn't, though. First he had to find out what in the world Amelia had been thinking. Probably nothing—she didn't know Cian herself, nor did she have any idea he and Jamie had a connection.

He flopped onto the couch, but he didn't even have the energy to turn on the television. It wouldn't be enough to distract him anyway. After giving it all of ten minutes, he texted Mack.

Date was a bust. Tell Amelia thanks anyway.

Mack replied right away. **What happened?**

Accidentally set me up with Brandon's friend Cian. You know, the dancer. Not her fault.

What? That makes no sense. I don't think Amelia knows Brandon's friends.

Jamie rolled his eyes. Of course it didn't make sense to Mack. **Not her. Some friend of hers from the orchestra knows him.**

I meant Amelia's met the guy you were supposed to go out with. Hang on, let me ask.

Setting his phone down, Jamie closed his eyes. The first thing that came to mind was Cian. Not dancing on stage but the version from tonight. Relaxed, casual, handsome. A nice, wine-colored button-down shirt, no tie, open at the collar. Dark trousers. A glass of water and an open menu on the table in front of him. When he looked up, Jamie had noticed the tiny laugh lines around his strikingly blue eyes.

There was no going back now. Jamie had effectively burned that bridge. They would get along for the sake of Brandon and Gemma, but after that, Jamie was done. He had to stay away from Cian.

His phone buzzed with a text, and he picked it up. Mack, of course.

Amelia says she didn't set you up with Cian and has no idea what you're talking about.

Jamie read the text three times before replying. **Then who did she set me up with?**

A short wait, and then, **Keith something. He says you never showed up. He met another guy there whose date didn't show either.**

Jamie quickly worked out exactly what had happened, but he didn't have anything else productive to say. He concentrated, thinking back to when he was leaving the restaurant, so sure his friends had set him up with Cian. Two men, standing by the host's kiosk. Blind dates. He hadn't caught the one guy's name, but the other one he was sure was named...

Jay or Jayden. Of course. It wasn't exactly the same, but the names were similar enough. Not only had Jamie ruined his date, he'd ruined Cian's as well. It sounded like Keith and Jay had lucked out, but they could as easily have been miserable too. One more indication that Jamie should stay the hell away from any attempts at a relationship, then or for the foreseeable future. Sure, he'd been planning to let Keith down. But they might've at least had a nice time, and he wouldn't have Mack and Amelia mad at him for his mistake.

Dude? Still there?

Jamie glanced at his phone. He'd almost forgotten about Mack. **Yeah, still here.**

You okay?

No, he wasn't okay. He was embarrassed and angry with himself and full of regret at losing his cool. He'd snipped at Cian, raged about his friends, stumbled over his words, and left everyone in a bad way. If he'd been listening, he wouldn't be in a position to need forgiveness. Sure, the host had led him to the wrong table. But how could she have known more than one couple was meeting there for a blind date on the same evening, at the same time?

I'm fine, Jamie lied, glad Mack couldn't see him through the phone. **Tell Amelia I'm sorry.**

I will. Don't worry about it. Shit happens. Sounds like Keith ended up having a good time anyway.

Jamie put his phone away and curled up on the couch. He wasn't sure how he could face Cian after this at all, even at the wedding. Maybe Sage was right all the times he said Jamie was nothing more than the same kind of screwed-up stock he'd come from. There was no point in resisting what he was, not if he was going to mess everything up all the time.

Before he could change his mind, Jamie flew off the couch and into his room, locking the door behind him. He'd left his phone on the coffee table, which was good. He didn't want anything to distract him while he fed his humiliation and sobbed himself to sleep.

Chapter Fourteen

In the back bedrooms at Gemma's parents' house, the wedding party was getting dressed. Jamie had a room to himself for the moment, until Brandon joined him. Brandon had chosen Jamie as his best man, and Jamie was both pleased and nervous. He and Brandon had been like brothers during the years Jamie lived with his family, and he was honored to stand as a witness.

Jamie stared at himself in the full-length mirror, angling his body before putting something on over his underwear. He no longer had bruises on his torso, but he still almost felt the pinch marks Sage had left more than six months ago now. Sage shouldn't have been on his mind on a day like this, but there he was. Jamie would've brought him to the wedding if they'd still been together.

He thought back to Trevor's engagement to Marlie before everything happened with them and Andre and the baby. Jamie had just broken up with Sage yet again, and the Creepy Crullers were playing for Valentine's Day. Sage had watched Trevor propose. Apparently so had Andre, but Sage was the one ducking backstage to find Jamie, drag him to a dark corner, and kiss him until his lips—and other parts—were swollen. Jamie hadn't taken him back immediately. He'd tried to stay away, really he had. But by the time they were celebrating the engagement with their friends, he was back with Sage and they were fucking in Jamie's bed while the others carried on with the party in the living room.

Both the engagement and now Jamie's relationship with Sage

were history. Jamie didn't like the way Izzy and Nate sometimes looked at him. They'd seen the places Sage had grabbed him, and Jamie knew they thought Sage was hitting him with something. Jamie could say honestly that Sage had never hit him, not in all the years they spent fighting and making up. No, it was only his way of measuring how much skin he could grasp between his finger and thumb, and how hard he had to go before the spot turned reddish purple. It was how he helped Jamie keep control of his eating; now there was no one to do that for him.

The door opened, and Jamie threw on a black T-shirt. He reached for his pants as Brandon brushed past him to grab his own clothes. If he had noticed Jamie looking at himself in the mirror, he didn't indicate it. Brandon was good that way, but then again, he didn't know how bad things had gotten with Sage in the few months before Jamie called it quits for good. He only knew what Jamie told him, and even that was enough for Brandon to hate Sage. There was no reason to give him more wood for that fire. Hastily, Jamie zipped his grooming bag shut so Brandon wouldn't see what else he'd hidden in there. It was foolish, really, but at least it was only a handful of granola bars and a bag of pretzels this time. They were the quickest and least messy things Jamie could think of, especially since no one had gone shopping in several days. He felt better knowing they were there, but he didn't need Brandon asking nosy questions.

Once they were both dressed, Brandon motioned Jamie over. He straightened Jamie's collar and grinned at him, resting a hand on Jamie's neck. Jamie wore a subdued pair of gray trousers and a deep purple button-down shirt, open at the collar. He'd let his hair grow out so it wasn't spiky anymore but instead lay mostly straight with a bit of curl around his ears and neck. It wasn't bottle-black, like Mack's, more of a muddy brown to match his eyes, though in dim light it appeared darker. As much as Jamie looked like his mother, he had enough of his father in him that people always assumed at first that he and Brandon were brothers rather than cousins.

Brandon had on a more traditional pair of black pants and a white shirt. Like Jamie, he didn't have on a tie. Jamie performed the same ritual on Brandon of straightening his collar and looking him over. Although he could see Brandon was properly dressed, he didn't know how to tell whether his cousin was ready to go out there and get married. He hadn't given it much thought since Sage, but Jamie figured it wasn't something he would ever do himself. Not even if he ever did find the elusive Mr. Right. No one had said so, but he had the impression that even his tolerant mother didn't know what to make of the idea of two men getting married.

Ready? Brandon asked.

I should ask you that? Jamie replied with a grin, and Brandon snorted a laugh.

Let's go, best man.

They returned to the front of the house, where the living room had been cleared out to make space for chairs. Fortunately, there was plenty of space for the guests, since it was raining and they'd had to move it all inside. Gemma and Brandon had opted for a casual affair, although Gemma's parents had gone a little overboard with the decorating. It was wild, with white, green, and purple twinkle lights everywhere and a rock music theme. All of it was perfect for Brandon and Gemma's laid back style. Still, it was a lot more than Jamie had expected. He'd half thought the two of them would opt for letting everyone sit around the living room with a beer or soda in hand while they watched the ceremony.

As Jamie peeked out from the hallway, he looked over the assembled friends and family. Mack was there. He had Amelia with him, of course. Their bandmate Cassie had brought her newish girlfriend, whose name Jamie had forgotten. He'd only met her once, briefly. None of their other roommates, former roommates, or their partners were there. Brandon and Gemma didn't know Nate, Trevor, or their families well enough.

Jamie almost groaned when his gaze landed on Cian. Of course he knew Brandon's friend would be there, but he hadn't wanted to think about it. Cian was still an irritation to Jamie, someone he would rather spend as little time with as possible. His mere presence—regardless of how attractive he looked—was enough to make Jamie's shoulders tighten. Not so tight that he missed the way Cian's muscles nicely filled out his shirt or the relaxed, happy expression on his face. More like enough to wish he hadn't noticed.

Cian was seated with a couple people Jamie didn't know, a woman and a man. The woman was visibly pregnant. She leaned against the other man and rested her hand high on Cian's thigh, and Jamie's eyebrows went up. Given the botched date, Jamie wondered if it was a situation like Trevor and Marlie's, where this woman was

Cian's girlfriend. Maybe the baby was his. The thought intrigued Jamie the same way it did with Trevor's family. He had to remind himself of exactly how well that had worked out for him with Trevor in order not to get caught up in the moment and the possibilities.

While he was busy watching them, he missed the JP moving into place along with the interpreter. Brandon nudged him, and Jamie put on his game face so they could take their spots at the front of the assembled guests. He couldn't resist one last look at Cian before concentrating on the ceremony. In a matter of minutes, he was so distracted by his duties as a witness that Cian's presence was overshadowed.

Watching Brandon and Gemma exchange their vows was emotional for everyone. He and Gemma were perfect together. Jamie's heart swelled when Brandon sniffled his way through the exchange of vows. Jamie handed over the rings, reading the love and respect in Brandon's expression as he accepted them.

Jamie brushed at the corners of his eyes with his thumb, overcome with happiness for them and another feeling underneath, something warm and sweet that he couldn't quite name. He startled himself on realizing the last time he'd felt it, he'd had baby Aidan in his arms. What an odd comparison, he thought, though it wouldn't leave him alone.

He glanced out at the assembled guests, and for a moment, his gaze connected with Cian's. Startled, Jamie wanted to look away, but he couldn't. The link between them wasn't broken until the JP announced Brandon and Gemma as married and the hearing half of the room broke out into cheers.

The whole entire mess at the reception was Cian's fault. When he looked back on it later, he was never sure whether he should laugh, cry, or be grateful to his own stupidity. In any case, things might have ended up differently if he hadn't had two shots of Red Bush neat—which he downed entirely too fast on an empty stomach—followed by champagne before *and* during dinner and the Sam Adams Summer Ale someone handed him during the father-daughter dance. If he hadn't been bored while waiting for the wedding party to finish photographs, he never would've started. He wasn't precisely drunk, but he'd lost a good deal of his usual filter in the process.

Up until that point, the day had been pleasant. The ceremony was very nice. Cian was happy for his friends, enough not to needle Brandon later for turning into an emotional puddle, barely able to sign his vows and slide the ring on Gemma's finger. Naturally, Gemma had lost it as well at that point. Skye had done a fine job as their interpreter, after which she returned to Eric, Nell, and Cian.

He should've known—and maybe did but blocked it out—that Jamie was Brandon's best man. Because of course he was. Not that Cian had wanted the honor himself. He'd promised Brandon he wouldn't do anything to cause a disruption. That wouldn't prevent him from enjoying the view, and the tension between them, a bit.

Jamie looked fantastic. He was more toned-down than usual, even his piercings. Somehow, they looked elegant with his button-down shirt and pressed trousers. Cian didn't know whether that surprised him or not. Jamie's formerly spiky hair was longer now, with just a hint of curl at the ends. Cian had to stop himself from wondering what it felt like.

Just as Brandon put the ring on Gemma's finger, Jamie had glanced out at the guests. His gaze locked on Cian's, and Cian couldn't have looked away if he'd tried. He'd had to breathe slowly, lost in the pure joy he saw on Jamie's face. If he could've captured it, he would have. The exchange only ended when the JP pronounced Brandon and Gemma married.

After the ceremony, they'd clustered around the bar while they waited for the wedding party to return from wherever they'd disappeared to for pictures. It was a huge house, so no doubt they'd set something up in the sunroom where the light was good. Cian had only been there once before, but he admired the design of the home. That wasn't his area of expertise, working for his father's contracting company, but he knew quality when he saw it.

Cian mostly tuned everything out. Weddings, and wedding receptions, generally bored him. He half wished something exciting like a zombie apocalypse would occur so they could all go home. Consequently, he wasn't paying enough attention to what or how much he was consuming in the alcohol department. As someone not prone to overdoing it, he missed the cues that he'd already passed that point.

The real trouble didn't start until after dinner and the customary scheduled festivities but before cake. Brandon and Gemma were working their way around the room accompanied by Skye. Everyone else was milling about and talking. It was too chaotic for Cian, and the excessive amounts of booze he'd consumed so far were not helping. He'd already lost track of Eric and Nell. He longed to go take his hearing aids out just to stop hearing the droning, headache-inducing conversation.

And then he spotted Jamie. Jamie, who looked far too appealing for his own good. Jamie, who made Cian feel hot and cold at the same time and made his head swim. All right, maybe that was the alcohol, but the worst of it had started to wear off finally. Cian deposited his empty Sam Adams bottle on a table and made his way over. An eighth of his brain told him it was a terrible idea. The rest, bathed in whiskey and champagne, urged him forward.

Jamie saw him before he got there, and Cian watched his whole body stiffen. That should've been a hint to stay away, but Cian was feeling bold—or possibly still tipsy—and didn't care. He meant to apologize for the mix-up with their dates. Those were the words in his head, anyway. They weren't the ones that came out of his mouth.

"Jamie," he said, and then when Jamie turned his attention to Cian, he continued. "I'm sorry about the—the thing. Y'know. At the thing."

The guy from the band, Jamie's friend what's-his-name, appeared confused. He looked from Jamie to Cian and back. It annoyed Cian, and he wished Jamie would say something. Instead, he just stood there, a glass of dark liquid in his hand. Probably Coke. Even in his slightly hazy state, Cian remembered Jamie didn't drink.

Finally Jamie said, "Uh...thanks, I think. You mean with the blind date?"

Cian intended to agree. It's what he'd come over for. Somehow, though, he ended up saying, "Brandon said we had to get along today."

Jamie looked amused. "I think we've managed so far."

It was too noisy in there, and Cian wanted to really talk to Jamie, not this thing where he couldn't concentrate or hear him properly. He needed an excuse to get Jamie on his own, somewhere he could appreciate the view while trying not to babble inebriated nonsense. He racked his brain to find a topic and then hit on something.

"Can we go somewhere else? I wanted to talk to you. Y'know, clear the air."

There it was, the door closing. The light had gone out of Jamie's beautiful, dark eyes. "Clear the air? I don't think—"

"About the other thing. From the engagement party."

Jamie looked to his friend, who shrugged and still looked utterly perplexed. "Fine," he replied. To his friend, he said, "Come get me when I'm needed for something."

Cian followed Jamie down the hallway to a back bedroom. Once inside, Jamie shut the door, blocking the sounds of the reception. Now that they were alone, Cian wasn't sure what to say. He looked around at the garment bags and other items and figured this must've been where some of the wedding party had gotten ready.

"You wanted to say whatever it was to me?" Jamie folded his arms. Always so reserved, holding something back. Cian wished he could see the spark from the night of their botched blind dates.

"I, uh." Cian licked his lips. He hadn't really, but now that Jamie thought that's why they were there, he had to go with it. "Yeah. We never got to finish talking at the party. You left."

"Of course I did. I mean, what did you expect me to say? You were going pretty hard on me for some stupid porn I did once."

Cian stared at him. "It wasn't stupid porn!" he insisted. "It was more than that. You were playing this character, and I—" He cut himself off.

The truth was complicated. Cian had strong opinions on representation in media, yes. He genuinely believed deaf actors should get deaf roles. But he'd also been sure Jamie was deaf. He'd assumed that, like himself, he hadn't been deaf as a young child, either. Finding out the truth had been disappointing. Cian, in spite of his partners, had never fully immersed himself in the Deaf community, not like they had. He'd made much more than grudging peace with his life; he was happy. But he supposed he'd wanted kinship with someone who felt and behaved as he did. Jamie had, by no fault of his own, let Cian down.

In his still not quite clear-headed state, Cian couldn't put that together in a meaningful way for Jamie. Instead, he continued, "Why did you do it? Play deaf, I mean."

"Excuse me?" Jamie stared at him. "Is that what you think I did?"

"Yes. Look, it's not just you. It happens all the time. And yeah, I get it that you're one person doing a thing, but don't you think it gets frustrating for us?"

"Did I do a bad job?"

"No, but it's the principle of the thing." Cian was warming up now, his tongue loosened and his confidence rising. "If people like you always—"

"People like me?" Jamie demanded. "What kind is that?"

Oh, now they were getting somewhere. Cian hadn't intended it to go this far, but now he saw the spark in Jamie, the thing he'd longed for every time they ran into each other. Good idea or bad, he didn't care anymore. He wanted to see what would happen if he pushed. "People who appropriate and fake shit because they think it's just fiction. This is real people's lives you're representing."

"Fuck. You."

Jamie's eyes were dark and angry, and the flicker in them made Cian's heart rate increase. He backed up a step, farther away from the heat radiating off Jamie. His back hit the wall with a soft thump. He stared at Jamie, mouth open and heart thundering from the adrenaline. He'd never seen this much passion from Jamie. Aside from the night of their missed dates, he was usually either cold or indifferent, to the point Cian had wondered if he had any other emotions. It shouldn't have been this appealing, having Jamie be so angry with him. Yet Cian was drawn to the fire in him; damn if it wasn't a turn-on to see Jamie standing his ground.

"You don't know anything!" Jamie snapped. "It's not—" He paused. "It's not your—not—not your—" Another pause, followed by an enraged noise deep in his throat. He balled his hands into fists. "It's not—oh, f-fuck this sh-shit!"

"Jamie?" Cian asked, reflecting his hesitation.

Jamie didn't respond at first. He glared at Cian and then his shoulders slumped. He let out a breathy and slightly irritated chuckle, startling Cian. "I can't—I can't—can't do words," he said. His half-amused smile turned into a frustrated expression.

Was this why Jamie was always so reserved? Cian regretted his ill-advised aggression. Cautiously, he touched Jamie's arm. *Sign it*, he told Jamie. *I want to understand.*

Jamie nodded. *It's not up to you*, he signed, a vicious bite in every motion. *Six months, I couldn't talk right after I lived with Brandon. He taught me sign so I can communicate without getting stuck on words. Not every person who needs to sign is deaf. I based my character on myself. You would know if you'd been paying as much attention to the plot as to my dick.*

Cian turned that over in his mind. He was right—Cian should've known better. And as much as he hated being wrong, he hated it more that he hadn't tried to understand Jamie's side of it.

You're right, Cian signed. *I'm sorry.*

Jamie's mouth dropped open, and Cian had a nice glimpse of his tongue stud. It only further aroused him, and he stepped closer again.

What? Jamie asked.

He spoke out loud, a way to reassure Jamie he knew why he'd made his choices. Cian had made some of his own over time. "I said, I'm sorry. For everything."

Jamie nodded. "Me too. I—" He sighed and went back to signing. *You caught me at a party to tell me what you thought of me. I liked it.* He licked his lips, which trembled a bit. *I like it now, too. I disagree with you, but it was so sexy. You weren't there to talk about my body or get my autograph. I was seeing someone. He didn't like it.* Jamie stopped and shook his head.

It's all right, Cian replied. *I get it.*

He was upset with me. Not about you. He got mad at me for talking to fans.

There seemed to be a lot of weight in that statement, but Cian didn't know how to deconstruct it. He wanted now to make things right between them.

I talked to you because I loved your work more than only your body. He let out a nervous chuckle. *You are very hot.*

Jamie shook his head, but his lips curled upward in a one-sided smile. *You too. You look good.* The smile faltered, and then Jamie signed, *I faked hating you. Easier than saying I wanted you. Less scary. Safer.*

Safer? Cian repeated. *From what?*

Me. Him. Jamie shrank back. *Nothing.*

It's okay, Cian told him, though he was a little confused. *Good now?*

Yes. Jamie straightened his back, and the tiny spark returned. Not anger but determination, as though he'd made an important decision. *I'm sorry too. Try again?*

That startled Cian. He wasn't expecting it when Jamie stepped in and put a hand on his shoulder, but he went with it. The next instant, they were kissing. Cian's breath was shaky, but so was Jamie's. His whole body vibrated as they kissed and kissed. Cian put his hands on either side of Jamie's face, and Jamie grasped Cian's hips. The pressure of their lips and the slide of their tongues—hell, that stud was sexy—increased.

Cian flipped them so he had Jamie up against the bedroom wall. Jamie was panting so hard that Cian felt it in his whole body. He couldn't fathom how they'd managed to hold a grudge against each other for so long. Apologizing and making out was so much more fulfilling. He lost track of the time, making up for all the lost opportunities. He wanted to fit months' worth of kisses and hot touches into a single, intense moment.

After who knew how long, he let go of Jamie, pulling back to give himself a few minutes to look Jamie over and see his jewelry up close—the horizontal barbell in his right eyebrow, the horseshoe ring in his nose, and his angel bites. He could smell the combination of Jamie's shampoo and hair gel; it was nice, tingling his nose with its almost spicy quality. Cian ran a finger down Jamie's cheek to his neck, following the path with his eyes before returning his attention to Jamie's face. He stepped back.

I'm so turned on right now. I don't want to stop.

Jamie's eyes were bright. *Me too.*

Cian went for it. *I want to put my hands on you.*

Yes.

We have to talk before we do in case you can't speak or I can't hear you.

Yes.

Cian drew in a deep breath. *I want to kiss you a lot more. I want my hands on that thick cock of yours, and I want your hands on mine.*

Okay. Yes. Jamie swallowed visibly. *I want that too. I have for a long time.*

They were kissing again after that, their bodies pressed together and their fingers in each other's hair. Cian felt a hand slither in between them and ground against it a little, hoping Jamie would get the hint and use more pressure. He didn't. Instead, his face screwed up and he made an indistinguishable noise. Cian put a hand on his cheek, and Jamie opened his eyes. He took a deep breath and spoke more clearly for Cian.

"I can't get my pants undone," he said.

"Let me."

Cian moved Jamie's hand out of the way, unfastening the hook at the top and tugging on the zipper. When he was through, he unbuttoned Jamie's shirt and shoved his T-shirt up under his arms, sucking in a breath at the sight of more hoops in his nipples and navel. Was there nowhere he hadn't pierced? He hiked up his own shirt; they were still dressed for the wedding, after all, and neither of them had an appropriate change of clothes.

Jamie's fingers were shaking as he tried to unfasten Cian's pants. Impatience warred with not wanting to seem like a jerk, so Cian allowed Jamie a few minutes of struggle before he helped him out. He let his pants slide to the floor. Jamie still had his on. Cian leaned in and ground firmly against him. He could make out what sounded like Jamie stuttering, "Oh, God" softly, over and over. He pulled back to look at him.

Half undressed and with his face flushed, Jamie was a thousand times more appealing than Cian had ever imagined. He was still trembling as he rushed to get his pants off. He looked about three seconds from coming, and that ramped Cian's arousal up several notches.

"Fuck…" Jamie complained. "I need to get my dick out…"

In one quick motion, Cian had Jamie's pants and briefs down to the floor. He pushed his own out of the way before grasping Jamie's gorgeous, thick cock. He was a lot bigger than Cian had imagined, even having seen him on camera. For half a second, Cian stared at the piercings. Holy hell, he had a fucking Prince Albert and two tiny pubic studs, and goddamn if that wasn't making Cian almost so hot he couldn't bear it. That answered his earlier question about how many more there were. Cian didn't recall whether they had been there when Jamie was filming, and he no longer cared. Jamie's small, warm hand wrapped around him, and anything else he might've thought went straight out the window.

Cian responded in kind, sighing at the feel of Jamie in his hand. He'd been right. Jamie was already so close to the edge that it only took a moment before he was urging Cian faster, thrusting into his palm. As soon as he felt the slick heat hit his skin, Cian's body went taut. The next thing he knew, he was groaning and releasing all over Jamie's fingers and his now-softening prick.

They gasped into each other's mouths as they cooled down. What a rush; trading hand jobs with Jamie was more intense and satisfying than bickering with him. The previous few minutes had assured Cian his first impression of Jamie had been the right one. If only it hadn't been clouded by misunderstandings and tension. Doing anything with Jamie other than holding him seemed like a complete waste of time now.

Before they'd fully recovered, the door swung open and a beam of light from the hallway illuminated the room. Cian swiveled his head, and his mouth dropped open at the lean, dark-haired figure in the doorway.

Jamie felt it when Cian tensed against him, both of them acutely aware that they were mostly naked in each other's arms. There was no possible way to interpret it as anything other than what it was. Cian turned and hid his face in Jamie's shoulder.

When Jamie saw Mack standing open-mouthed in the bedroom doorway, he almost laughed. Payback was fair; he'd spent ages listening to Mack and Amelia, and catching Mack drilling the blond from Starbucks was hardly the first time he'd gotten an eyeful. He only wished the other guys were there too.

"I came to tell you they're about to have cake. You look like you've already had dessert, but maybe you still want cake. Do you want cake? I sure want some. Mm, frosting." He blinked a few times. "I mean...no, not frosting...cake...oh, my God. Fuck this."

Now Jamie really did laugh. "Shut the fuck up. I just had the best goddamn hand job in the last...I don't know, several years. So hell, yeah, I want some fucking cake. Go away so I can clean up."

"No problem. I'm gone." Mack slammed the door shut.

Once he'd left, both Jamie and Cian broke into gales of laughter until they were wiping tears away. Jamie shifted so he had use of his hands.

Thank God it was only Mack, he signed.

Still embarrassing. Cian leaned in and kissed Jamie. It quickly escalated, although everything remained above the waist. "Mm...who needs cake," Cian mumbled against Jamie's lips.

For a fraction of a second, Jamie contemplated skipping the cake-cutting and staying locked in the bedroom with Cian until they were both ready to go again. Brandon probably wouldn't care, especially since it meant Jamie and Cian would be able to sit in the same room without shooting daggers at each other. Gemma, on the other hand, would kill them both. He pushed a little until Cian straightened up and backed off.

We need to go, he signed.

With a sigh, Cian backed up and looked around until Jamie

spotted a box of tissues on the nightstand and pointed it out. That would have to do, and they would both have to hope they could make themselves presentable enough to keep the other guests from developing a clue what they'd been up to.

Jamie tucked his shirts back in and zipped his trousers. He wrinkled his nose; they probably both smelled like sex. Cian obviously had the same thought because he was making a face as he got himself dressed again. In spite of the situation, Jamie wasn't sorry for anything they'd done. The only thing on his mind now was when they could do it all again.

His stomach fluttered. Cian was hot, sure, and this was a fun diversion at a boring wedding reception, nothing more and nothing less. At least, that's what he tried to tell himself. He could pretend there was nothing more to his pre-hand job confession than an admission he found Cian hot. Surely it didn't carry any more weight for either of them than that. Maybe Jamie should stop it now before it had the chance to go anywhere.

He meant to. He intended to tell Cian he wasn't interested in dating. Instead, what came out was, "You want to meet up again?"

Cian held motionless, his fingers on the button of his trousers. Still looking in the mirror rather than at Jamie, he didn't answer immediately. While Jamie held his breath, Cian finished fastening the button. He finally turned around.

"Yeah," he said. "I'd like that." There was a pause long enough to become awkward before Cian added, "I'd like to take you out first next time."

Jamie had the chance to say no. Cian was watching him expectantly, and from his open posture, he'd have understood. Yet there was something else there too—a wary, hesitant look in his eyes. With a shock, Jamie realized Cian was mirroring the same feelings Jamie had always had around him: interest, desire, and a fear of the unknown. No one, not even Trevor and certainly not Sage, had ever looked at him that way. Cian might be worth taking a risk for after all. One date; he could back out at any time afterward. Jamie took a deep breath, counted to ten, and let it out slowly before answering.

"Okay. Um...yeah. Okay."

Cian's eyes crinkled like he was amused, but he didn't laugh at Jamie. He stepped closer and kissed him, mouth closed but it was still enough to make Jamie's knees turn to jelly.

"We'd better get out there," he said.

Right. Cake. Jamie sighed, and this time, Cian did laugh. He supposed only time would tell how right Brandon was, but Jamie wasn't looking forward to the smug reaction he was sure to get the minute Brandon found out what they'd been up to. He just hoped they could make it through the rest of the evening first.

Gentleman that he was, Cian opened the door and let Jamie pass before stepping out and shutting it behind them. One more exchanged glance and they were on their way back to the main room.

Chapter Fifteen

They were finally having the long-awaited—or dreaded—real first date, the one Cian had agreed to at the wedding. Having their hands all over each other at a time when emotions were already high was one thing. Being able to sit and have a conversation without arguing was something else entirely.

Jamie had his game face on. He had gone over the list of off-limits topics, and he had mentally prepared himself for their date by choosing where he wanted to go. They were at the coffee shop around the corner where Nate worked one of his three jobs. Jamie had made sure it wasn't his shift. A familiar place was good, but a nosy roommate was not.

This was the safest sort of date he could create. No need to have a whole meal together. Jamie couldn't have eaten anyway, and that would've raised too many questions. Cian had been puzzled by Jamie's selection of venue, but he'd also been polite enough not to press the issue.

Cian set his latte on the table and slid into the booth across from Jamie. He flashed his charming grin, and Jamie couldn't help smiling back. While Jamie had very few preferences when it came to men, he couldn't deny Cian was one of the most attractive guys he'd ever seen.

"So..." Cian began, but he trailed off.

Jamie sighed. Less than five minutes in, and it was already almost as awkward as his date with the investment banker. Neither of them seemed to know how to start a real conversation.

After a pause, Cian tried again. "I am sorry about what I said to you at the wedding, you know."

"I know." He grinned and signed, *Coming all over our hands made things right.*

Cian laughed. *True.* He turned serious before speaking out loud again. "I'd had a bit too much to drink, and I wasn't keeping myself in check."

"You weren't wrong about everything, just wrong about me. Anyway, that's behind us now." Jamie stirred his cocoa with a swizzle stick, and Cian raised an eyebrow at him.

"No coffee?"

Jamie shook his head. "It makes me jumpy. I—" He tapped a finger on the table then realized what he was doing. "I have some health issues, and it messes with them."

"Ah, I see. So that's why no alcohol, either?"

"Kind of." It was only one of many reasons, but those all seemed like too much for a first date.

"I didn't mean to poke around too much." Cian took a sip of his drink, obviously stalling. Finally he said, "Look, all I know of you is the argument we had, your web series, and the fact that you're damn hot. Maybe we can trade some info, here."

"Okay." Jamie sat up a little straighter.

"I don't even know what kinds of things you like. Movies?"

Jamie flushed. Would Cian think he was silly? "I like romances."

Cian cringed visibly. "So the latest superheroes are out of the question, then. Does that go for books, too?"

"No, not really." Jamie was too embarrassed to tell Cian that he still preferred young adult fiction. He didn't know if Cian would think he was stupid or not. "You?"

Leaning forward, Cian said, "I don't usually like to tell people I prefer science fiction. They get ideas about me, you know?"

Jamie smiled in spite of himself. "I guess I can understand that. I'm not judging." It was a start. Some of Jamie's favorites were young adult gay science fiction novels, but he wasn't ready yet to mention any by name.

"Okay. So far, we're zero for two. Sports?"

It was Jamie's turn to cringe. "No. Except there's this one baseball player I think is really hot."

Cian gave a name, but it was meaningless. "How the hell does he make adjusting his cup sexy?"

"Right?" Jamie grinned.

"Okay, so that's one we agree on," Cian said. He moved in again and signed, *Unless we're talking about porn.*

Jamie snorted, flushing and hoping no one else in the cafe knew ASL. *I was in it. I don't watch it.*

Cian nodded. His cheeks turned rosy. *Yours was the first gay porn I watched on purpose.*

That was definitely a surprise. *Really?*

Yes. I don't like it. I'd rather watch het or girl-on-girl.

Jamie's eyebrows shot all the way up and he was so startled he spoke out loud. "Seriously?"

"Is that going to be a problem? You'd better say so now."

"No," Jamie insisted. "I didn't realize, that's all." He went back to signing. *You're bi?* At Cian's agreement, he hesitated and then continued, asking what had been on his mind since the wedding. *Pregnant woman is your partner? With you at Brandon's wedding?*

Now it was Cian's turn to look surprised. *Yes. Baby's not mine. Our male partner's.*

Man who was with you?

Yes. Their interpreter is our other female partner. They have three-year-old twins together. Cian looked uncomfortable. *I should've told you. I'm sorry. What made you ask?*

Jamie had suspected, seeing them sitting together. He had to know if this was going to be Trevor all over again. He thought about how to say what was on his mind without sounding needy or pathetic or accusing. They sat there for several minutes without speaking or signing at all. Jamie took it as a good sign that Cian allowed him some time to process the information, but he figured he should say something before Cian made assumptions and left.

My friend, Jamie signed, then stopped when a pang of regret hit him. At Cian's puzzled frown, he shook it off and continued. *He has boyfriend and girlfriend and baby. Why are you here with me not them?*

They live in Springfield. I live here. I only see them a few times a month. Cian looked tense, as though there was more to the story than he was letting on.

Jamie sat back, considering it. He could press Cian for more details, but it obviously wasn't the same situation as Trevor, Marlie, and Andre. He wondered why Cian didn't live with his partners.

Whatever the arrangement was, Cian didn't seem to want to divulge the details. The thing between him and Jamie was too new, maybe, or poorly defined. Jamie didn't even know yet what he wanted or expected. How could he pressure Cian into making that kind of statement?

Okay, he signed.

Okay? Cian looked confused.

Yes.

Jamie hoped that was enough. He'd never had a problem with any of it, as long as everyone agreed. He wasn't ready to tell Cian about Sage and the ways that had messed him up, the expectations of exclusivity on Jamie's part while Sage could lie and cheat and come back begging forgiveness. Hell, Jamie barely dated after each breakup, knowing they'd be back together eventually. Every time he had, Sage wouldn't let it go. He had a constant need for reassurance, for proof that Jamie wasn't leaving him or screwing someone behind his back. Never mind how often he failed on that front. Jamie had thought offering an open relationship might solve the problem, but it had only made it ten times worse.

You're all right with things?

I am. Jamie reached across the table and touched Cian's arm, hoping to reassure him.

Cian relaxed. *What were we talking about? Aha. Books, movies, sports. What else do you like?*

Cian didn't want their night to end. They'd spent what felt like hours talking, speaking some but mostly signing. Jamie, like Cadence, switched fluidly between the two, which amused and pleased Cian. He hated admitting how right Brandon had been after all and how wrong he'd been to charge headlong at Jamie the first time they met. He thought back to what Denver had said at the bar—that Jamie'd had it rough and needed someone patient. He wanted to be that person.

After the cafe, Cian had invited Jamie to come home with him. Now they lay in bed on their bellies, naked but not yet touching each other. Cian had already taken out his hearing aids. Having them make noise or slip during sex wouldn't be attractive or romantic, and he wanted this to be good. They needed to talk beforehand, but for now he only wanted to look at Jamie. He was so gorgeous. Cian traced the three curved bars on the back of Jamie's neck. Jamie's only tattoo was in the same spot, a black and silver ribbon drawn to look like shoelaces as paired with the piercings. Cian wondered how he'd done it. He sat up, and Jamie rolled onto his back.

Tell me about all these, Cian signed, then touched the row of hoops in Jamie's left ear and then the bar over his eyebrow. *What do you do with them at work?*

I trade for less obvious ones. They let me keep them because I don't work in the kitchen.

It made sense. Cian leaned in and kissed each of Jamie's angel bites and then his lips. *I love them all. How did you decide to get them?*

Jamie didn't answer for a moment. Eventually he sat up. *I have one piercing for every breakup.* He smiled and tugged one earlobe. *My first. Got them when my high school boyfriend broke my heart.* Jamie laughed. *He didn't want me, but suddenly I had girls all over me.*

Cian laughed too. *Lucky you!*

Jamie nudged him with his toe, but he was still smiling. *Then this one.* He fiddled with the eyebrow bar. *I dated that guy for two weeks before we figured out it was never going to work.*

Why not? Cian wanted to know.

We were on set together. He was cameraman. He said he was into me emotionally, but anything more than kissing he couldn't do. He was so upset. Didn't want to hurt me. I heard he got engaged to one of my costars. They are agender.

Maybe you opened his mind, Cian suggested.

Maybe, Jamie agreed. He shrugged and moved on to touching the hoops. *All the rest.* He wouldn't meet Cian's gaze for a moment, and Cian saw the way his eyes shimmered. *They're all from the same guy. Not this one.* He touched the daith. *It's new. I'm not sure we broke up. We weren't official.*

The same guy? Cian blinked, going back to what Jamie had told him. That was a lot of breaking up.

He hated them. I got one done and told myself it was the last time. We were apart for a week each time, two at most. He groveled or I called and begged.

It clicked. *The one I saw you with at the engagement party.* The one Jamie had said was angry with him when he talked to fans. Some of the pieces were beginning to fall into place.

Yes. Jamie closed his eyes briefly when his finger came to rest on the pubic studs. *He saw these. He stopped us in the middle of sex. Didn't *touch me for two weeks after.* He swallowed visibly and flicked his PA. *He told me if I got this one, I'd never see him again. I waited a month after our last split, and then I got it. I had to be sure he was never coming back.*

Did it work?

Jamie took a while before he answered. He looked like there was a lot there, hiding just below the surface. At last he signed, *I haven't seen him in more than six months.*

Cian signed, *Can I touch you?* At Jamie's assent, Cian ran his thumb over the PA. It was so sexy, and it excited Cian, but he wasn't trying to get a reaction from Jamie. He sensed there was a lot of hurt from whatever had happened with Jamie's ex, and Cian wanted to ease it with sensual touch. He wanted Jamie to know he loved the piercings and would never shame him for them or tell him what he could do with his own body. He knew what it felt like to have someone else believe it was their right to make those decisions, and he never wanted Jamie to think Cian would do such a thing.

Jamie closed his eyes, and a single tear slid down his cheek even as his cock grew firm under Cian's fingers. Startled, Cian withdrew his hand and cupped Jamie's cheek. He swiped away the tear, and Jamie opened his eyes.

You miss him? Cian asked.

He wasn't good for me.

That didn't really answer the question. *It doesn't matter. You can still miss him.*

No. Jamie closed off, and it was clear the conversation was over. When Cian reached for him again, Jamie shifted away. *I don't want to have sex tonight.* He shivered. *I'm sorry.*

It's okay. Cian only touched his hand this time. *We don't have to.*

Jamie relaxed. *I want to be here with you. Can I stay?*

Of course. Can I kiss you goodnight?

Yes.

Cian gave Jamie a gentle kiss, making it as tender as he could. Some things couldn't be said with words or with sign, and the affection he felt now was one of them.

They lay down, and the minute Cian was on his side, Jamie scooted closer so his back was pressed to Cian's chest. Cian curled around him and closed his eyes. He felt Jamie shaking, but the only thing he could do was press his cheek to Jamie's shoulder and hold him a little tighter. This was too new to push for answers, but he hoped Jamie would trust him. Cian pulled the covers over them both and drifted off into troubled dreams.

Cian woke and rolled over. The bed next to him was empty, the covers wrinkled and drawn back. He yawned and stretched before rising from bed, putting in and adjusting his hearing aids, and throwing a knee-length bathrobe over his nakedness. When he stepped into the hall, he saw the bathroom door was closed. Breathing a sigh of relief that Jamie hadn't left, he wandered into the living room.

He stood at the glass balcony door and looked out over the city, at the dark street far below. The sky had lightened since Cian had woken, and he could make out the shapes of the buildings. His mind traveled to what he would be doing at the end of the summer, and he wondered again if he would be happy giving up this view and the life he'd built. He'd put off thinking about it, telling himself it could wait until after the wedding. Now here he was, over a week later and no closer to a decision.

Cian thought about Nell and the baby, due early in September. He could be there, living with them, just in time. It wouldn't solve his problem of finding a day job or of reopening his studio or any number of other things, but most of those weren't going to be resolved by staying here, either.

The bathroom door opened, and Cian's heart leapt. The other person he now had to consider emerged. Jamie was clad only in a T-shirt and his boxer briefs, looking sleep-rumpled but no less sexy for it. Cian had never had much in the way of specific preference. From Eric's big, hairy frame to Skye's fairly average curves to Nell's willowy build, he liked all of it. He was sensual and sexual with a high drive, and not much turned him off if it was attached to someone he cared about. Jamie, though—he was something special, and it was far more than what Cian had seen of him on film.

Yet along with a flash of desire, Cian also had nagging regret and worry. They hadn't even properly talked about—well, anything, if Cian were honest. Jamie wrapped his arms around his waist and stood by the couch. Cian's stomach dropped; Jamie was still so closed off. He looked like he wanted to say something but didn't know how.

Before approaching, Cian cleared his throat. Jamie gave him a faint smile, but there was sadness and pain underneath it rather than happiness. Cian stepped toward him, and at last Jamie moved. He came over to the window and stood next to Cian, looking out at the dim gray dawn. Cian shifted so he was behind Jamie.

"Is this okay?"

Jamie turned his head to look up at Cian. "Yeah."

Cian folded Jamie into his arms. Jamie leaned back with a sigh, and Cian kissed his neck. When Jamie hummed, he did it again, this time moving his hand to rest on Jamie's stomach. He swayed a little, rubbing slow circles over the top of Jamie's T-shirt before sliding his fingers underneath to dance along the soft skin there. He liked it, the way it wasn't completely flat. Jamie stiffened in his arms as Cian explored his belly, and Cian paused.

"Still okay?"

"I—" Jamie's breaths were shaky, and Cian felt the shivers. "Can you not touch me there?"

"Of course." Cian pulled his hand out. "Where would you like me to touch you? Or do you need to stop?"

"I want—I w-want—" Jamie made an irritated noise and took several slow breaths. "Here." He moved Cian's hand to the waistband of his boxer briefs. "And—and lower. You—you can—you can—"

"It's okay," Cian murmured. "Just say yes or no. I can touch your dick?"

His answer was too quiet for Cian, but he repeated it louder when asked. "Yes."

While Cian continued kissing and tasting Jamie's neck, he dipped his hand lower, cupping Jamie through his boxer briefs. He pressed and released gently until Jamie swelled under his fingers, then he traced the outline with his thumb. At the groan vibrating against his chest, Cian slipped inside the soft cotton, his breath catching when Jamie arched against his palm. He continued with deliberate strokes, his own cock filling where it nestled just above the rise of Jamie's ass. Jamie's moans thrummed against Cian, and he'd have reacted to them even if he hadn't been able to hear. Under Cian's other hand, Jamie's chest rose and fell rapidly.

"D'you want to come like this?" Cian asked, his mouth against Jamie's ear.

Jamie nodded then shook his head. He tugged at his boxer briefs, making them ride lower on his hips. The shiver running through him as he did so transferred to Cian, making his body hum with pleasure.

Cian withdrew his hand from the front of Jamie's underwear and dragged them down, freeing his thick, full length. Cian couldn't hold back a groan of approval. He opened his robe, letting his naked dick press against Jamie's ass. Pushing a little, he guided Jamie until his palms were flat against the glass of the balcony door. He widened his stance, offering himself to Cian.

"I will stop any time you need me to. All right?" Cian said.

Jamie nodded, and Cian adjusted. He slid between Jamie's thighs. Slowly and carefully, Jamie closed them tighter together around Cian's length. He was shaking, but he didn't give any indication Cian should withdraw. Cian remained steady, resting with his chest against Jamie's back, despite his building urge to thrust, to feel the friction of skin-on-skin. He was waiting for Jamie's signal.

After a moment, Jamie said something, but it was muffled. Cian cursed the position they were in that it was no good for signing to each other. He could hear, but not if Jamie didn't speak clearly. He was on the verge of pulling away and asking to go back to bed when Jamie turned his head and spoke more clearly.

"I want this," he said, though he still trembled.

"Only if you're sure," Cian answered. The way Jamie was shaking made Cian hesitate. Something told him he had to say it again, had to remind Jamie he had the right to say no. "Tell me the minute you need to stop."

By way of an answer, Jamie began to move. He rocked his hips, pushing back against Cian. Keeping one hand on the glass door, he reached back and grasped Cian's hip, pulling on him.

Taking the hint, Cian matched the rhythm Jamie had set. They gained confidence, and their motions synchronized. Jamie stroked himself a few times before almost losing his balance. He caught himself by returning his hand to the door. Cian reached around and down, finding Jamie's cock and wrapping it with his fingers. Pleasure tingled across Cian's skin at watching Jamie let go, and they thrust together harder, faster.

Cian was close. He opened his eyes just as Jamie leaned his head back against his shoulder. Jamie's whole body tensed, hot streams of ejaculate hitting the glass as he almost sobbed his orgasm. The sight sent Cian into his own climax, chanting Jamie's name like a prayer as he spurted between his legs. Jamie's chest heaved, and Cian clung to him through the aftershocks. They remained joined until their breathing had slowed and their shaking had steadied.

Arms tight around Jamie's chest, Cian chuckled against his neck when he saw the thick fluid dripping down the door. "Well, that'll be fun to clean," he remarked.

Jamie stiffened. He shoved at Cian until he backed up, then he turned around. Jamie's eyes were wide with fear, and his lip trembled. He said something too quietly for Cian to hear it, but he was sure he'd caught it watching Jamie's mouth move.

"What?" he said anyway, then signed it.

I'm sorry, Jamie signed. *I'm sorry.*

He turned and ran, ducking into the bedroom and slamming the door. In confusion, Cian remained where he was until Jamie emerged a few minutes later, fully dressed and with his bag in hand. He swept up the T-shirt and underwear, tossing them inside. Frustration rose in Cian. They'd had months of misunderstandings, and there was no way Cian was letting him go without sorting it out. His impulse was to demand what was wrong with Jamie, but he knew it wouldn't do any good.

"Wait, please," Cian begged. When Jamie stopped in his tracks, Cian swallowed both his spit and his pride. "Tell me what I did wrong."

Jamie's mouth dropped open. "You? No. It's me. I—" He looked from Cian to the glass balcony door.

Now Cian was well and truly befuddled. "I don't understand."

"You're n-not upset?"

Cian wanted to shout, to demand what he should be upset about. Except that was obviously what Jamie had expected, even though Cian had no idea why. He followed Jamie's gaze to the stained door. That? But why would he—

"Oh," Cian said, softening. "Because I joked about the door?"

Jamie didn't respond.

"It's nothing. I was kidding. Why would I be angry about it? That was brilliant, if I do say so myself." He flashed Jamie a smile.

Jamie's shoulders relaxed, but he didn't smile back. "I'll clean it for you."

Cian stepped closer, pausing to see if Jamie would back away. When he didn't, Cian came all the way over to him. "I'm sorry for making a joke. It's not a big deal. Did you think it would be?"

"My—my last—my—" He was stumbling again.

Sign it, Cian said.

I've been with people who said it was gross. Jamie looked like it had taken everything out of him to explain that far, and it clearly wasn't the whole story.

I'm not like that.

Like the way he sensed Jamie had to be told clearly he could say no, Cian understood Jamie now needed reassurance he'd done nothing wrong. Cian put his arms around Jamie and rested his cheek on Jamie's head. It struck him again how the image of Jamie he'd built up in his head was so different from the real man he was now holding. Something in him seemed so unlike the self-assured man who had appeared in videos or the capable drummer he was with the band. It was as if someone or something had bled all that confidence out of him. What would it take to find that person again?

He had an idea, the one thing that had given him his confidence back and drained away his pain and anger. Backing up slightly, Cian studied Jamie. "Come somewhere with me," he said.

"Where?"

"My dance studio. You can watch one of my summer classes, maybe try it out."

Jamie finally smiled. "I'm not really a good dancer."

Hoping it was the right thing to do, Cian leaned in. "But you have such good moves."

Now Jamie laughed, and the tension at last lifted. "You're only saying that because you got off. You might not feel that way if I step on your feet."

"I'll take my chances." He closed the gap and kissed Jamie. "Now, are you staying for breakfast?"

CHAPTER SIXTEEN

CIAN HAD told Jamie to meet him at the Dyer Theater at one on
Saturday. Fortunately for Cian, it had worked out for him to hold his
summer classes there. He'd been able to clean out the other dance
studio early, leaving the rest of the details to Marta. It hadn't made
him less uneasy about the situation. If anything, the switch had made
it worse. He felt as though he had no home now, and yet he still
struggled with the idea of moving. No matter what angle he examined
it from, the outcome wasn't different.

He arrived a few minutes early and waited for Jamie outside.
Around the corner, between buildings, he saw the shadow of a person.
Cian huffed. It was probably the same guy who'd been lurking there
on and off for a couple of weeks. He wasn't really doing anything, but
Cian had no idea what he was there for or if this was just another one
of the theater's quirks.

Jamie showed up just before one o'clock. Cian greeted him with
a kiss, but Jamie pulled back and looked him up and down.

"What's wrong?" he asked.

"Nothing. Just sort of annoyed by some random guy hanging
around. Is that typical?"

Jamie shrugged. "My roommate works here. You'd have to ask
him. I've never seen anyone." He drew his brows together. "He's
probably harmless, and you're sounding kind of...I don't know. Judgy.
Why does it matter if a homeless man hangs around here?"

Cian backed off. "It's not that. For all I know, he's not homeless, and that wasn't my concern. He watches me when I get here, and then he disappears. I thought it was weird, that's all."

"I wouldn't know."

"Never mind, then. Let's go inside. Class starts at one thirty."

Cian held the door open for Jamie. He was wrong-footed again, not quite sure what he'd said to upset Jamie this time. He hadn't been making any accusations, but Jamie had somehow read it that way. For the time being, Cian chalked it up to whatever Denver had meant about Jamie's life before. While he didn't want to feel like he was constantly watching everything he said, he also didn't want to make Jamie upset or uncomfortable.

They entered the building, and any other thoughts about what had happened outside vanished. Cian loved the Dyer Theater. It was an older building, and it had gone through multiple stages of remodeling. The owner/manager had tried to preserve the character of the place, so it had an old-fashioned feel to it. The walls in the main foyer were covered in posters and cast photos from many eras.

Jamie paused at one picture and smiled. He pointed to it. "This one's new," he said.

"How do you know?"

Tapping the center of the picture, Jamie said, "This is my roommate. He directed the performance. I saw it—something called *The Pearl Fishers*. It's pretty good, for opera."

Cian squinted at the photo, but it was hard to see much individual detail of the cast and crew. "Maybe I'll look up the story later. C'mon, let's go into the auditorium."

They followed the signs to the interior stage entrance, and Cian led Jamie out onto the stage. The squeak of Jamie's sneakers echoed in the empty auditorium so loudly even Cian heard it. He laughed, and Jamie flushed. Gorgeous. Cian wanted to kiss away any embarrassment Jamie was feeling, but they were about to be surrounded by middle schoolers.

Cian had invited Jamie to watch his intermediate class. Not only were they his favorite, he thought they would be the most fun. They were competent dancers, but not as serious and focused as the older students. He gave them their instructions and put on the music, motioning for them to do their warm-ups.

The expression on Jamie's face was delightful. He was caught up in the simple steps of the exercises. They weren't even anything complicated, just the sort of thing Cian had grown up knowing in the same way he knew how to breathe. His American students had to learn them; aside from Cadence, none of them had Irish roots. Even she was the product of families who had lived for more than a century in the US. For Cian, though, these steps were as natural as anything.

When the students had finished, Cian gathered them and signed their instructions. They were in the midst of putting the final touches on their dance for the end-of-summer show. It was going to be fantastic, but Cian was keeping everything under wraps from their families. He wanted the whole thing to be a surprise. It didn't matter that Jamie was seeing it because he wouldn't have any idea what it meant.

Cian danced with them, following their lead this time. There was nothing like feeling the vibrations and moving his body in time with them. He liked to joke that exercise was a bore but dancing was like having a céilí every class. Like his students, he was swept up in the rhythm and the storytelling, all else fading into the background.

They finished, and Cian stole another glance at Jamie. The way he was so into it made Cian feel as though he was flying, taking him to a high that even the dance hadn't quite achieved. When at last Jamie's gaze met his, the gentle, childlike wonder in his eyes caused a rush of intense feelings—surprise, joy, affection. He'd made Jamie happy, and there wasn't a way to capture how good it made him feel.

In a blink, the moment passed, and Cian turned his focus back to his students. *One more time,* he signed. *Then get your hard shoes.*

After the class left, Jamie waited for Cian to tidy the stage. He'd been to the Dyer Theater before, to watch Nate. Not that Jamie was a huge fan of opera, but Nate and his co-director, Del, were outstanding at what they did. Whether Jamie liked the music or not, queer opera was unique and fun.

Jamie stood at the edge of the stage, looking out into the empty auditorium. He couldn't picture himself in such a venue, doing what Cian or Nate did. Sure, he'd been on stage plenty of times, both in school and at the various bars where the Creepy Crullers played. He'd also been a model/actor, but that was a much different set, and they had multiple chances to get their performance right. This was different.

There was a clacking against the floorboards behind Jamie, and he turned around. Cian still had on his jig shoes, and when Jamie looked at him, he showed off a few lively steps with a twinkle in his eye. Jamie had seen tap dancers before, like Izzy when he was performing as TaTa. The sound of the jig shoes was different from the bright clicks of the metal taps. The fiberglass was richer, more full. Somehow, though, it was lighter the way Cian did it, every step paired with a little jump.

His posture was different too, Jamie noted. Narrower, with his shoulders, hips, and feet lined up vertically rather than horizontally. He kept his arms still at his sides and his back straight. After a moment or two, Jamie could tell the difference when Cian switched from tapping only on the balls of his feet to using the whole shoe to stomp.

Want to try? Cian signed after he came in for a landing in front of Jamie. He still had his hearing aids out.

No! Jamie tried to shift away, to make it clear he wasn't up for such a thing. He couldn't possibly hope to learn that skill.

Cian grinned. *Please? It's easy. I'll show you after I change shoes.*

Jamie looked at his own feet, thinking it didn't look particularly easy. *Should I change?*

You don't have to. I have extra if you want. Cian ducked into the wings and grabbed his bag. *What size?*

Do I have to wear the ones with all the ties? Jamie couldn't picture himself trying to get them done up without getting tangled in the long laces.

G-h-i-l-l-i-e-s? Cian finger-spelled it, and Jamie wondered how it was pronounced. *No. Only girls, unless you're in Scotland. Here.* Cian reached into the bag and tossed over a pair of soft black shoes. *Try those.*

Jamie toed off his sneakers and slipped on the black shoes. They were a little loose, but they fit well enough and conformed to his feet. The thin material felt strange after wearing street shoes. He faced Cian and waited for instructions, his heart beating rapidly and his palms sweaty.

Cian explained the steps and what he called them, then demonstrated for Jamie. He made it look easy. Cian was muscular but not lanky; he wasn't built the way Jamie envisioned most dancers. Yet he was light on his feet, almost springy. He always looked to Jamie as though he was flying when he danced at Grand Slam. Here on this stage, he toned it down a bit for Jamie's benefit, the same way he did with his students.

Jamie tried to imitate the pattern of steps. The first one he got all right, but by the second set he'd somehow ended up on the wrong foot. Cian didn't make fun or chastise him. He showed Jamie again then motioned for him to try. In a short time, Jamie had picked up one of the basic forward steps.

They played around for a bit longer, at which point Jamie'd had enough. He truly wasn't any kind of dancer, no matter what Cian had tried to tell him. He asked to stop, and Cian praised his effort before accepting the shoes back and tucking them away. He slid his hearing aids back in and sat down to put his street shoes on.

"Not bad, for a first time," he told Jamie as he laced his sneakers.

"I guess. I don't think I'm cut out for it."

"Maybe you don't think so, but it takes more than one short lesson to pick it up. You could learn, I promise."

"I'm not graceful like you or my friend Izzy." Jamie shrugged; he wasn't bothered by it.

"I'd say you're very graceful," Cian objected. "I mean..." His face went red, and Jamie laughed.

"You said that before, about when I was in the web series."

They hadn't really talked about how Cian had known who he was, aside from their argument and an offhand comment or two from Cian. Jamie didn't think he had expectations, and so far, sex between them had been good. Still, he wondered if it bothered Cian the way it had bothered Sage. Or if it bothered Jamie, come to think of it, to be with someone who'd enjoyed his series.

Cian leaned back and propped himself on his hands, his feet dangling off the stage. He was scrutinizing Jamie, making him feel exposed and uncertain.

"Does it upset you?" he asked. "I mean when I talk about it."

"Not really." Jamie imitated his posture. "I guess it's more that I wonder how you feel about it."

"Other than what I told you before about the casting, I liked it. The camera angles, the way the sex was directed...it was beautiful and artistic. And you." He smiled. "You're gorgeous, Jamie. I don't just mean your penis, though that's damn impressive. I mean you. How you moved and how you made it look like there was nowhere you'd rather be. I don't care about the specific acts, but damn...to be loved like that? It would be amazing."

Jamie was hot and cold simultaneously, embarrassed and yet glowing from Cian's praise. No one had spoken to him like this about it. Either they were matter-of-fact, like Mack, or they were uncomfortable. Or they were like Sage, but Jamie shoved those thoughts away.

"I don't know what to say. Thank you."

Cian leaned in for a light kiss. "You're welcome. How did you get started, anyway? And why did you stop?"

Jamie did a bit of condensing in his head. Cian only needed the short version, the one that didn't involve Sage being Sage. "There's not much to it. When I was eighteen, I wanted to be out on my own. I had my job waiting tables, but it wasn't enough to pay rent. So I answered an ad for one of those 'hot college guys' things. I didn't get hired—they were looking for jocks, and I was too...well, not. The casting director had some connections and thought I might like something else. I did a couple of things, got an agent, and then landed the web series. I stopped because the band was doing more, and I decided to focus on that."

"Oh, right." Cian laughed. "I don't really know whether the band is good or not."

Jamie grinned. "Mostly not. We would be, if Mack got off his lazy ass and wrote us more original stuff. His songs are great, but I don't think he believes that."

"You've known Mack a while?"

"Since high school. We started the band with Cassie and a couple other people."

Sage, before he and Jamie got together. He'd played keyboard. Cian didn't need to know that detail. Sage hadn't played with them in years, not since the first time he walked away and left both Jamie and Mack in the lurch. That's when they'd gotten Gemma. Jamie took Sage back, but Mack wasn't so forgiving. Or maybe he wasn't so easily manipulated. Jamie didn't know.

"Are you hungry?" Cian asked, jostling Jamie back to the present. "We could go somewhere."

"Um..." The mild anxiety was back, though not as strong as usual. For Cian, Jamie might be willing to try.

"Or just back to my place?" Cian put a hand under Jamie's chin and brought their lips together. Quite a long while later, he let go. "I think that answers it. I'll cook for us after."

"Mm. Sounds good to me." On a whim, he said, "I've seen your class. Next time, you'll have to come with me to one of our practices."

"Oh yeah? I'd like that." Cian's surprised delight made Jamie glad he'd offered.

Cian stood and pulled Jamie to his feet. He shouldered his bag, and they linked fingers as they exited the theater. The jitters in Jamie's belly were back, and he almost let go. He'd never meant to let things go this far between them, not to the point of holding hands, for fuck's sake. At the same time, something about it made Jamie feel as though he'd been missing out. Sage had never touched him like this; it was always more aggressive, like he owned Jamie. Trevor had certainly never done it, as they'd never been out in public together. And no one else Jamie had ever been with had lasted long enough for this stage.

Jamie blinked for a moment in the mid-afternoon sun. Once his eyes had cleared, he thought he saw movement between the buildings. When he looked, there was nothing but a shadow there. He wondered if it was the person Cian had said was hanging around the last couple weeks. Maybe later, he would ask Nate about it. He spent enough time at the theater that he would know if there was anyone nesting there.

Cian didn't appear to have noticed. Jamie had taken the train, but Cian had his car, so they headed for the parking lot. At the last minute, Jamie looked back again. His heart dropped into his stomach. For a fraction of a second, he was positive he'd seen Sage. It didn't make sense, though, so he brushed it off as his mind playing tricks. This thing with Cian was new enough that anxiety was making Jamie see what wasn't there.

To distract himself, when they got to the car, Jamie took a chance. Before Cian could get his key out, Jamie pushed him up against the driver's side door and kissed him. Cian's surprise gave way to a gentle laugh against Jamie's lips. Jamie let go and winked.

"Well, then," Cian said. "Guess we'd better get home sooner rather than later."

###

When Jamie woke on Sunday morning, it took him a few minutes to figure out where he was. He had on nothing but a pair of sweatpants that weren't his. He stretched, yawned, and rubbed the slightly itchy spot above his navel ring. For a second, he panicked, worried he'd missed the band's practice. He searched for his phone, finally finding it on the nightstand. Only nine. Plenty of time for a relaxed morning. He extended his legs and lay back down, the previous night coming back into focus.

Jamie'd had the dinner shift the night before, so he gone late to stay with Cian afterward. It had been less intense than after Nate's cafe or the dance class. Maybe it shouldn't have been a surprise, but Cian wasn't pushy at all. Jamie had been exhausted after being on his feet for hours, despite having had a good shift. His mind was willing, but his body simply wouldn't cooperate. Instead of being angry, Cian had taken it in stride. They'd kissed softly with the patchy moonlight shining on the bed and the gentle whirring of the window fan in the background. Jamie had fallen asleep in Cian's arms.

Cian wasn't in bed now, but it was late enough Jamie wasn't shocked. He swung his feet over the side of the bed and sat there for a few minutes, feeling relaxed and comfortable. Then he stood and stripped off the sweatpants, which were quite a bit too big on him. He'd showered the night before—no way was he making Cian's bed smell like clam chowder—so he dressed in the fresh clothes from his overnight bag.

He messed with his wild mop of hair. Sage never would've liked it the way Jamie wore it now, all grown out. In fact, there wasn't much left of the Jamie that Sage had sculpted into his own image. The face staring back at Jamie in the mirror now was the same, but so many other things had changed. It was hard to say whether he liked it or not.

Sage had no business being on his mind anyway. Jamie hadn't heard a peep from him since changing his number. Even emails to the band's page had stopped. Today was not a day for thinking about him. It was a day to enjoy bringing Cian to watch the band rehearse. Mack had a new song he wanted to try out, so they were meeting up in the disused recording studio owned by Cassie's brothers. Jamie only had so much room in his head, and he wanted his attention only on the band and Cian.

While he was applying product to his hair, Jamie listened for any sound in the apartment. It took him a minute to realize the thumping he heard wasn't coming from outside the window but from the other room. Curious, Jamie tucked his things back in his bag and opened the bedroom door.

He followed the sound out to the kitchen. Cian stood at the counter, his laptop open and Irish pop music with a lot of drums playing. He had one hand resting on the countertop while he drummed a rhythm with the other. Periodically, he would stop and jot something in a binder. He'd showered, and his hair was still damp. When he danced, he usually slicked it back. Now he had it parted neatly on the side. He was wearing khakis and a plain white T-shirt, looking as relaxed as Jamie felt.

Cian didn't have his hearing aids in, so Jamie went over and touched his arm. When Cian looked up at him, Jamie almost stepped back, startled by the happiness in Cian's wide smile. He looked Jamie up and down, and Jamie flushed. He wasn't wearing anything special, just a pair of jeans and a tank top that faded from pink to orange with a black palm tree in the center.

WOW, Cian signed, using both hands. *Sexy.*

Jamie ducked his head and signed a timid thanks. Cian moved a little closer and took Jamie's face between his palms. He motioned with his chin, asking if it was okay. Jamie nodded, and Cian kissed him, apparently unconcerned that Jamie hadn't yet brushed his teeth.

He ended the kiss all too soon and stepped back. *When do we leave?*

Jamie peered around him at the clock over the stove. *Ten thirty.*

Breakfast?

OK. Thanks.

After they'd eaten—more accurately, Cian ate and Jamie picked—they left the apartment and went around back to the small parking lot. Jamie's car was parked about four spaces away from Cian's. They were driving separately, a fact for which Jamie was grateful only a moment later.

Tucked under his windshield wiper was a small piece of lavender paper. Jamie pulled it off as soon as he was sure Cian was inside his own car. He unfolded it and sucked in his breath. Just five words were enough that Jamie had to sit in his car until his heart rate had returned to normal. Under no circumstances would he show it to anyone, especially not Cian. He had no idea what he was going to do about it, but whatever it was needed to wait until they weren't on their way to rehearsal with the band. Jamie read it one more time before crumpling it and shoving it in the glove box.

I saw you with him

Still shaking, Jamie backed out of the parking space and sat there until Cian was behind him. There was no way he would get Cian involved in this mess. Jamie would find a way to deal with it himself, even if he didn't yet know how he would accomplish that. It was going to have to wait. He breathed slowly, distracting himself with a cheery wave at Cian before they pulled onto the main road.

Cian definitely needed his hearing aids out for the band's rehearsal. It wasn't that they were bad, exactly. They were just loud in a way that jarred his nerves. He tucked his hearing aids away in their case and settled himself on an old sofa.

The whole room looked like something out of the 1970s. In fact, it probably was. Jamie had said this place belonged to Cassie's—the bass player's—brothers. They didn't use it for recording; they had a much nicer space for that. Instead, they rented it out for a minimal charge to small-time bands like Jamie's, people who had nowhere else to rehearse.

Jamie and his bandmates had spent a good while going over a new song, apparently something Mack had written. Cian recalled Jamie saying he was good but lacked confidence in his skill. Mack didn't seem like the sort to go hard on himself that way, but Cian didn't know him well enough to be sure.

They worked on the song for a long while. Cian sat forward on the sofa, bracing his arms on his thighs and keeping his eyes on Jamie. He was fully immersed in the music, his focus solely on what he was doing with his sticks. He had an air of total devotion to the rhythm. Sometimes, if Cian was lucky, Jamie looked like that when they were making love.

It didn't happen often. A lot of the time, he was still as timid as a rabbit with Cian. Letting go like this, with his eyes closed and an expression of rapture on his face, was a rare thing. It wasn't quite the same, of course, but when Jamie concentrated like this, when he shut out everything else, he was so fucking gorgeous. Watching him was almost too intense.

Art, Cian had said of his sex work, and this was much the same. He looked like there was nowhere else he wanted to be than behind the drums, with his sticks in his hands. He played as if they were an extension of himself. There was no question that Jamie was Cian's favorite part of the band, and he almost had himself convinced he wasn't biased.

Cian lost track of time. He'd expected to watch for a bit and then get bored, so he'd brought a book. He never opened it. Instead, he absorbed the vibrations of the music, almost until he felt in sync with it. Rhythmically, it was similar to what he danced to. Jamie had called their band folk-punk, and he wondered if they'd borrowed at all from traditional Irish tunes. He would ask when they were done, since he couldn't really hear it.

While he watched, he tried to memorize the way Jamie looked. He wanted to capture it and try to imitate it later, to bring him to that place when they were together. He recognized the way Jamie must have been feeling because Cian felt it too when he was moving his body with the music. It would be fun sometime to see if they could make magic like this together—the beat of Cian's shoes against the wood matching the thunder of Jamie's drumming.

He was so caught up in it that it startled him when they finished. Cian put his hearing aids back in, mostly for Mack's and Cassie's benefit. He knew it wasn't necessary with Jamie or Gemma. There was a bit of light chatter among the band members, but Cian missed most of it. He had a brief signed exchange with Gemma about the honeymoon—he hadn't seen her or Brandon since the wedding—and they parted ways.

Jamie signed that he'd be right back before helping Mack load equipment into a van. When at last the dust settled and Cian was alone with Jamie, they sank down on the old sofa together. Jamie rested his head on Cian's shoulder, and Cian slid his fingers to loop with Jamie's.

"Thanks for coming." Jamie yawned. "Sorry."

"Do you have to work tonight?"

"Yeah, dinner shift again, but I have a little while." Jamie shifted and sat up. He had a gleam in his eye and a wicked little smile curled one side of his mouth. "You made me dance. Let me teach you what I do?"

Even though he was teasing, there was a charming hesitance to the question. Jamie had a way of putting Cian at ease. He would never demand more than he was willing to give. This wasn't about payback for Cian making him dance. They were trading, like schoolchildren sharing secrets. It made Cian warm all over.

"Sure," he said. "But didn't Mack just take your drums?"

Jamie laughed. "I didn't start out on a kit like that. Here." He pulled his sticks back out of his bag along with a couple of small discs.

"Practice pads. I played percussion in school, which is a bit different in some ways." He laughed. "My mother said it was the only way to keep me from beating out a rhythm on anything I could find."

"So, basic band stuff?" Cian had never played anything. His body was his instrument.

"That's what I did at first, yeah."

Jamie played a half dozen different patterns, none of which Cian quite distinguished and all of which had names that sounded like nonsense to him. What the hell was a flamacue or a paradiddle? Before he could make sense of it, Jamie handed over his sticks.

"Uh..."

Grinning, Jamie said, "Just try a basic right-left tap. Go on."

They spent the next ten minutes on it. Cian picked up—very slowly—a few strokes. The minute Jamie tried to coax anything faster or more complicated out of him, he ended up with his right and left backwards and no rhythm at all. Cian groaned and handed the sticks back.

"Thanks, but no thanks. I'll stick with dance. I think I'm beginning to see how you felt."

Jamie laughed. "I can coordinate the hi-hat, snare, and kick drum, but I have no idea what to do if you give me—what did you call those dance steps? Something with numbers. Do they all run that way?"

Cian couldn't help barking out a laugh. "No. The steps are not all numbered. Those aren't names, threes and sevens are how many times your feet hit the floor. So, how did you end up playing drum kit, anyway?"

Jamie half-shrugged. "You know I lived with Brandon for a while, right?" When Cian nodded, he continued, "The school had both a concert band and a jazz band. It's the only reason I graduated. I wasn't too good at school, and I didn't like it much. But I wanted to play, so I did the best I could."

"I liked watching you play." Cian ran his fingers over the back of Jamie's hand.

There was that sexy blush again. Cian plucked the sticks out of Jamie's hand and placed them on the table. He shifted closer and touched Jamie's lips with the tip of his thumb. Jamie closed his eyes and leaned in. Cian slowly brought their mouths together, relishing Jamie's shaky exhale into the kiss.

Cian's focus narrowed to Jamie and the glorious things he was doing with his lips and tongue. They kissed endlessly in the musty old room. At some point, Cian tore his mouth away to ask Jamie if he thought anyone was coming back. The minute Jamie assured him they weren't, he picked up where they'd left off.

Jamie shifted to straddle him, and Cian panted as Jamie kissed and nipped his neck. They were now half undressed, hands down each other's trousers. They tore at the rest of their clothes, both anxious to have fewer barriers. Cian opened his eyes, and it was as though the whole earth stood still. Jamie had *the* look, the one Cian loved. The utterly blissed-out, lost-in-the-moment expression.

It was too much and not enough all at once. Cian reached back with one arm and anchored himself on the sofa, arching into Jamie as heat and energy shot through him. He kept his gaze on Jamie, watching him come unraveled with a sharp exhalation.

Their breathing was noisy in the silent room. Jamie slid off, and Cian ran a hand through his now-sweaty hair. His head buzzed a little; he would need a few minutes before he could move, let alone get up and find somewhere to clean off. He rolled his head to the side and looked at Jamie. He had his eyes closed and mouth open. His head rested against the back of the sofa, and his heart was still pounding hard enough Cian saw the pulse in his neck. He was sure he was in the same state.

After what felt like a very long time, Jamie got up. He didn't tuck himself away when he ducked into the nearby bathroom. Cian groaned and stood, following him. When they'd sufficiently cleaned up, they returned to the main room. Jamie, still flushed and with his hair mussed, went to the door. He opened it, and a cool breeze brought the scent of rain with it. Cian joined Jamie, and they stood facing each other and leaning against the frame of the open door.

There didn't seem to be a whole lot to say. Jamie had closed off again, and Cian's high faded. He seemed far away as he stared out at the rain-slicked street. After a bit he turned his attention to Cian.

"We should probably go."

"Yeah."

Cian thought about reaching for him, reassuring him with a kiss. Instead, he stayed where he was and watched Jamie retrieve his drumsticks and practice pads, tucking them back into his bag. He slung it across his shoulder and returned to the door. They stepped outside, and Jamie pulled the door shut. Sticking close to the building under the awning, they stayed there until the last minute, finally dashing across the parking lot to their cars. Cian watched Jamie drive away, wondering if he would ever discover what was under all those layers.

CHAPTER SEVENTEEN

AN INCOMING text caused Jamie's phone to vibrate against the coffee table where he'd left it. He jumped a little now every time he heard the phone, whether from anxiety or excitement. There was no such thing as relaxing. Sage hadn't done anything in a while, but that meant very little.

Warily, Jamie picked up the phone. Not Sage; Cian. Jamie sighed anyway, tempted not to respond. They'd struggled after their first couple of dates. As Jamie had feared from the night in the cafe, they had little in common. His mind drifted to an unwelcome thought of Trevor and the night they'd played together at the church. It had felt natural, as though their music was meant to be. With Cian, every move, every step was a struggle to stay on his feet. It was Sage all over again. No common ground would inevitably lead to endless fights over petty things and breakups as numerous as the stars. By the end of it, they'd both be shattered.

Jamie looked at the message. **Want to come over?**

No, Jamie didn't want to. Or he did. He wasn't sure. What would they do? Not a meal. Surely Cian hadn't missed the way Jamie pushed food around on his plate, not really eating it, or the way he took a small amount and cut it so it looked like more. He'd been trying so hard, but enjoying a meal with someone else made his stomach tense to the point he couldn't put anything in it. Not until he was home in the safety of his room and could pull out the bin under his bed.

There weren't many other options either. They'd established they didn't like many of the same things. Jamie's sloppy attempts at dancing and Cian's equal frustration with drumming meant one more thing they couldn't share. Cian likely wouldn't even want to, not after that. Jamie stared at his phone, shaking, recalling the time Sage had spent an entire evening yelling at the walls about how he would never live up to Jamie's standards. It wasn't true, but that was the last time Jamie dared ask Sage to do what Jamie wanted for once.

He should tell Cian it was over now. He should've ended it the day they were in the old studio. He'd wanted to, but he'd thought following sex with a breakup was probably bad form. God knew, Sage had done it to him more than once. Sage would fuck him, tell him how lousy he'd been in bed, and then throw his clothes at him with a demand to get out. Of course, he always followed it up with a pleading phone call and a promise he didn't mean it. Without a second thought, Jamie would take him back every time.

Jamie shuddered. Meeting Cian to break things off was a good idea. Better than doing it via text. They would remain fully upright and clothed. He wouldn't even have to go inside Cian's apartment.

He texted back, **When?**

Almost as soon as Jamie sent it, he had a reply. **Now? Or are you busy?**

Not busy.

Great! I want to show you something.

OK. On my way.

What in the world would Cian want to show him? Now Jamie was stuck. How was it that he was the one feeling awful when it was he who wanted to call it quits? He couldn't fathom how Brandon could've missed the mark so spectacularly. He'd chosen the last two people who should ever try to make something work long-term. Shouldn't they have at least one thing in common?

Jamie grabbed his keys and wallet. He didn't take an overnight bag, even though he suspected Cian would ask him to stay. There was no point. Once he'd said everything, Cian was sure to realize Jamie was right. Somewhere in his vague childhood memories, Jamie recalled his mother telling him about her grandmother's words of wisdom. She'd once said, "There's a lid for every pot." Jamie wasn't Cian's lid, that much was obvious, but surely someone else was.

When he arrived at the tiny visitor parking area near Cian's apartment, Jamie texted to say he was there. Cian replied with, **Come on up.**

Jamie sighed. He had intended to do this somewhere neutral, but he supposed inside was better anyway. No public scene that way. He got out of the car and entered the building. Cian was waiting for him, and Jamie was temporarily thrown by how excited he seemed. His enthusiasm was making it difficult for Jamie to focus.

Inside the apartment, Jamie stopped dead with his hand on the doorknob. There was a book on the coffee table, a copy of *The Drummer's Bible* identical to the one Jamie had on his shelf at home. Next to it were two CDs. Jamie looked up at Cian in confusion, only to finally notice he had a small wrapped box in his hand. Temporarily at a loss for words, Jamie froze, staring.

Cian set the box on the back of the sofa so his hands were free. *Say something,* he signed. His expression was pleading.

Jamie signed the first thing that came to mind. *Is that my band?* He waved at the coffee table. *You did this for me?*

His face turning red, Cian replied, *Yes.*

Instead of being glad or excited or grateful like he should've been, a wave of anger hit Jamie. Rather than talking to Jamie, Cian had gone and done this thing. It reinforced what Jamie'd thought to begin with—that they had nothing in common. Jamie had spent too many years on and off with Sage's resentment, and he couldn't do it again. He stood there, clenching and unclenching his fists.

What's wrong? Now Cian looked upset and worried, and it fueled Jamie's panic.

I can't do this.

I don't understand.

This! Us! Jamie's hands shook.

Are we breaking up? Cian still seemed confused rather than angry. *You're breaking up with me?*

You're pretending to like the same things as me. He waved at the coffee table again. *It won't work.* He shook his head and made as firm a "no" as he could.

What? Make sense! Now Cian seemed frustrated, but underneath it Jamie still felt his confusion.

Time to lay it all out on the table. *Why did Brandon think we should date?*

I don't know! Cian huffed. *Maybe he thought we would like each *other.* With a sneer, Cian added, *I thought so too. What is your problem?*

Jamie shrank back. Fear replaced his anger, and he remained motionless. He'd screwed everything up, exactly the way Sage said he would. Cian was angry with him, and Jamie warred with himself on how to respond to it. He wanted to run, to escape out the door and not look back. But Cian pinned him with his gaze. Jamie had to give him something.

Brandon only thought we would work because you're deaf and I know ASL. We have nothing in common. You can't pretend forever. That was the best Jamie was going to do.

You're holding back, Cian signed. When Jamie shook his head, trying to deny it, Cian stepped closer. *Go on. Do it. Get pissed off.* He took another step. *Let it out, Jamie. Tell me why you're mad at me.*

With a frustrated cry, Jamie let loose. *This isn't what I want! It's fake. You didn't ask me what I need from you.*

Then tell me! Tell me what you need.

Jamie's shoulders sagged. *We don't like any of the same things. I can't dance. You can't drum.* He poured his hurt into the next sentence. *We can't make music together.*

Half the intensity drained from Cian's expression. He waited, studying Jamie. After a moment, he signed, *What do you mean?*

My friends do it with their boyfriends. They play together.

Jamie thought about Nate and Izzy, the way they sometimes sang show tunes in the kitchen when they were both there. Or Trevor, how he and Andre loved playing jazz duets. A lump rose in his throat when he remembered testing it out with Trevor at his church and how well they fit. *We can't do that. I don't make the kind of music you can dance to.*

And that's what you want?

All Jamie could do was nod.

There was so much raw pain in Cian's eyes now. A long stillness followed during which they faced off, neither ready to make the first move.

At last Cian tore his gaze from Jamie's. He ran a hand over his face, at a loss for how to respond. Jamie didn't want to live in Cian's nearly-silent world. It had never occurred to Cian how important that one thing might be. Jamie was right; Cian hadn't asked.

You need music to be happy.

Jamie's shrug rippled his whole body. Dismissive, as though he couldn't bear to answer properly. He looked away.

Hey. Cian waved to get his attention again. *What aren't you telling me?* When Jamie tried for the second time to deny it, Cian wouldn't let him. *I don't play games,* he signed. *We talk or it's over for good. I mean it.*

For a moment, Jamie stared, but then he assented. *My ex-boyfriend. Nothing in common. Couldn't make music together.*

Cian remembered the first night Jamie stayed with him and the little bit he'd revealed then. He reached out. Jamie flinched, but he didn't move away when Cian's fingers brushed the bar in his eyebrow then touched his nose and his angel bites.

The man you got these for? Cian asked. Jamie nodded again.

One reason we broke up so much. Jamie's eyes darkened. *Don't fake it for me. Don't expect me to fake it for you.*

There was so much more than Jamie was telling him, but it was clear Cian wasn't going to get it out of him yet. Whatever had happened, he wished he could erase the naked hurt he saw in Jamie now. The most he could do was reassure him this wasn't the same thing.

You're wrong about me. Let me show you.

He took Jamie's hand and led him into the living room. Jamie sat on the couch, staring at the glossy cover of the book Cian had left on the coffee table. Next to it was the only CD Cian had been able to find of the Creepy Crullers. He'd wanted Jamie to know he cared, not that he was trying to change for Jamie or expected Jamie to do the same. Cian brought over the wrapped package and set it down on top of the book. Then he knelt in front of Jamie.

This is something you love. I wanted to understand you better. He swallowed against the painful lump in his throat. *I know we can't make music like your band. We make music with our bodies. Rhythm and timing. I wanted to learn about your art. We don't have to be good at the same things.*

He picked up the box again and held it out to Jamie. Accepting it, Jamie hesitated before pulling off the paper. Inside was a brand new drummer's multi-tool. He traced the picture on the box with his finger.

I love it, Jamie signed.

Do you have one?

No. I take tools with me. This is better.

I'm not going anywhere, Cian told him.

He took Jamie's hand and kissed his fingers. Hauling himself up, he sat next to Jamie and put his hand on the back of Jamie's neck. He offered a questioning look, and Jamie leaned in. The brush of their lips was soft, seeking, until it found its outlet in a proper kiss. When Cian touched his tongue against the seam of Jamie's mouth, Jamie pulled away. Cian let go of him, but he adopted as relaxed a posture as he could. He never wanted Jamie to feel coerced in any way.

They'd been signing, in part because Cian understood how easily Jamie's words became jumbled when he was upset. Now that he'd calmed down, Cian spoke aloud, a way to reinforce the point he was about to make.

"This is what people do," he said. "It's not important if we like all the same things. Haven't you ever done something just because someone you care about wanted to?"

Jamie's mouth twitched like he might smile, but he didn't. "I watched baseball with my friend Trevor."

"See? You hate sports, but it meant something, right?"

The sexy blush made an appearance. "We spent about a third of the game..." He bit his lip. "...making out."

Cian raised an eyebrow. He had a feeling there was a bit more to it, but he didn't press. "That's all I'm doing."

"And you want to make out with me?"

Thanking whatever gods might exist that Jamie seemed to be teasing him, Cian mentally crossed his fingers before answering. "Well, yeah. But that's beside the point."

Jamie's laughter was soft. He didn't seem to be quite past whatever had gotten him so upset, but at least he'd begun to relax. "Maybe later."

An idea occurred to Cian. "If you're worried about stuff, would you like to come somewhere with me?" He hesitated. "I hope you say yes. I won't be angry if you say no."

"Where?"

"There's an Irish pub, Sharkey's Snug. They have a céilí every month. There's one tonight. Cian paused, but when Jamie didn't react right away he went on. "It's a party with dancing. Not the kind I do. You don't need steps. They'll have live musicians, and it's really fun. I know you said you didn't like dancing, but—" Cian cut himself off before he kept babbling.

Jamie toyed with the box still in his lap. "Okay."

Cian couldn't help the relief washing over him. "Good. There's one more thing, though."

Jamie eyed him sideways. "What?"

"You'll probably have to partner with women for the two-hand dances."

Now Jamie did laugh. "I think I can manage their cooties for one night." He poked Cian in the ribs.

The thought remained even as Cian pulled him to his feet. "Grab a bite to eat first?" he suggested.

Jamie bit his lip even as he agreed to dinner. Cian had to work to keep his face neutral. Jamie possibly thought he was concealing something, but it hadn't escaped Cian's notice. For whatever reason, Jamie didn't generally like to have meals together, especially in restaurants. When they did, Jamie tended to pick, push food around on his plate, or arrange it so it looked like twice the amount. There was more to that story too, but Cian would settle for managing one issue at a time. It wasn't as though he hadn't been warned. Denver's words—that Jamie'd had it hard—came back to him.

Baby steps, though. "You know, you're probably sick of eating out, working in a restaurant and all. Maybe something quick here? I have some soup in the freezer my stepmother sent home with me."

Relief was obvious in Jamie's expression. "I'd like that," he said.

Cian wanted to do more, say more, something. Instead, he settled for a gentle kiss before getting up and heading to the kitchen. This was enough for now.

###

Having been startled out of an incoherent dream, Jamie lay awake next to Cian. The combination of oppressive heat and being in someone else's bed kept him from falling back asleep. There was a fan in the window, but it wasn't helping much. He kicked the sheet off, exposing his bare skin to the hot breeze.

They'd have been more comfortable in Jamie's air-conditioned apartment, but he wasn't ready for that yet. Having to either avoid or introduce his roommates made a convenient excuse why Cian's apartment was a better choice. At some point, Jamie would need to bring Cian there before he began asking uncomfortable questions. After the previous couple of dates, things had taken a more serious turn. Maybe it was time Cian did meet his friends. If Jamie could sit in the same room with both Cian and Trevor without feeling tense or awkward, then maybe they had a chance at making things work.

Jamie's mind wandered to what they'd been doing the last few days. Cian had taken him to the céilí, which ended up being more fun than Jamie had thought it would be. The dances weren't hard; Cian hadn't exaggerated that part for Jamie's sake. For most of them, he'd been in what Cian called the "gentleman's position." There was one where they didn't trade partners, and for that one, he got to dance with Cian.

Even though they'd hardly touched due to the nature of the sets, Jamie had felt close to Cian. Joy had radiated off him at being able to share something he loved. When they'd joined hands and moved in sync with each other and the music, Jamie felt how powerful Cian's muscles were and how much control he had over his body. It was as much a turn-on emotionally as physically, something Jamie could connect to in a different way. Cian had said they both made their music with their bodies, in rhythm and timing, and he'd been right.

Cian had been right about something else too, and the follow-up date had proved it. They didn't need all the same interests; it was exciting to share what he loved with someone new. Jamie's surprise for Cian was taking him to meet one of the percussion players for the South Boston Community Orchestra. Amelia, who played flute, set the whole thing up. Instead of trying to learn the basics of snare drum patterns, Cian had been able to experiment with a variety of instruments. It brought back a lot of memories for Jamie of playing in his high school band.

Afterward, they'd found a vendor selling overpriced ice cream and bought cold treats. For once, Jamie allowed himself the pleasure of enjoying the rapidly melting chocolate. They'd eaten them while watching a group of street performers doing some sort of acrobatic dance. A woman dressed up like a clown with a handful of balloons had tried to give them a pamphlet on the dangers of eating animal products. It still sat out in Cian's living room, and Jamie wondered what he was going to do with it.

Now here they were, sleeping off their post-sex haze with the whir of the fan and the whoosh of passing traffic in the background. Jamie turned onto his side and watched Cian. His lips were parted, his chest rising and falling in rhythm. Jamie wanted to reach out and touch him, but he restrained himself.

Cian was gorgeous like this. He was on his back, one leg

outstretched and the other bent, the sheets bunched at his feet. Even in sleep, he seemed so confident, unashamed to be fully exposed. His black hair was messy and sticking to the damp skin of his forehead. Jamie's gaze traveled the length of his body. He was hairier than Jamie, but that was partly a function of all the personal grooming Jamie still liked to do. Cian had a good bit of hair on his chest, and he left his pubes to grow as they pleased. Jamie wanted to touch him there, to run his fingers through the thick, black patch.

He had, earlier. Cian encouraged him to touch and examine, even guiding Jamie's hands to show him what he liked. This was all new territory for Jamie. With Sage, there was never much discussion. They did what Sage wanted, and if Jamie was lucky, he at least got off. With Trevor, it was more a matter of a quick check-in about what they were in the mood for.

Not with Cian. He needed everything clear beforehand because he didn't like to keep his hearing aids in. Signing was difficult unless they were in a position which allowed it. Always, though, Cian was willing to use his expression or his body language to communicate. It fascinated Jamie that Cian hardly made any sound when they made love. Random grunts or labored breathing, but none of the usual vocalizations hearing people used to express pleasure.

Everything he needed to say was written all over his face, and Jamie was learning to read him. The way his nose scrunched and his lip curled when Jamie hit an especially good spot. How his eyes widened and he licked his lips when he discovered a new way to make Jamie come undone. The round, startled O of his lips and the tilt of his chin in the seconds before he came. Jamie treasured each and every one.

There was never any pressure, either. Cian was open about his desires, and he expected Jamie to be the same way. It had taken some getting used to, being free to say yes or no or please. As Jamie turned that over in his mind, something struck him: Cian always asked. It wasn't a demand, nor was it a hint with the underlying implication he'd punish Jamie for refusing.

It extended outside the bedroom, down to Cian's invitation to the céilí. Jamie was free to do as he wanted, and he could have said no without fear. Cian was pushy, yes, but not like Sage. Not even like Mack. They'd fought that day, yet Cian had still respected him. Jamie sucked in a breath at the realization he'd been allowed, maybe for the first time ever, to get mad. And Cian, as promised, hadn't left.

Now Jamie finally allowed himself one small touch, something that wouldn't wake Cian. He put his hand into Cian's and let his eyes drift closed again. He descended into a contented, dreamless sleep.

The soft pressure against his hand made Cian stir. He opened his eyes and glanced over at Jamie, smiling when a tiny snore escaped. Cian held still, not wanting to wake Jamie by withdrawing his hand. He closed his eyes again but didn't go back to sleep.

After a few minutes, Jamie snored softly again and rolled onto his back, letting go of Cian's fingers. Cian was fully awake now, and he shifted onto his side so he could have a better look. Jamie was so sexy, even when he was dead to the world. Cian hoped the visual would provide him pleasant dreams.

Jamie's face was relaxed, his plump lips parted and his skin free of the worry lines that sometimes plagued him. He'd cleaned off the little bit of makeup he often wore. He still had shadows under his eyes, dark smudges Cian wished he could wipe away. Jamie had taken out some of his jewelry, but most of it remained. Cian's favorite were the angel bites; he loved to kiss them during their most intimate moments.

His gaze drifted down, over Jamie's smooth chest and the piercings in his nipples and navel. He kept himself nearly hairless. Cian didn't have a particular preference either way. He didn't shave or wax or do anything else to remove hair, and he didn't expect his partners of any gender to do so. But Jamie enjoyed it, and for that reason, so did Cian. Not to mention it made his pubic piercings stand out. Those, too, were sexy as hell.

Jamie had shoved away the sheet at some point, which meant Cian could see all of him. He'd been surprised when Jamie remained naked after sex. He usually preferred to put something on. Tonight, they'd cleaned up and then gone back to kissing and light touching before settling down for sleep. Jamie had never even put his underwear back on. That meant Cian was now treated to an excellent view of Jamie's long, thick penis and his beautiful PA.

Cian was mildly aroused now and feeling good. Mostly he was enjoying the freedom of lying naked next to Jamie. Their lovemaking had been slow and gentle yet intense, as though in some way Jamie had been trying to open himself more fully to Cian. It was as though he'd let go of something and allowed himself to be fully present.

It was like the day they'd gone to see the percussion player with the orchestra. Afterward, they'd stopped at one of those little street ice cream vendors, and Jamie had gotten some chocolate thing on a stick. He'd actually eaten it, which surprised Cian so much he hadn't even laughed when Jamie'd had to scramble to stay ahead of the melting so he wouldn't lose it to the sidewalk.

Whatever was tangled in Jamie's psyche was loosening bit by bit. It was frustratingly, painfully slow, but they were getting there. Cian could only guess at what lay beneath the surface. As much as he wanted Jamie to be honest with him, Cian's gut tightened at the thought of everything spilling out one day and the mess it might leave them both in.

He'd seen it already, the evening they went to the céilí. Jamie had tried at first to escape, but Cian had demanded the truth—or some part of it, at least. There was much, much more than Jamie was letting on. Still, it was progress. Cian couldn't be with someone who refused to communicate. On the other hand, he knew a bit about bottling up all that pain and anger and why Jamie might be reluctant to confront it.

Cian sighed and turned his attention to happier thoughts. They'd had fun at the céilí. Jomari had been there, playing fiddle with the other musicians. When Cian introduced them, Jomari had asked if Jamie was "Brandon's hot cousin." Cian almost laughed now, remembering Jamie's flaming cheeks and his own embarrassed flush. Later, Old Davey had patted Jamie's cheek and said he was special. He'd told Cian not to let "such a pretty young thing" go. Cian had always assumed Old Davey was straight as an arrow and just about as tolerant, but perhaps he'd been wrong on at least one of those.

The thought made him smile. He looked again at Jamie's face, so peaceful in a way he usually wasn't while he was awake. It made Cian feel protective. He wanted to be the person Jamie trusted with his whole self. Maybe more than anything, Cian wanted to see *that* expression on Jamie's face. The one he wore when he was performing, whether on-screen or behind his kit. The one that said he was right where he wanted to be and it was everything.

It was too hot for spooning, and he didn't want to disturb Jamie anyway. Like Jamie had done, Cian reached for his hand. Jamie's eyes flew open, and he turned his head. For a moment, Cian felt bad for having woken him. A heartbeat later, though, Jamie turned onto his side. He reached up and brushed the hair from Cian's forehead then linked their fingers again.

Cian felt the puff of air from Jamie's sigh, and he mirrored it. A wave of drowsiness hit Cian, and he yawned. He watched Jamie's eyes close again before allowing himself to be pulled under as well.

Chapter Eighteen

In the days following their overnight, Cian and Jamie texted back and forth. Nothing more was said about their prior argument, and Jamie's melancholy seemed to fade. Now Cian was here at his apartment, waiting for him before their next date. At some point, they were going to have to be adults about this. Cian was rapidly becoming absorbed in spending all his free time with Jamie, to the exclusion of other important matters. Jamie was never cool or unkind, but he was still so damn shuttered. Cian was used to being around people who didn't hold back, and this was an adjustment. And yet, he couldn't help how drawn he was to Jamie, compelled to coax the fire and passion to rise to the surface.

When Jamie emerged from his building, Cian couldn't keep his eyes off him. He always looked good, but this was different—black trousers and dress shirt with a bright blue vest. He had no jewelry or makeup aside from his piercings. Even those were subdued, probably the ones he wore to work. Usually his hair was a bit unruly, but tonight, he'd even tamed that.

Cian smoothed his own clothes, hoping he was dressed appropriately. Jamie had said to wear something he might put on for church, which had made Cian laugh. He hadn't been to any kind of church since coming to the US, and he had no idea what would be customary. When he'd texted that to Jamie, all he'd gotten in reply was, **Try business casual but less stuffy.**

So there Cian stood, in pinstriped gray trousers and a collared shirt somewhere between maroon and magenta. Jamie finally noticed him and waved, hurrying over. He leaned in for a quick kiss that sent an electric thrill up Cian's spine. Damn if Jamie didn't get to him every time.

"Where are we going?" Cian asked.

"A little jazz place near Grand Slam. My friends Trevor and Andre are playing tonight." Jamie blushed, and Cian wasn't sure what had caused it until Jamie added, "Is—is that okay?" He stole an unsubtle glance at Cian's hearing aids.

At least he'd asked. "Sure. Just curious, but why there?"

That blush again. "I, uh, want you to meet them."

Cian couldn't help grinning. Jamie didn't have a lot to say about his life, but the band and Trevor's family topped the list. He worked for them, caring for their infant son. For no good reason, that was one more thing about Jamie which Cian found to be a charming and odd juxtaposition with his rocker persona. It also said a lot about what sort of man he was, that his friends trusted him with the care of their baby and the degree to which he clearly loved the arrangement.

They took the train into the city, arriving at the cafe just as Trevor and Andre were setting up. Including Trevor, that made exactly three white people in the entire place, which was much busier than Cian had anticipated. Jamie drew him aside, pulling his attention from their surroundings.

We're guests here, Jamie signed. *This is safe place for queer black people. Trevor is here because he's Andre's boyfriend. You and I are here because of Trevor. Understand?*

Cian did. He let Jamie lead him to the low stage where they were setting up, and he hung back a bit while Jamie greeted them. Andre was a wiry man with glasses and a small, neat beard. He had close-cropped hair, smooth, brown skin, and nice full lips with an enthusiastic smile full of perfect teeth. Andre was handsome in a business-professional way, like some of the men at Dad's company.

Trevor was quite a contrast—thick build, dark blond hair, and deep gray-blue eyes. His laid back manner was also the opposite of Andre's quick, energetic movement. In a thousand years, they were not people Cian would've paired up, but the affection between them was so obvious even Cian felt it. He realized their faces were familiar, possibly from Grand Slam. Jamie had said they all frequented the bar.

Cian emerged from his musings about Jamie's friends as soon as

Jamie touched his arm. To Cian's relief, Jamie understood it would've been difficult for him to hear with all the ambient chatter, even with his hearing aids. Jamie interpreted Andre and Trevor's greetings and polite inquiries. The sweet blush was back, which intrigued Cian all the more.

After their brief exchange, he let Jamie make all the decisions and place their order for dessert, assuming Jamie had been there a time or two before. They chose a table with a good view of Andre and Trevor. The two of them moved around each other with practiced ease as they set up.

Music was a touchy thing for Cian. He often didn't use his hearing aids if he was going somewhere like Grand Slam. Even here, where the music and conversation were both much softer, he wasn't inclined to listen. Filtered through his hearing aids, music didn't have the same resonance for him it once had. He'd gotten used to it, at least as much as he could over the years, learning how to feel it in the rest of his body instead of hearing it.

When Andre and Trevor began to play, Cian felt the vibrations. The cafe came alive around him, and he understood that they were good. He turned to Jamie, and they kept up a lively signed conversation throughout the first few songs.

The musicians began a slower tune, and a number of couples got up to dance. Cian thought about asking Jamie, but when he turned to him, Cian was surprised at what he saw. Jamie was watching his friends. More specifically, his gaze was on Trevor. There was a look in his eyes that Cian could only describe as pure adoration. All the blushing now made sense; Cian had no doubt he was watching a man in love.

He sat back, startled but not, to his amazement, upset. Instead, it turned him on. Cian glanced back and forth between them, first to Trevor and Andre. They communicated wordlessly through the music and a handful of gestures. Something in Andre's expression made Trevor laugh, and Cian saw them exchange the same adoration. When Cian returned his attention to Jamie, he didn't see any hint of jealousy, only the same sweet smile and dreamy gaze. The whole thing took place in less than a minute, but it was enough for Cian to feel the effect on his body.

Before Cian could say a word, Jamie turned to him. To Cian's surprise, Jamie was looking at him with the same tenderness. It was *the* expression, the one Cian had been hoping to see. Jamie reached over and rested his hand on top of Cian's. It almost sent Cian through the roof with a combination of physical and emotional desire.

Something of that must've showed on his face because Jamie signed, *Want to get out of here at break? We can say quick goodbye to them. They don't care.*

God, yes. Yes, Cian did want to go, and blessedly, Jamie had read him easily. Cian had never been good at hiding his feelings anyway, but to have Jamie pick up on it so fast only made the need stronger.

Yes, please, he signed back, half eager and half relieved. Jamie's face went from soft and sweet to mischievous and hungry. It made Cian laugh, taking the edge off his want.

He barely contained himself, keeping his eyes on Jamie, who had gone back to watching Trevor and Andre. They finished the set, and Jamie was on his feet before Andre had even set his saxophone down. Jamie pulled Cian out of his chair, and they weaved their way through the other patrons toward the stage. Cian pleaded with whatever powers there were that neither of Jamie's friends would notice anything amiss.

Cian had calmed down enough to exchange a pleasant goodbye with the others. He caught a bit of Jamie's praise for their skill. As he observed Jamie's interaction with them, he didn't get the sense there was anything other than friendship between Jamie and Andre. He did see a flash of the same adoration for Trevor he'd caught earlier. It intrigued him anew.

At last they were on their way. It wasn't late, but the street was much quieter than the cafe had been. Cian strolled beside Jamie in silence. There wasn't the same urgency he'd felt a short time ago, but he would still be glad to get back to Jamie's apartment.

"So," he began. "Uh...you and Trevor?"

Jamie didn't respond right away. He touched his daith then stopped walking and turned to face Cian.

Yes. It didn't work out. He clearly wasn't going to elaborate.

OK, Cian answered. *You still have feelings for him.*

Jamie touched his arm. *I'm sorry. Is it weird?*

Cian's mind went back to how he felt seeing Jamie react to Trevor, and a spark of desire warmed him again. He wanted to kiss Jamie, but they were out on the street, in full view of anyone passing by. He settled for a brief, light touch to the back of Jamie's neck, enjoying the way it made Jamie smile and shiver.

No, it's fine, he assured Jamie, whose face briefly displayed surprise followed by relief.

Let's go, Jamie urged, and Cian couldn't agree more.

They arrived back at the apartment, and Cian was ready to tumble inside and push Jamie up against the door. He'd held it in the whole ride back, and he was more than ready.

Unfortunately, when Jamie opened the door, there were already two people in there. Cian saw Jamie's shoulders tense with annoyance. Both of the other men were tall, must've been over six feet each. The taller one had sand-colored hair and broad shoulders. The other man was slim with nearly-black hair and dark olive complexion. They looked up when Jamie and Cian stepped inside.

"Hey, Jamie," the sandy-blond said. "Sorry. We didn't expect you so soon. I forgot a few things. We'll be out of here in a sec." He stepped closer to them. In painfully slow and formal ASL, he said, *My name is Nate. This is my boyfriend, Izzy.*

Fiancé, Jamie corrected, but Nate just looked confused. Jamie said, "He's your fiancé."

"Oh. Right. Well, I didn't know the word for that."

"I'm Cian. It's probably faster if you just talk. I can hear with these in if you don't all speak at once." Cian indicated his hearing aids then shook Nate's hand. "Jamie, did you teach him that?"

Jamie blushed again. Adorable. "Yeah. We see Brandon so much, and he doesn't talk at all. I thought the guys should at least know some. Trevor's pretty good now, and I'm even teaching the baby."

Izzy shook Cian's hand as well. "I've seen you dance. You're really good."

Cian frowned. "You look familiar to me. Have we met?"

Nate laughed. "Probably. We all did that benefit thing last fall at Grand Slam. If you're a regular there, you might've seen Izzy when he's performing."

After studying Izzy for a minute, Cian said, "Ah, that's it. You're TaTa Latke."

Izzy's smile was sad. "Used to be, yeah. I don't do drag anymore. It's a little hard on my body these days."

"I'm sorry to hear that." Cian didn't press for answers. If it was any of his business to know, Jamie would fill him in. "And you, Nate.

You perform too?"

"Only the once at Grand Slam, for the benefit last fall. Not much call for an opera singer at a queer bar." He laughed.

"I suppose not. But..." Cian tilted his head, trying to puzzle out where else he'd seen Nate. "The Dyer Theater. One of my troupe's fiddlers plays with the South Boston Community Orchestra."

"Right!" Nate snapped his fingers. "That's my opera company's theater. We're on break for the summer, but some of the community orchestra's members play with us for our shows."

"Ah, got it. Well, it's good to finally meet you."

When Cian returned his attention to Jamie, he almost laughed. Jamie seemed pleased that Cian was getting on so well with his friends, but he also had an underlying air of irritation. They'd come back here for a reason, after all, and he appeared to be losing patience with the conversation.

Nate obviously saw it as well. He glanced at Jamie and then brushed Izzy's arm. "We should go."

"Right," Izzy agreed, picking up on the atmosphere. "Nice meeting you."

Like Jamie's adoration for Trevor, this dynamic intrigued him too. These were open-minded people, clearly used to navigating around one another. He admired the closeness they must've shared in order to create that. And yet, now he did feel those pangs of jealousy. They all knew Jamie in a way Cian wished he did. He hoped it would come in time.

Nate and Izzy made their goodbyes, and at last Cian was alone with Jamie. It took all of fifteen seconds of quiet for them to decide the others weren't coming back in. Then Jamie grabbed his hand and hauled him into the bedroom. The door had barely shut before mercifully, blissfully, Cian's hands and lips and dick were occupied with his very sexy man. All his other jumbled thoughts were swallowed up by Jamie's deliciously talented mouth.

###

The drive to Springfield was long. They were headed there so Jamie could meet Cian's partners. Jamie was nervous, but he tried to hide it for Cian's sake. These were people he loved, and Jamie wanted to see how they fit together.

He was more anxious that they wouldn't like him than the other way around. If Cian loved them, then they must be good people, he told himself. Someone like him wouldn't settle for anyone unkind. Still, Jamie didn't know if he would fit into their world. His life had never been anything like as stable as theirs.

Cian had his hearing aids in and the radio off so they could talk, but Jamie couldn't think of much to say. Instead, he listened to Cian sharing about his job and his family and his classes.

"Not all my partners are deaf," Cian explained. "Eric has some hearing, but he doesn't wear hearing aids. Skye is hearing, and she works as an interpreter. They have twins together, Sammy and Scarlet. Nell's the only one who's been deaf her whole life. She's the one who's pregnant. She has Waardenburg syndrome, and the baby probably will too. Do you know what that is?"

"No," Jamie said.

"It's a genetic condition, and it affects a lot of things, mainly her facial features. You'll see. Some people think she looks like an elf or an angel. She's really beautiful." He laughed. "But I forgot, you don't like women."

Jamie snickered. "I can tell when someone is pretty, you know."

"Fair enough."

Jamie loved Cian's mild accent; he thought he could listen to it all day. He'd never been one to swoon at the sound of someone's voice, but Cian was a man he appreciated for many things. The accent was so much a part of him that Jamie couldn't separate the two.

There was a brief pause, and Cian looked out of the corner of his eye at Jamie. "You're quiet."

"And you have a lot to say." Jamie grinned, hoping to make it clear he was teasing and not annoyed.

Cian chuckled. "Go on, then. Ask."

"Ask what?"

"Whatever's on your mind. I see you want to."

"Um...okay." Jamie flushed. "I was thinking how I like your accent, but I didn't want to be rude."

Cian laughed and applied a much thicker version, saying, "If you're lucky enough to be Irish, you're lucky enough."

Jamie snickered. "Where are you from originally?"

"A tiny town in County Galway," Cian said, dropping back to his normal accent. "My mother still lives there."

Jamie frowned. "How come you ended up here?"

Cian pursed his lips in thought. "I got sick when I wasn't quite thirteen. Meningitis, lost most of my hearing. Mam was sick too, but not as bad. She put up with me for another year and a half, but I was...angry and unruly. So she shipped me here to live with my dad."

"How in the world—sorry, but how did your parents end up together?"

"Oh, that's a story!" Cian said, laughing. "Honest to God, it's a clichéd romance novel with a bad ending. Dad was studying abroad and had a fling with Mam. She was a local with a reputation, if you know what I mean. Got her pregnant, she never told him before he went back to the States. He only found out I existed when she'd had enough of me and sent me here."

"Damn," Jamie said. "That's...wow. So, you've lived here since then? You've never been back to Ireland?"

"Twice," Cian said, his tone turning darker. "A mistake both times. Mam and I don't see eye to eye on a lot of things."

"I'm sorry." Jamie thought about his own mother. He didn't know what he'd do without her. "You have an accent, but you talk like a local."

Cian was back to amused, the tiny laugh lines around his eyes reappearing. "I learned fast that I'd get made fun of if I used my own slang. Even so, I had some kid call me a leprechaun for half a year before he finally quit."

"Oh, that's mean!" Jamie tried not to laugh, but he wasn't successful. Cian didn't seem too upset, though. "I had a kid call me that at one of my schools because I'm so short."

"One of your schools?"

"We moved around a lot when I was younger."

"For your parents' jobs or something?"

Jamie didn't answer right away. He looked out the window, silent until he heard Cian's apology. Jamie turned back to him. "No. Not jobs." He took a deep breath and let it out slowly. "We were mostly homeless. For almost ten years, we lived in different people's apartments, just me and my mother."

Cian looked shocked. His knuckles went white, gripping the steering wheel. "You don't have to talk about it if you don't want to."

He did, though. Jamie had never spoken much about it. Mack and Brandon knew, and the others had no need. "I want to tell you."

So he did. He took Cian on the short tour of his childhood, leaving out some of the worst of it. There was no need to mention that most of the places they'd stayed belonged to his mother's boyfriends or anything about Jamie's myriad small ways of coping. He finished with escaping from Mama's terrifying boyfriend and his months on the street.

"When I couldn't find her, I looked for my father. I didn't know until I lived with Brandon that he'd been dead five years. Heroin overdose. I don't know whether Mama has any idea and just never said, or whether she still thinks he's out there somewhere. I didn't ask."

"Christ, Jamie," Cian said when he was done. "I don't even know what to say."

"It's okay. You don't have to."

Cian reached over and put his hand on Jamie's. He ran his thumb over Jamie's fingers then withdrew. The gesture comforted Jamie, and his affection for Cian grew. He hadn't gushed pity, nor had he commended Jamie for his heroic escape from his shitty childhood. He'd only offered him gentle empathy. Neither of them said another word about it for the rest of the drive. There wasn't any need.

They pulled up to a beautiful old colonial-style house. Jamie got out and stretched while Cian pulled their duffel bags from the trunk. They'd been invited to spend the night, since it was such a long drive. Jamie wasn't sure what that meant. Cian had explained their relationship, making it clear that they were often sexually intimate all together. Jamie didn't think they would ask him to join them, but he didn't know what their expectations for Cian were.

They'd talked about everything; Cian had said there was no other way. He'd made it clear his partners were a non-negotiable part of his life, and in theory, Jamie was all right with that. What did surprise Jamie was that Cian was open to Jamie having other partners. Sage's jealousy had extended not only to relationships but to Jamie's sex work, to the point he'd finally had to quit. In contrast, Cian's generosity appeared to extend to include anything Jamie needed.

Now here they were, and it was all a full-color reality. Jamie's nerves caught up with him, and he waited for Cian to lead the way up the porch steps. Cian pressed the bell, and Jamie saw the lights flicker inside. They didn't wait for someone to answer. Cian opened the door and took Jamie's hand to pull him inside.

A burly, hairy man came out to greet them. He was built a bit like Trevor but more muscular, with ruddy skin, brownish auburn hair, and a full beard. He greeted Cian with a kiss and Jamie with a crushing hug that left him laughing and shaking. When he finally put Jamie down, he signed his greeting.

Eric. You're Jamie?

Yes. Jamie was still a little wobbly.

Eric led them into the kitchen where there were four more people. The adults all looked vaguely familiar. It took Jamie a moment to realize they were the people he'd seen Cian with at Brandon and Gemma's wedding. Cian pointed them out to Jamie. Skye was the one at the kitchen counter, and Jamie recalled she'd been the interpreter. She was average height and very curvy. She had a light peachy-brown complexion and a lot of springy curls piled on top of her head. The twins were playing with some plastic cups on the floor at her feet. Eric stepped up behind her and touched her shoulder. She turned and stepped around the little ones.

Jamie, yes? Her hug was much less terrifying than Eric's had been.

The woman seated at the table rose and came over to them. Her whole body swayed. She was otherwise slender, and her belly was so perfectly round she looked like she'd tucked a basketball under her dress. Cian had been right; Nell was lovely. She had wide-set eyes, which Jamie was startled to note were two different colors. Her long hair, which flowed around her shoulders, was dark except for one perfectly white streak in front.

She greeted Jamie with a gentle kiss on the cheek then turned to Cian and gave him a long, full kiss on the mouth. Cian's body relaxed, and Jamie was startled to find that the intimacy between them gave him a pleasant tingling in his stomach. They were achingly beautiful together. When she let go of him, Cian turned to Jamie and held out his hand.

Instead of the jealousy Jamie had expected to feel, he had a sense of being welcomed in. Cian was looking at him in the same way he'd looked at the others when he greeted them. It was mildly disorienting; Jamie had never experienced anything like it. He recalled the way Cian had watched him at the jazz club, when Jamie had unintentionally been so drawn to Trevor. Now he thought he understood the look in Cian's eyes that night.

To avoid the strangeness, Jamie took on a much more familiar role. He knelt down on the floor to say hello to the twins. Both of them looked at him wide-eyed, and he signed his introduction to them. After a tense few seconds, one of them handed him the plastic cup in her hand, and he accepted it. He spent the next few minutes getting acquainted with them, paying little attention to the four other adults in the room.

Cian's hand on his shoulder startled him, and he looked up. *You're good with them,* Cian signed.

Jamie ducked his head, flushing. He stood and followed Cian to the table. Skye set food out, and Eric brought over plates. While they ate, they conversed. Despite having lived with Brandon, it had been too long since Jamie had been in the company of so many people signing. He lost track of things a little, though he joined in occasionally.

At some point, Eric's attention fixed on him. He grinned. *You sign like Skye,* he told Jamie.

The others all seemed amused, and Jamie's face went hot again. He never could hide his blushes. Looking to Cian, he signed, *I don't understand.*

Cian laughed. *He means he can tell you're hearing but you spend a lot of time with deaf people.*

He should keep it to himself. Nell shot Eric a look that was half humor and half exasperation.

You're lucky, Skye told Jamie. *He likes you or he wouldn't say that.*

Now Jamie laughed too. He liked this little family and their easy way with each other. Cian touched his shoulder affectionately, and Jamie finally relaxed. These people were Cian's family of choice, in the same way Jamie had his family. Their relationships may have been different from his, but there was a lot of love between them. He began to hope there was room somewhere in there for him too. Conversation moved on, and this time, Jamie wasn't too distracted to keep up.

Chapter Nineteen

A NASTY summer cold took Jamie completely out of commission for several days. He couldn't swear he'd gotten it from being around any of the kids, but both Aidan and one of Skye's preschoolers had been sick. One week later, Jamie was finally feeling human again, his ears and sinuses mostly clear at last. He'd texted with Cian, but they hadn't seen each other because Jamie hadn't felt well enough to go out aside from work. He supposed Cian could've come over, but Jamie had been too exhausted to want company. Who knew a simple cold could take so much out of him? He tried not to think about all the other germs he might pick up from the baby.

It was his day off, and Jamie had done a bit of grocery shopping. He and Cian had plans now that Jamie was healthy, so he wanted the chores out of the way before lunch. He headed up the stairs to the apartment with the bags. As he reached his door, a voice behind him said, "I signed for this for you."

He turned around to see their nosy downstairs neighbor. In keeping with their habit of not using the real names of people they disliked, Jamie's roommates called her Mrs. Crotchety. Her real name was Mrs. Phelps, and she'd turned out to be all right, if still a bit moody about how much noise she thought they were making. Trevor said that she once caught him making out with Andre in the parking lot and left them a copy of a smutty note Mr. Phelps had written her.

"You're a popular fellow," she said, holding out not one but two floral arrangements.

Jamie smiled. The note on the first bouquet wasn't in an envelope, and Jamie saw Cian's scrawling signature on the get-well card. He didn't know whether Cian had sent two bouquets or if the second was from a fan. Not that the Creepy Crullers had that many, but a time or two had found them on the receiving end of nice things.

He accepted the flowers, juggling them with the grocery bags. Mrs. Phelps winked at him before she stumped away with her cane. Jamie shook his head and opened the door. He set the grocery bags and the flowers on the counter and took the note from the first bouquet. Cian said he hoped Jamie felt better, and he was looking forward to their planned date that night.

Before Jamie could open the second card, Mack came out of the bathroom, wiping his freshly shaved face with a towel. "What's all that?"

"Cian sent them." Jamie grinned in spite of himself.

"Nice." Mack thwacked Jamie's ass with the towel on his way past. He tossed it onto the back of a chair and started unloading the grocery bags.

Mack had his head in the fridge and therefore didn't see Jamie's reaction when he opened the second card. For a moment, Jamie thought he might collapse right there on the kitchen floor. He gripped the counter, trying—and failing—to take steady breaths.

"Hey." Mack's voice sounded funny, and Jamie wished the ringing in his ears would quit so he could hear properly. "Hey, Jamie. Breathe."

Mack's hand was on his neck, massaging. Jamie shuddered, his whole body seizing up. He shoved at Mack. Before he could stop himself, Jamie hurled the second bouquet across the room. The glass vase it was in shattered on the hardwood floor, and the pieces went everywhere.

"Fuck him!" Jamie yelled. "Fuck him. Fuck him. Fuck him…" He repeated it over and over until the words didn't make sense anymore. He fell onto his knees.

"Let me see." Mack's fingers closed around the card Jamie was still clutching. He pried it away. A few seconds later, he muttered, "That absolute asshole. How long has this been going on?"

What Mack had said was true; Sage was an asshole, but he was one with a remarkable ability to know what would go straight to Jamie's heart. He had all the right words, every *I miss you, baby* and *I'm no good without you* and *I swear I can't go on.* What scared Jamie wasn't the thought that Sage would make good on his threats to hurt himself. It was how tempted Jamie was to go back to him. How many nights, even after Trevor and Cian and all the dates in between, he still ached for Sage. Still wanted the familiarity, even if it came with all the pain. He could forget for a little while, but now it all caught back up to him in a rush.

"It hasn't—it's not—" Jamie tried.

Mack shook his head. "He didn't just start by sending you flowers eight months after you left him. How long, Jamie?"

Jamie was shaking all over and couldn't string a sentence together. Mack reached for him again, but Jamie swatted him away.

"Stop. S-stop—stop it!" He clutched his head in his hands. "N-not a baby!"

"Jamie." Mack knelt down next to him. "I know you're not. You can do this. Come on, breathe with me."

Jamie was babbling, and in his head he knew he had to calm down so he could talk to Mack, but he didn't want to. He was tired of it all. Instead, he shoved Mack hard. Mack toppled backward, and Jamie heard the thud as his back hit the cupboard door behind him. Before Mack could do anything, Jamie was on his feet, running for the door. He fumbled for a moment, long enough to hear Mack pleading with him not to drive in that state. He ignored it and tumbled out the door the minute he had it open.

He hadn't given a lot of thought to where he would go, but something in his subconscious urged him to take the most familiar route he knew. Trevor didn't live far, and Jamie convinced himself it would be safer to go there than to attempt a longer drive. Trevor wouldn't judge him, not for his state of freaking out and not even if he confessed he was ready to call Sage. Cian still didn't know a single thing about Jamie's volatile ex. Jamie latched onto anything to justify why he was headed there instead of pulling over and texting Cian or going back to the apartment to let Mack take care of him.

Jamie was shaking head to foot by the time he stood on Trevor's front stoop. Trevor answered the door still looking sleep-rumpled. He let Jamie in and shut the door.

"What's wrong? Did something happen?" Trevor asked.

"Wh-where—where—"

"Marlie's sister took her and the baby shopping, and Andre's at work. Jay, what's going on?"

"S-Sage," Jamie said. It was the only thing he could manage before he was half-sobbing.

Trevor pulled him close, folding him into a warm, solid hug. At last, Jamie's breathing slowed in the comfort of Trevor's big arms. Jamie relaxed his hold on Trevor and shifted to look at him. He meant to say something, but instead every last rational thought slid away and he yanked Trevor down to kiss him. It took just long enough for Trevor to respond so that Jamie's brain caught up. By that time, Trevor was kissing him back, and Jamie didn't want to stop.

He shouldn't have done it. He should've asked first or banished any notions the way he always had before. But if he'd been stupid and impulsive, Trevor was definitely along for the ride by then. Jamie caught it in the way Trevor breathed *yeah, yeah* into his mouth between kisses and the way he grabbed Jamie's ass and ground against him.

They stumbled through the house, pulling at each other's clothes, stripping down as fast as they could before tumbling into one of the bedrooms. Jamie didn't stop to question why Trevor was allowing him into what he'd called sacred space. Trevor was Jamie's sacred space, occupying a position in his soul that no one else was allowed. He was going to land there, secure in the fevered kissing and groping.

Naked, they fell onto the bed and shoved the covers down. Trevor pulled Jamie onto him, but Jamie needed to feel Trevor's weight covering him, keeping him safe. He rolled so it was Trevor on top. As they writhed and groaned, each motion taking them closer, Jamie sensed the enormity of everything that had happened. He sobbed even as they both crested, pouring out relief and desperation and loneliness.

Trevor slid to the side, panting hard. He ran his hand up and down Jamie's trembling arm. "Hey. Hey, it's okay."

Jamie took several deep, slow breaths until he was calm enough to speak. "I'm sorry. I don't want you to get in trouble."

Withdrawing his hand, Trevor rolled onto his back. He turned his head to look at Jamie. "I won't. I'll need to tell Marlie and Andre about this, though."

"We shouldn't have—I shouldn't have—" He swallowed. "Please, don't tell anyone."

Trevor sat up. "Jay, I don't keep secrets from them. They're not gonna be pissed at me. Well, no, they might be, but they know how much I love you. They just wanted me to do better at talking about shit instead of keeping it all stopped up till I explode. I was ready to tell you about it, but then you were with Cian, and I thought it might be too soon." The color vanished from his previously flushed cheeks. "God. He doesn't know about us, does he? Jamie, are you cheating on him?"

Jamie sat up too, shocked and dismayed at Trevor's words. He loved Jamie? He'd said it so casually, like Jamie should've known it all along. And then in the same breath, he'd asked if Jamie was cheating on Cian. Was he? Cian had other partners, and he'd assumed Jamie would too. Did it count as cheating if they weren't exclusive? Or only because it was with Trevor and not a casual one-time thing? Jamie might have spent time on a web series with a lot of different kinds of people, but he had no idea how to do relationships. Sage had seen to that.

Everything came full circle the moment Sage reappeared in Jamie's head. He thought about what Cian would say and how upset he might be if he knew what happened and what Jamie had done—was doing. Jamie stared at Trevor, then looked down at his naked, sweat-and-come-covered body.

"I have to go."

He slipped out of bed and began hunting for his clothes. Hastily, he cleaned himself off the best he could before throwing his jeans and T-shirt back on. Just like he'd ignored Mack when he tried to speak, Jamie now ignored Trevor's pleas. He'd screwed up everything with everyone, just like Sage always said he would.

For the second time that day, Jamie ran out the door and away from anyone who might have stopped him from what he was about to do.

Four hours. That was how long it took Jamie before he broke. He'd tried. All day, he'd stayed away from the apartment, not wanting to run into Mack. Even long after he knew Mack would be at work, he avoided going home. If he stayed away, maybe this time he would be all right. This time, he would keep himself under control.

He'd been so good since the last time he'd promised himself to start over in the morning. No listening to Sage's old messages on repeat. No pining after Trevor. No filling the gaping hole with whatever would make the pain go away. He hadn't needed to. Being with Cian, being good for his sake, had been enough. Now in a single day, everything had gone down the drain. Part of him figured he might as well go all in.

He didn't, though, not right away. Not until he'd fought the urge as hard as he could. A drive through town, a sun-baked walk through the park, sitting in his car in the parking lot and sweltering even with the windows down—none of it was enough distraction. Out of ways to resist, Jamie went into the apartment and shut himself away.

He was glad he was alone. No one was home to ask questions or wonder why the hell Jamie was locking himself in his bedroom, yanking a bin out from under the bed, and giving little or no thought to what he was pulling out of it and eating. It wasn't ever about enjoying it. The goal was to put as much of it in his mouth as he could until he hovered on the edge between pain and puking.

All his thoughts were on the years he'd wasted on Sage. Jamie should've known Sage would never let him go, not even after Jamie changed his phone number and blocked everything else from him. He knew why Sage had started calling three months ago. No doubt Sage's new man had called it quits, as well he should have if he was smart. Sage would've been furious and looking to Jamie to come back and fill that void.

He would never, ever do that again.

Sage had brought New Guy with him to one of the Creepy Crullers' gigs at Grand Slam back in January. It was maybe four or five weeks after they'd broken up. Sometime after Jamie was out of the hospital for getting dehydrated in his quest to stop exactly what he was doing now. Sometime after he'd tried—and failed—at going to a twelve-step group at Mack's urging. It wasn't that simple.

Thank God for Denver, the bar manager, and Jack, the bartender on duty that night. Denver had offered to throw him out, which Jamie declined. She did tell Sage not to distract the talent. Jack had kept him occupied by turning the charm up to a ten and flirting with Sage's guy. For a probably straight man, Jack was hella cool.

None of that had prevented Jamie from going home that night and shutting himself away, nearly making himself sick. Again. The same thing he did every time. He'd never told a soul what had happened.

It was why he'd finally broken it off for good with Sage. None of Sage's other behavior had been enough for Jamie to stay away. Not the pinching or the cracks about letting himself go. Not the complaints about how Jamie wasn't working hard enough to get the band noticed. Not making him quit a job he loved or demanding he stop masturbating because Sage insisted Jamie wasn't keeping up with his needs. Not the parading him in front of friends as a power play. Those were enough for Jamie to walk away multiple times, but never to stay gone. Every time, one or the other of them would make contact again, and they'd end up finding somewhere to fuck each other senseless. Not that last time, though. They'd fought, and Sage had crossed a line.

He hadn't hit Jamie. He'd threatened to spill his secrets, and not in the sense that he was concerned about Jamie's wellbeing. They'd been fighting, and Sage had used it as a weapon. Said he'd tell Jamie's friends everything, and they wouldn't be so understanding as Sage was. Jamie suspected he was right. They never would've gotten Jamie's secret binges or the real reason for his speech difficulties.

When Jamie was with Sage, he could control it better. Sage would distract him. It was part of what he always meant when he said he would "try harder." Be more attentive. Lavish Jamie with gifts. Tell him how good he was and how proud he was that Jamie had managed for another day. Sage wasn't monstrous down to his core, no matter what the others thought.

Unless he didn't get what he wanted, and what he always wanted was Jamie—mind, body, and soul. The flowers weren't about being sorry or showing affection. They were about making sure Jamie couldn't ignore him.

All of the history and the anguish rattled around in Jamie's head, even as he tried to force it out. The others had never understood any of it, especially why Jamie went back over and over. All except Trevor. He didn't like Sage, but he'd never pressured Jamie or called Sage names. He hadn't ignored everything like Nate. In fairness, Jamie didn't think Nate knew enough to have an opinion, and he was wise to keep his mouth shut. He'd tried once, and it hadn't gone well.

Thinking about Trevor and how monumentally stupid Jamie had been that morning woke him up a little. He looked at the floor, which was now littered with wrappers. His gut cramped, not just from how much he'd eaten but from the visual. He hadn't realized the sheer volume of it. He rolled off his bed to collect it all before Mack showed up and found him like this. Jamie groaned, not from pain but from the realization Mack wasn't coming home until late. Jamie was alone, and all he wanted to do was sleep it off. Everything from Sage's stalking to sex with Trevor to the scattered packaging on the floor.

He stood, pain flaring in his stomach. After managing to sweep everything under his bed with his foot, Jamie stumbled out to the living room. The first thing he saw was the vase of flowers from Cian, and his heart sank as his gut twisted. He'd forgotten their date. A few seconds of maneuvering and he had his phone out of his pocket, sending a text to Cian. Afterward, he sank to the floor and curled into a ball, which was exactly where Cian found him thirty minutes later.

You and Jamie are serious, huh?

Cian grinned at the text from Brandon. He hadn't said "I told you so," which was a plus. Cian had finally come clean about taking Jamie out to see Eric, Skye, and Nell. Cian had never brought anyone to meet them, certainly not after such a short time. Brandon knew that.

It looks that way.

A poor attempt at being casual. Cian hadn't seen Jamie in a week, due to the nasty cold Jamie had picked up, but he couldn't wait to go over tonight. He didn't think he would ever come down from the joy of watching Jamie connect with his family of choice.

I told you so. Followed by a grinning emoji.

And there it was. Cian rolled his eyes, even though Brandon couldn't see him, and laughed. Oh, well. He could withstand a bit of teasing. Brandon had been right, after all, even if Cian and Jamie had wasted a good chunk of time before figuring it out.

Yes, O Wise One, Cian texted. **Hang on, getting a text from Jamie now.**

He switched over to read the incoming message but frowned as soon as he saw it. The text from Jamie made no sense to Cian. He'd said not to come over, but it didn't read like he was simply still not feeling well from his cold. Something about it bothered him, the way it was too many words. It almost read to him as frantic.

Don't come tonight. Not feeling good. Something came up and I can't do this now. Don't call.

The message was out of the blue, not even in response to

anything. Cian hadn't contacted him. He was too busy getting ready and texting with Brandon. Sure, he was hoping they could talk about things while on their date, but nothing he'd mentioned yet to Jamie. Maybe just over a month in was too soon, but he had to make some decisions about where he would be in the fall. He couldn't put his students off any longer. The recital was a few weeks away at that point, and he was no closer to a solution than he had been in June.

And now here was Jamie's random text, half a day after the one saying he was looking forward to their date. Cian texted Brandon back. **Did Jamie message you or anything?**

No. Why?

Fuck. I don't know. Weird text from him saying not to come over. Says he's sick.

Wasn't he feeling better?

I thought so.

Did you call?

He said not to.

There was a longish pause, then Brandon texted again. **He's not answering. I'll see if his friends know anything.**

Cian tried calling in the meantime, despite Jamie's plea for him not to. Naturally, he got no answer. Instead of sitting around waiting for Brandon to text him again, Cian headed for Jamie's apartment.

No one answered the door buzzer. Cian ran a hand through his hair, gripping it and tugging impatiently, now out of his mind with worry. He fervently pleaded in his head that someone would come out of the building, preferably with some information. After fifteen minutes of texting and calling, to no avail, the building door finally opened.

An elderly woman hobbled out, leaning on her cane. She eyed Cian suspiciously. "Can I help you?"

"Please," he begged her. "My—" He stopped. Was she the sort to care? He certainly no longer did. If she was going to fuss over it, so be it. "My boyfriend lives here. He won't answer the door."

"And just who would that be?" The woman stretched herself up, her gaze fierce.

"Jamie. Uh, Jamie Cosgrove." He couldn't help an anguished cry. "Something's wrong, and I need to get to him."

The woman relaxed ever so slightly and glanced around. She came closer. "I'll let you in this once, but don't you breathe a word of it." She patted Cian's arm. "You take care of that sweet young man."

Cian nearly collapsed with relief. "Thank you."

She held the door for him, and he slipped inside and up the stairs. He banged on the apartment door, but as he expected, no one answered. When he tried the knob, it was open, and he exhaled forcefully.

It was silent inside, and it took a moment of looking around before Cian spotted Jamie on the floor at the near end of the hallway. He lunged forward and knelt down, checking to see if Jamie was breathing. The minute Cian touched him, Jamie stirred. He groaned and looked up, his eyes glassy. Cian was afraid he was hurt, but he might have been under the influence of something. He remembered that Jamie didn't drink, and a stab of recognition hit him. Except he didn't smell alcohol anywhere.

Perplexed, Cian said, "Jamie? What's happened?"

Jamie folded over on himself, holding his stomach. Maybe he really was sick because in the next instant, he gagged and struggled off the floor, bolting for the bathroom. For a fraction of a second, Cian stared after him. He stood and followed the sound of Jamie's retching, passing the open door of his bedroom. The sight left him no less confused—the area rug by his bed was littered with wrappers from prepackaged food.

Cian remained where he was, still trying to figure it out, until he heard Jamie sobbing. Whatever was going on mattered far less than the distress of the man he loved, so Cian left his confusion behind and turned back to the bathroom.

When Cian stared at him, it made Jamie's whole body tense up. His stomach throbbed; he crossed his arms over it, trying to soothe the ache. The sudden rolling made him afraid he was going to throw up. He gagged and scrambled to get off the floor, rushing into the bathroom just in time.

He lost track for a few moments in the violence of his vomiting and the deep sobs that followed. It wasn't until he heard Cian's voice that the pounding on the door registered. Jamie gasped and coughed, but nothing else came up. He wiped his sweaty forehead with a piece of toilet paper and tossed it on top of the mess. Closing the toilet, he flushed and laid his cheek against the cool lid. He'd stopped crying, but he was still shuddering. His eyes slowly drooped shut.

"Please," Cian begged on the other side of the door. "Come out or let me in. I can't help you this way."

Jamie crawled to the door and stretched up just enough to open it. Cian tumbled in and almost tripped over Jamie. He caught himself against the sink and looked down. Jamie peered up at him, willing himself not to vomit again. His stomach still felt tender. It was the first time in years he'd gotten sick after, but this time was mostly due to his humiliation at having Cian uncover his secret.

Cian leaned against the cabinet under the sink, and Jamie pressed up against the wall opposite. They were both silent. The only sound in the room was the toilet refilling. When it stopped, they were alone with the sound of their breathing.

I saw your bedroom. I'm not mad, Cian signed. He seemed to understand that's what Jamie needed right then rather than speaking aloud. *Confused. Help me understand?*

He'd obviously realized what Jamie had done. Jamie knew there was a word for it, but he could never bring himself to say it—not even in his head. Cian probably could have, if Jamie let him, but that wasn't what he was asking. He wanted to know why, and that was something Jamie couldn't begin to untangle on the floor of his apartment bathroom.

Jamie knew he couldn't talk. He was too wound up, and his words would end up as garbled nonsense. There was only one way to communicate all the complicated reasons Jamie had for his behavior. This time, he couldn't sign it, either. It was too much, a lifetime of hurts and fears and Sage-in-his-head. If he could tell Cian just one thing, he wouldn't have to search for words even he couldn't bear.

He swallowed, hating the raw feeling in his throat and the acidic taste. Making a C with his hand, he brought it to his chest and signed *hungry*. He did it again with more force.

Cian frowned. *Not a good idea.*

Jamie shook his head vigorously in exasperation. He tried again, not even sure if he was getting across what he meant. He didn't know how to tell Cian about the vast cavern inside, the one that would never be filled no matter how hard he tried. He blinked away tears and signed *empty*. He did it again.

Hungry, he signed, his hand shaking.

Something clicked, and Cian's mouth opened in an O of understanding. He held his arms open, inviting. Jamie scooted across the floor and collapsed into Cian's arms, shivering. His head hurt, and nothing made sense. Jamie tried to clear the fog, but he shook harder and his vision was spotty.

"Jamie? Jamie." He heard Cian's voice, but it sounded far away. "Stay with me, okay?"

That was the last thing he was aware of before the world went dark.

Chapter Twenty

JAMIE EMERGED into consciousness. It was dim in the room where he lay, and for a moment, he wasn't sure where he was. His first thought was, *not again.* A few hard blinks, though, and he realized he was in his own bed, not the hospital, surrounded by half a dozen people.

He wasn't injured, as far as he could tell. Whatever had preceded his blackout remained a mystery for the time being. He kept his eyes closed as he tried to remember what happened. Cian had sent him flowers because he'd been too sick to go out. Jamie was better now, and they were supposed to have a date. He concentrated, trying to recall the details. Sage—that was it. A rush of memories flooded in. The second bouquet, Sage's disgusting note, Trevor, and then making himself sick...

Oh. Cian knew. Jamie had left him a message not to come, but either he hadn't gotten it or he'd ignored it. He'd been the one to find Jamie. Too many things swirled inside Jamie for him to pick any one of them to concentrate on. Mostly he was embarrassed and angry at how Cian had caught on to his problem and apparently alerted all his friends.

His stomach didn't ache as badly anymore, but he had the lingering mild cramps which always followed. If he hadn't accidentally made himself puke, his body would've found another way to empty itself after a day or so. He'd probably have to deal with that anyway, same as always.

Now Jamie focused on the faces around him: Cian and Trevor closest, Izzy and Marlie at the foot of the bed, Brandon and Gemma by the door, and Nate and Andre against the wall. Andre had Aidan in his arms. Jamie pushed himself up a little.

"Hey," he said, his voice cracking.

"You okay?" Izzy asked.

"I guess," Jamie answered, glancing down at himself. "How did you—"

"I think between Brandon and Cian, they texted everyone in your emergency contacts."

Jamie nodded. He wasn't fine, even if his body was recovering. There wasn't a way to describe the deep shame, especially now that all of them had found out what he'd been hiding. Jamie looked to the others, wondering which of them was going to tell him he'd screwed up. He didn't think he could stand it, and he wanted them gone. Except he knew he had to tell someone what was going on.

"Marlie," he said. "I want to talk to Marlie. Alone."

He didn't miss the looks exchanged all around the room. Gemma signed to Brandon, and he acknowledged her. They stepped out first. Trevor and Cian both looked like they might argue, but Marlie shook her head. Everyone else cleared out, Izzy last.

"You need anything?" The question was directed at Marlie.

"No, I'm good. Just give us a minute. I'll let you know when we're done, and you can check in on him."

"I'm right here," Jamie said, irritated at being ignored.

Marlie squeezed his hand, and Izzy pulled the door shut behind him. She dragged over a chair and sat beside Jamie. He looked up at her, searching for the words. He and Trevor had gone behind her back, and now he was in no shape to take care of Aidan. Marlie probably wouldn't want him to anyway, not with his mess of problems.

"I'm sorry," he said. "I—"

Marlie interrupted him by leaning over and drawing him to her. Jamie couldn't fight it, and he sobbed into her shoulder. Somehow, she'd understood without him having to say a thing. Eventually, he let go of her, and she sat back.

"Can you talk about it?" she asked. "I assume that's why you wanted me to stay and not the others. You know I'm bound by confidentiality."

"Yeah." Jamie cleared his throat. "I think—I think I need the kind of help they can't do."

"Do you need to go to the hospital?"

"No!" Jamie softened his voice after Marlie leaned away from the force of his denial. "I mean, I don't think so. Can't you, like, refer me to someone?"

"Not really," Marlie said. "I'm not that well connected yet. I can help you find something, though."

"What about, um, Aidan? I know I'm not in good shape now, but I promise, I'll work on it. I want...I need..." Jamie swallowed back more tears. "I gotta be there for him."

Marlie took his hand again. "You will be. We'll manage until you're doing better enough. Did you think we wouldn't want you around him?"

"Yeah." The word was almost a whisper. "Not just this. I mean about Trevor, too."

"Oh, Jay." Marlie hugged him again "I meant what I said before. He loves you, and he said he told you so. We're all going to have to talk about this sooner or later. It was probably a mistake to ask you two to stay apart." She tilted her head. "What about Cian?"

"I don't know. I haven't told him what happened."

Now that Jamie's head was more clear, he thought about it. He didn't know whether Cian would be angry with him or not. Jamie had seen how Cian looked the night they saw Andre and Trevor play. Cian hadn't missed the way Jamie had been so captivated by Trevor. Something about it had sparked him, and there was no mistaking the bald lust in Cian's eyes. They'd gone back to Jamie's and fucked for what seemed like hours. Jamie'd had the same intense feelings the next weekend when they went to see Cian's partners.

Marlie interrupted his thoughts. "About Trevor, or about your bingeing?"

She'd said it out loud, and it hurt a lot more than Jamie had anticipated to hear it. "Both, I guess," he answered. "But I think Cian's figured the second one out by now."

Marlie sighed, raw and anxious on Jamie's behalf. "I won't push you, but it might help just to say it, to name what you're doing. I'm not judging you, Jamie. A lot of people have things they have to manage around food." Picking up on Jamie's confusion, she said, "I can't diagnose you with an eating disorder. But I can tell you that what you're doing isn't good for you. You'll need a professional for an official word on what to call it."

Oh. That did explain her word choice. "I've done it—" He cleared his throat. "Bingeing, I mean—since I lived with my aunt and uncle." He peered up at Marlie. "I was really good until a few months ago, though."

It had been an accident, that first time. He hadn't known—and they apparently hadn't either—that food could make him sick after so long at near-starvation. He'd liked it, though, the comfort and pain of too much and the experimentation with the right amount to hurt without vomiting. The secret thrill of hiding food even in the face of having plenty. The tight ache that dulled his mind and kept him from thinking about anything.

"That's a long time to have to hold in something like this," Marlie said. "It's not about being good. You're not an awful person, just someone who needs some help to figure it out."

Marlie's face showed no sign that she was angry or confused or judgmental. For once, Jamie's instinct had been right. He looked at her and only saw love and tenderness in her eyes. Not even pity. He saw now why Trevor adored her. Jamie would never be attracted to her the way Trevor was, but he had a sudden rush of love for her that he couldn't explain.

Before he could say another word, she leaned in again and kissed his forehead. "You're family, Jamie. Please don't forget that you can always talk to us." She stood. "Do you want to speak to Cian?"

The way she said it sounded less like a question and more as though she was giving him the go-ahead. He nodded, and she turned to go. Jamie stopped her as something occurred to him.

"Where's Mack?"

At that, her face fell. "I—"

"What happened?" Jamie's heart thudded. Was Mack okay? Had he gone out looking for Jamie and had an accident or something?

"We weren't going to tell you," she said. "We all thought Mack should be the one to do it, and we thought he'd be back before you woke. He went with Amelia to see Sage."

Jamie couldn't formulate a response. Dazed, he nodded. It made sense, really, but he hoped Mack hadn't done anything stupid. Then he reminded himself that he wasn't one to talk. Mack would be all right; Amelia would see to it. They'd both known Sage longer than

Jamie had. If anyone had a right to do something, they did. Still, he wished they'd at least asked him first what he needed from them. They'd gone without telling him because Mack knew Jamie would've begged him not to.

Marlie waited a moment, but when Jamie didn't say anything else, she slipped out of the room. Jamie lay back, eyes closed. The bed shifting stirred him, and he opened his eyes.

"Hey," Cian said.

Jamie hauled himself up so he could sign properly. He didn't think he could use words yet. *I'm sorry.* He tried to convey it with his whole body.

Tell me, Cian urged.

I can't say everything yet. Jamie fought the rising emotional tide. When he was more or less under control again, he signed, *I had sex with Trevor. My ex sent me flowers. I panicked.* He couldn't stop the tears. *I went to Trevor because I love him.*

I know, Cian signed. *I saw when we were at the cafe.*

Cheating? Jamie wondered if he looked as miserable as he felt when he signed it. He shivered, but Cian didn't reach out to him.

Not sure, Cian replied. His mixed feelings were plainly displayed. *Maybe. You think it is.*

What about us? When Cian didn't answer immediately, Jamie hesitantly signed, *You angry?*

Cian let out a long, slow breath. *No. I understand. I love my other partners too. Not angry. Sad. I wish you talked to me. Can we work this out?*

I want to, Jamie told him. *I need help for my problems. I have to deal with big stuff.*

Will you tell me?

Yes. Give me time? Jamie made it into a question and then touched Cian's cheek. *I'm tired tonight. Come see me soon. I'll tell you everything.*

Cian finally cracked a smile. *Everything?* He exaggerated the sign. *That will take a long time.*

Jamie relaxed. *I'll make coffee for you.*

Like Marlie, Cian bent to kiss Jamie's forehead. He ran one finger through Jamie's unruly hair, and like a cat, Jamie leaned into the touch. It was brief but reassuring. Cian wasn't going to leave, not even after hearing the whole story. Not because of that, anyway. Maybe they wouldn't be able to make things work between them. Or maybe they would. It wouldn't be because of what Jamie had or had not done, and that more than anything else was enough to give Jamie courage.

"Goodnight," Cian murmured against Jamie's cheek. He stood.

"Goodnight," Jamie answered before closing his eyes once more. He hardly heard the click of the door as he slid back into dreamless sleep.

It ended up being a few days before they saw each other again. Jamie needed time to heal and to see a doctor to make sure he was all right. He went to Cian's apartment this time. They sat facing each other on Cian's bed, knee-to-knee. Jamie toyed with the cuff of Cian's jeans, searching for a way to begin. He finally withdrew his hands so he could sign, *I need to tell you something. Lots of things.*

Cian reached out and took one of Jamie's hands in both of his. "You can talk if you need to. I can hear you well enough."

Jamie shook his head and pulled his hand away. Signing was better because he didn't have to fumble for the individual words and explanations. Cian would be able to gather the whole story better and more quickly, and Jamie wouldn't have to try to describe the feelings—he could show Cian instead. He inhaled, drawing his shoulders up, held his breath a few seconds, then blew it out slowly.

Hurts, he signed.

I know, Cian replied. *Take your time.*

I told you about when I was homeless, he began. *You know about the web series. You saw what I do to my body.* He swallowed, trembling. *Now I'll tell you about Sage.*

Jamie didn't leave anything out. He explained the best he could about escaping Mama's boyfriend and getting so sick he almost died. About what he'd done to survive the streets and how they'd never figured out if his speech problems were psychological or the result of brain damage. About getting into the web series and Sage and why he'd tried to hide him from Cian. Most of all, he explained the one thing no one ever understood, his craving to fill the emptiness and focus on the pain in his stomach instead of his mind.

Cian didn't flinch. He nodded and put his hand on Jamie's calf. The warmth of his palm anchored Jamie, and he continued, pouring out the whole history of what had happened. For as many years as he'd been communicating with Brandon, Jamie had never fully been able to capture the range of emotions Brandon expressed when he signed. Brandon's whole body moved, and Jamie had always marveled at the way he could say so much with his face and his posture and especially with his eyes. Now, telling Cian about his life, Jamie let go in a way he never had before. He let his body speak, conveying everything he'd held in while his hands provided only the few words he needed to tell the story.

The whole time, he focused on Cian's blue eyes, tracking them as Cian followed Jamie's visual cues. When Jamie was through, he slumped, drained but relieved at finally having confessed to Cian. He squeezed his eyes shut, not daring to see Cian's reaction once his life was out there, laid bare between them.

The hand on his cheek caused him to open his eyes. He was glad he'd been around Brandon and Gemma so much; he was easily able to read Cian's shifting expression: sorrow, rage, confusion, worry. The one thing he'd expected to see—pity—was nowhere to be found. Instead, Jamie saw love and tenderness as Cian's hand drifted from his face down to his shoulder, pressing and releasing.

Jamie drew his lower lip between his teeth, contemplating whether he should say what was on his mind. He shook as he warred with himself.

Cian tapped his shoulder to get his attention. *I love you. You're brave.*

No! That was one thing Jamie had no problem using his body to express. *Don't say that. I'm not brave at all.* He breathed rapidly.

What is it?

Jamie had to say it. He owed Cian the truth, the thing he'd tried to tell Trevor with sex. It was one of so many ways he'd driven a wedge between himself and everyone else. He'd tried to tell Sage, too, but he'd controlled everything Jamie did and claimed it was for his own good. Jamie had let Sage use him long after he was done working, drawing on his ability to do what he needed to in order to get the job done. Jamie was caught in Sage's need for him to be desirable yet unavailable. He knew he needed to stop what he was doing to himself, but he didn't know how. He'd never told anyone the truth, including himself.

Now, with Cian here beside him, Jamie thought he could say it safely, wordlessly. He poured all his pain into his expression, watching Cian's eyes widen as he signed.

Marlie took me to a doctor. He faltered a moment, and then discovered he didn't know how to sign it. He put his head in his hands, covering his face so he wouldn't have to make eye contact. He was only partially aware of Cian reaching for him, folding him into his arms and holding on tight.

Cian said over and over, "It's okay. It's okay."

Jamie lost track of time, unsure how long he clung to Cian before he stopped shivering. He'd had no idea how frightening it would be to admit everything so directly. Even after he'd calmed down, he remained in Cian's arms, simply breathing, until he finally felt safe. He sat up, daring to meet Cian's eyes. Cian put his palms on Jamie's cheeks, drawing him closer to nudge Jamie's nose with his. He sat back and let go.

We will help you. I promise. Doctor said what's wrong?

Jamie nodded, at last finding his voice. He gathered his strength, and spoke out loud, unsure how to convey the specifics of his diagnosis in ASL. "Binge eating disorder. It's unofficial until I see a psychiatrist and have a bunch more tests done. Do you know what it means?"

"I'm not sure. Is it like overeating?"

"Not quite. It's hard to explain, but when I do it, I can't stop until I make it hurt. I keep—kept—a bin under my bed full of packaged stuff, like what kids put in their lunch boxes. When I can't handle things any other way, I pull stuff out and eat it until I'm almost sick."

Cian opened and closed his mouth a few times before he finally spoke. "I thought before you might have a problem, but I wasn't sure what. I've seen you do this thing where you try to look like you're eating, but you're really not."

"Yeah. When I...binge, I sometimes can't eat regular food after. Or I worry about how much I'm allowed to have, so I pick to avoid eating too much. I don't really like it when other people can see what's on my plate. Most people assume what I do—the bingeing— means you'll be fat, but I'm not, so no one thought anything was wrong. I wouldn't have cared if I was, though." Jamie wanted to look away, but he forced himself to meet Cian's gaze. "Sage did. It's one reason I stayed with him so long. He said he was helping me. He used the threat of being 'fat and ugly,' but at least it kept me from hurting myself."

Cian's lip curled with obvious distaste. "That's the kind of help you can do without. I meant it when I said we'll take care of you." He took Jamie's hand. "I'll take care of you."

Jamie nodded; he didn't want to discuss it further. Any aid Cian might have offered could be off the table by the end of their conversation. They had to talk about what happened after Sage sent the flowers.

"The other day," he began, "I went to Trevor because he already knew everything I just told you about Sage—except for the part about my disorder. I didn't want to tell anyone he was still calling me, especially not you." He sniffled, and Cian passed him a tissue.

Cian sighed, and Jamie heard the distress underneath it, something he'd caused. "I do understand." He stood and paced, finally turning around to look at Jamie. "I'm not pissed about the rest, but it hurt that you went to him, you know?"

"I know." Jamie slid to the edge of the bed and swung his legs down.

"We'd already said we weren't exclusive, and I can hardly fault you for seeing someone when I have other partners. But the fact that you yourself thought it was cheating...I don't know what to do with that. I can't build a relationship with you if we can't trust each other."

"I said I didn't know if it was. Trevor thought so because I hadn't said he and I might still see each other. I thought it might be because I'd told you Trevor and I didn't work out." Jamie kept his eyes down, unable to bear looking Cian in the eye for the next part. "Sage used to call me names and throw it back in my face that I was doing sex work. He said it was cheating."

Cian's expression turned angry. "I can't believe he said that."

Now Jamie looked up. "You don't think it was."

"No, of course not. Look, I know I can be a bit heavy-handed with my opinions—" Jamie snorted, and even Cian cracked a tiny smile. He took Jamie's hand. "—but that's one I think even you should be able to agree with. I don't see anything wrong as long as you feel good about it. Do you know what I liked about your web series?" He cleared his throat. "Besides the obvious."

Jamie shouldn't have found it funny; Cian was obviously trying to be serious. He had to bite his cheek not to smile. "Tell me."

"You always had this look, like that was your favorite place to be. I've been trying for months—maybe foolishly—to get you to see me that way."

Too shocked now to be amused, Jamie said, "But...I do. I thought you knew that."

"I hoped." Cian ran a hand through his hair and sighed. "I would've been fine with keeping our relationship open, but you withheld so much more than a single time with Trevor."

"I did, and I'm sorry."

Jamie never would've gone back to Trevor if he'd been truthful with Cian about Sage. Or if he'd told anyone at all, especially Mack. Hell, he could've told Trevor long before Sage sent him flowers. Even Nate or Izzy would've been there for him. It was easier to see it now than it had been in the moment.

Cian sat next to him. "I haven't been fully honest with you either."

Jamie was fairly sure Cian didn't have any abusive exes who had been texting him for several months and sending him flowers, though he couldn't say for certain. He wondered what Cian had been hiding.

"I don't get it."

"The dance studio where I work closed. The owner, Marta, had to move home, and I can't afford rent by myself. I had use of it in July, and then I moved over to the Dyer Theater so we could practice there before the summer recital." He hesitated then put his hand on top of Jamie's. "I was thinking about moving out to Springfield, since that's where Marta went."

"And where your partners live." Jamie was beginning to understand.

"Right. But then you and I...and I couldn't imagine leaving..." Cian looked away. "Even if it was only in my head, I used being with you to justify staying here. It was a way to make the decision easier. That isn't fair to you, especially since I didn't tell you what was on my mind. I still don't know what to do, but it's come back up. If we can't be together, then I have to go. I have to try."

"Do you want to?"

"No," Cian said, looking over at Jamie at last. "I never did. But what else can I do? I don't have anywhere to take my students."

Jamie gaped at him. "What in the world do you mean?"

"I just told you, didn't I? My studio closed. I can't pay rent."

"I know, but you're wrong. You do have a place. You said it yourself."

"No..." Cian was frowning at him.

Excited, and happy for anything to get his mind off his own problems, Jamie grinned. Here was his chance to do something for Cian. "Yeah, you do. The Dyer Theater. They have classrooms, and they're looking to rent to someone. It's right in South Boston, not that far from where you were before. Let me talk to Nate, okay?" His smile faded. "Even if we're over, let me do this for you."

Cian ran a hand over his face. "I don't want us to be over, Jamie. I only want us to be honest with each other. If we can't do that..."

Nodding, Jamie said, "You're right. I do want us to try." He paused. "I still want Trevor to be part of my life too. He said he loves me, and Marlie confirmed it. We're not ready yet, but I can't pretend what he and I did means nothing."

"I know." Now Cian shifted to face Jamie, and the tenderness was back. "It's going to be a while. We need to deal with what's going on with you first, but then we all have to decide what we want and what we can give. I went through negotiating this stuff with my partners, and it'll take time."

"Time," Jamie repeated. "Yeah, I think we can do that."

Cian kissed him. It wasn't the bittersweetness of goodbye, but it wasn't full of raw passion, either. It was more like an agreement to see where this went. Jamie could live with that.

Chapter Twenty-One

CIAN FIDGETED while he waited for Skye to return with his glass of water. He'd never felt like a guest in their house before. Always when he came, he was considered family. It was no different from visiting his father and stepmother or Brandon and Gemma. Now he felt like a stranger, someone there to talk business or deliver a message. He supposed in a way that's what it was, and maybe that's why he was so uncomfortable.

Eric and Nell were quiet too. Nell rubbed her belly. She was only weeks away from delivering the baby. Cian wondered if he would still be welcome then, after telling them what he'd come to say. They might not want to open their home to him anymore if he wasn't going to become a permanent force in the new baby's life.

Skye set the water down on the table, but Cian didn't take a sip. She sat next to him, which was unusual. Skye had taken longer than the others to warm to him, and their closeness over the summer was relatively new. He wondered if she would be glad about the decision he'd made, possibly hoping it was permanent. It would be if Eric and Nell were angry with him.

I need to talk to you about us, he signed.

Nell and Eric exchanged a glance. Cian looked over at Skye, but he couldn't read her expression.

Is everything okay? Nell asked.

Yes. Cian gripped his knees to stop both them and his hands from shaking before trying again. *I need to take a break for a while.*

Another traded glance, this time with a lot more meaning in it.

Cian frowned.

We thought you might, Nell replied.

What? Cian was confused.

Eric told him, *We always said our home is open. You liked our arrangement as it was. We wondered when you would feel ready to move on.*

No! Cian realized the misunderstanding. *That's not it at all.* He took a slow, deep breath. *It's complicated.*

Skye tilted her head. *How so?*

Remember Jamie?

The others all indicated they did. Eric said, *Your boyfriend. Of course we remember him. We all liked him very much.* He smiled, and Cian could tell it was meant to be reassuring. Somehow, it only made him feel worse for what he was about to say.

Yes. He's not doing well. Cian thought about everything Jamie had been through in his life, challenges far removed from anything Cian had faced. *Jamie and I need time. He's healing from a lot of trauma. We want to concentrate on us for a while until he's better.* He didn't want to admit he was afraid to lose his closest friends in the process.

Skye's brow creased, and Cian couldn't discern if it was worry or disappointment. Maybe a little of both. She shook her head. *You're taking a break to focus on the two of you?* she asked.

I guess so. Yes. Cian looked at each of them in turn, trying to figure out what they were all thinking.

Nell glanced at Eric then returned her attention to Cian. *Tell us what's going on?*

Cian didn't want to break Jamie's trust, but he had nowhere else to go. He wrestled with it and finally began telling them the whole story. When he was through, he sat back and waited for their reactions.

That's a lot for one person to take on, Nell told him.

I know. He stopped himself from telling them he could manage it all. It was a lot, and he'd shouldered it all himself. He hadn't realized how sick and worried he'd been and how much he'd held back from Jamie so as not to make him feel guilty. Jamie had so much shame, and he hadn't even wanted to tell his friends or family the whole truth for fear of hurting them. He'd gone out of his way to protect Cian from Sage. He didn't need to feel as though he had to bear this too. *I love him so much,* Cian signed.

He put his head in his hands, shaking. He couldn't even look at the others, even though he knew they needed his eyes on them. It was too much, and he didn't know what to do about any of it. Skye's gentle tap on his arm caused him to raise his head at last.

Let us help both of you, she signed.

How?

There's an outpatient program here. It's at the clinic. Skye looked at the others, and both of them nodded. *He can stay here where he'll be safe.* She took his hand briefly and pressed it between hers before letting go. *I promise, we'll look out for him.*

Nell added, *Let us take care of him for a while. You don't need to do this alone.*

Even with the new baby? Cian asked.

Yes, Skye assured him. *There are three of us plus you when you can.*

Cian's eyes stung. Instead of letting him go, they remained steadfast. They were family, and without question, they were welcoming in someone Cian loved. They didn't even know Jamie very well yet, but they were willing to open their home to him. He trusted them with his life. Now it was time to trust them with Jamie's.

If he agrees, yes. Cain dropped back against the couch, relief pouring out of him. He hoped he could convince Jamie it was the right thing to do.

###

Jamie stepped inside Mama's apartment, inhaling and searching for the familiar smells. He still caught a whiff of her cigarettes, but the rest had been replaced with the scent of air fresheners and some kind of cleaning product. Maybe Bruce liked things a little cleaner than the other people living there. The absence of familiarity only served to make Jamie feel even more removed from Mama.

She hugged him as always. Maybe it was his imagination, but he thought she held on longer and tighter than usual. He pulled away. It wasn't going to be easy to tell her everything, but he thought he owed her at least most of the truth. He probably wouldn't ever tell her about the web series, and he didn't think he could bear to repeat the details about what Sage had done over the ten years they'd known each other. He could give her the most recent news, which was really why he was there.

"Come on in. Did you have lunch yet?" Mama asked.

"Yeah. I, um..." Jamie cleared his throat. "Can we sit down? I need to talk to you."

Mama eyed him curiously, but she led him into the living

room. She sat down on the ancient futon, and Jamie parked himself in a chair across from her.

"I'm listening," she said.

Jamie took a deep breath. He needed to tell her about it without hurting or blaming her. She'd always done the best she could. It wasn't her fault, all the things that had gone wrong in his life.

"Mama, I have to go away for a little while. I'm going to stay with some friends of..." He couldn't help flushing. He'd never mentioned boyfriends before. "Friends of the man I'm dating."

Mama seemed not to have heard the going away part. At the mention of Cian, her eyes lit up. "You have a boyfriend?"

"Yeah." He smiled, but it quickly faded. "Mama, that's not the important thing. I'm going away to get help for—for my problem."

Her mouth dropped open, but she shut it just as fast. "Oh, baby. Please tell me it's not—"

Jamie cut her off. "Not drugs, Mama. You did a good job, helping me stay away from that. I, um, have an eating disorder." His gut churned with a combination of anxiousness and shame.

Judging from Mama's expression, she was about to say she was sorry. Jamie shook his head, fighting the urge to comfort her and rescue her from her guilt. As hard as she'd tried, she couldn't do everything. There wasn't much question that Jamie's rough childhood was a factor, and he couldn't sugarcoat it for her. She closed her eyes and sat back.

When she looked at Jamie again, she nodded. "Okay, baby. So you said they're going to help you?"

"Yeah. Cian—that's my boyfriend—has family in Springfield." Jamie didn't think Mama would take it too well if he tried to explain who they were to Cian, so he didn't. Besides, family was exactly who they were. It didn't matter how that worked. "There's a special program there where you just go during the day for a few weeks. It's real intense, but I know I can do it." He got up and came to sit next to her. "Just like you did."

She put her hand on his knee and gazed at him intently. "It's not quite the same thing, is it?"

"No. It's not an addiction, Mama." He sighed. "I have to tell you some more things before I go."

"Okay." She sounded wary.

"Before Cian, I was seeing someone else. He wasn't nice to me." Jamie bit the inside of his cheek. He was hedging again, trying to spare her the worst of it. "No, wait. He—he never hit me, but he was abusive." He let out his breath in a rush, shaking from having said it.

"Oh, Jamie."

Mama put out her arms, and Jamie scooted forward so she could enfold him. He rested his head on her chest like he had when he was little, almost climbing into her lap like he was a small boy. Mama simply held him, stroking his hair and rocking a little. Jamie closed his eyes and let her warmth fill all the empty places he still had inside.

When Jamie sat up, Mama took his face in her hands. "You listen to me. I'm sorry I didn't protect you from all of this. But we're survivors, you and me. I'm still here for you whenever you need me."

"I know that." Jamie pulled back and gave her a smile he hoped would put her at ease.

He really saw her for the first time in ages, studied her. She looked a lot older than her late forties, which didn't surprise Jamie too much after all she'd been through. He realized something else. As much as she'd tried, she'd never been able to take care of him. He didn't know if this made him sad or relieved to admit it. Brandon's family—his father's relatives—had been the ones to take him in and make sure he was safe. He'd made a mess of their generosity, but he would make it up to them. He would make it up to everyone he'd shut out for trying to help.

That was where he was going next. He'd arranged to see Brandon and his family to talk to them about what was going on. Brandon at least deserved an explanation after what happened. Jamie was still trying to put together what he would say so they wouldn't feel as though he blamed them. They'd tried, but he'd rejected their efforts. Unlike with Mama, he hadn't wanted to be alone. Cian was coming with him, mostly because he'd known Brandon for longer than Jamie had.

His mind wandered to his tentative relationship with Cian. Jamie wanted to be the kind of man Cian deserved, someone who got his life on track not for them but for himself. He'd loved Cian enough to try to protect him from knowing about Sage, and that had to mean something. Now he had to care enough about himself to get well.

"I have to go," Jamie told Mama. "I have a lot to take care of. Cian is a dance teacher, and I'm going to watch his class dance before he drives me out to Springfield. My program starts right after Labor Day, and they thought I'd like the long weekend with Cian there to help me adjust first." He stood.

Mama got up too and gave him another hug. "Come see me when you get home, okay?"

"Sure, Mama."

He didn't tell her he needed more than just the few weeks of the program before he would be able to talk to her again. He had to have time and space away from all the things that set him off, including being at her apartment. He would call her when he was strong enough, but he needed to learn how to manage triggers—that's what the doctor and Cian's partner Skye called them—before he could handle experiencing them. That meant he might need to be away from Trevor for a bit too, but he thought that might be different. Trevor wasn't part of the source of his trauma.

Jamie stepped out of the apartment, pulling the door shut on his way. He stood in the hallway for a few minutes, collecting his thoughts. At last he turned and descended the stairs to the car where Cian was waiting.

###

Jamie set clothes out on his bed, then put them back in the drawer, then got them out again and folded them. He didn't know what he would want from home. He'd made sure to change to his more subtle body jewelry, the sort he would wear for work. To his knowledge, there weren't any rules at the outpatient program, and he didn't want his piercings to close. On the other hand, he didn't want to stand out too much. He was having the same problem with his clothes.

While he worked through his crisis of wardrobe, there was knock on his open bedroom door. Jamie turned to see Mack, two glasses of water in his hands.

"Thought you could use this." Mack brought them in and set one down on the nightstand.

They hadn't talked much since the day Sage sent the flowers. Only the quick exchanges required for hello or goodbye. Mack had canceled the band's most recent gig. As much as Jamie knew it was all right to concentrate on his health, he still felt bad.

Picking up the glass, Jamie said, "Thanks." He took a sip and set it down before going back to sorting and folding.

After an extended silence, Mack said, "You know Amelia and I went to see him."

"Marlie told me." Jamie kept his back turned.

"He had no right to do what he did."

"And neither did you," Jamie snapped. He finally faced Mack. "I never asked you to play bodyguard."

"Damn it, Jamie, someone needed to! You never fucking ask for anything. I've tried. God knows, I've tried. I put up with his shitty treatment of you for your sake, not his."

"You don't get it, do you?" Jamie breathed slowly, trying to stem his rage before he wasn't able to speak. Mack needed to understand, and Jamie couldn't tell him if he was too busy finding words.

Mack put his glass down and folded his arms. "You're right. I don't get it, but I want to."

"Sage has been the most stable thing in my life. I don't want to wind up like her, living boyfriend to boyfriend in an endless loop." He waited for Mack to digest that. "He said I would. I was too needy, too unstable. Only he could fix everything."

"Satan's left nut," Mack muttered. "That asshole is the gift that keeps on giving."

Jamie snorted at Mack's weird oath. "It was pretty easy to believe him, especially after that many years."

"Do you see why we went to him? We had to stop the cycle, Jamie. Cian made you the happiest I've ever seen you."

"No." Jamie shook his head. "It wasn't just him. It was a lot of things. You know what I learned?"

"What?"

"I can't really love him until I'm okay with me. I did so much stupid shit when I was with Sage, including quitting a job I loved. Yeah, I said it. I got paid to fuck hot men on camera, and I'm not sorry. It was a quality job with people I liked."

"Jesus, Jamie. I know that. I always wondered why you stopped. You were really good." He went red. "Not that I, uh, have an opinion on your work. Nope."

Jamie grinned. "Always knew you watched it, whatever you tried to say."

"Yeah, well, don't get a big head about it."

"Nah." Jamie's amusement receded. "Sage used to call it cheating. He tried to make me feel like I was doing something filthy, but then he'd act all proud that he'd gotten someone like me. Do you know what Cian said?"

Mack shook his head. "No. You never told me any of this."

"Cian said I was making art and that it was beautiful." Jamie flushed. "He didn't make me happy. I was happy because I'd stopped fixating on Sage for the first time in years. I had Aidan and—" He cut himself off. Mack still didn't know about Trevor.

Or maybe he did because he said, "And Trevor."

"You knew?"

"How the fuck did you think we all missed it? You used to go all moony-eyed over him every time we were over there." He snorted when Jamie gave him an incredulous look. "Fine, it was Amelia and Nate who pointed it out to me. You know I can't tell that shit. I did figure out you two were fucking, though. She thought you were pining, and the last time Nate talked to Trevor about it, he said you were only friends."

Jamie sat down on the edge of his bed. He rested his trembling hands on his knees. "With Sage, it was just fucking. Not with Trevor."

"Or with Cian?"

"Yeah."

Mack sat next to him and bumped his shoulder. "You'll work it out."

"Cian said it'll take time. I haven't talked to Trevor yet."

"You probably should before you go." Mack stood. "I know I can be a dick sometimes, but I'm here for you."

Jamie rose from the bed and picked up a T-shirt. "I know."

Mack patted his shoulder and ducked out of the room. For a moment, Jamie stared after him, wondering if there was more they should've said. He thought about going out to the other room and asking exactly what Mack and Amelia had said to Sage, but he decided he didn't really want to know after all. It was enough they'd done it. He set the shirt in the duffel bag and picked up a pair of jeans.

As Jamie was picking up his car keys to go see Trevor, the phone rang. "Hello?"

"Is this Kit Carter?"

Jamie hadn't been called that in years. He nearly tripped over himself saying, "That depends. Who's calling?"

"This is Dirk Bloom from Spider Industries." The man's voice softened. "I'm not sure if you remember me."

Jamie's legs wobbled, and he had to go sit down on the couch. "Yeah. I remember."

"Look, I know this is a long shot, but I've got a new production in the works, and one of your former costars said he saw your band perform recently. It took me a while, but I finally tracked down your band's front man. He didn't seem to think you'd mind if I called."

"What kind of production?" Jamie's heart thumped. He wasn't sure he wanted to go back to anything quite like the web series, but his interest was piqued.

"It's a little different from before. We've expanded, you know." He sounded proud.

"Expanded?"

"We developed a secondary channel with different programming. For youth, education, and general programming. That one's free. The new series is for a third channel under the same umbrella. New concept, new show. It's about a group of friends living and loving in Boston."

"I don't know..."

"Look, if it helps, there's nothing as explicit as the other series. Although, that one is still going, and if you wanted back in..." He trailed off.

"I don't, not right now. I've been out of the industry so long, and I don't even have an agent anymore."

"Don't worry about that right now. There are plenty of people who can help you out there if you need. At this point, I'm simply feeling out the people I think might be a good fit for this project."

Now Jamie was curious. His original series had been meant for specific tastes, and it wasn't for everyone. If he'd wanted, he could've looked for other work. He'd have considered it, if not for Sage. After talking to Mack, he'd entertained the idea of going back, except he'd been away for long enough and didn't know if he'd be welcome. Dirk was offering something he hadn't considered, and it appealed to him.

"Can you tell me more?"

"I'd love to. Over coffee? Or you can meet me at the studio?"

Jamie's shoulders slumped. "I'm sorry. I—" He'd been about to make an excuse, but he thought better of it. "Look, I have to be honest. I'm dealing with some personal issues, and I'm going to be away for a few weeks to learn how to manage them better. I don't know when I'll be up to something like this. I appreciate the offer, but this might not be a good time."

"Oh, that's no problem," Dirk assured him. "We're only in the planning stages now. Production doesn't start for months yet.

Listen, I'll give you my contact information, and you get back to me when you're in town again."

"All right."

Jamie took Dirk's info and then ended the call. He sat staring at his phone for a few minutes before slipping it back in his pocket. He didn't know if he would take the offer. It was tempting, and he was flattered that his former costar thought he'd be a good candidate, though he did wonder what else might've motivated Dirk to call. There was very little chance that there was nothing extra in it for him. The company was doing fine, and Jamie's star status—or, more accurately, his cock's star status—were probably not quite enough of a draw. Still, it was worth considering, and it was nice to know he still had friends in the business.

For now, he still needed to go see Trevor, who was waiting for him at the house. Jamie wasn't sure it was the best place to meet, but for a single conversation, he could manage. His inner storm was down to a category one at the moment. He left the apartment and the strange conversation with Dirk behind for the time being.

Trevor was on the front stoop when Jamie arrived. He stood as soon as Jamie pulled into the driveway and came toward the car. Jamie remained seated and rolled down the window.

"Hey," Trevor greeted him. "Did you want to come in, or would it be better to go somewhere? I hadn't thought about how it might be for you after everything."

"It's fine. I can't stay long anyway."

He got out and followed Trevor into the house. None of the others were home except Aidan, who had somehow fallen asleep in the middle of the floor. Jamie smiled; he was as cute as ever.

They sat on the couch, carefully not touching. It was weird the way he both wanted Trevor and didn't. Like with Cian, they needed time to sort through what they meant to each other and why.

Trevor cleared his throat. "Do you remember when I came home from Andre's the first time? This has to be more than a year ago now."

"Yeah, I remember." Vividly. Trevor had been so upset and worried about Nate.

"You massaged my neck and talked me down from freaking out." Trevor glanced over at him. "That's the first time I remember feeling anything for you. It wasn't much. Mostly I was grateful you weren't being an ass about the whole thing. But, uh, I did wonder. You know. What it would be like with you."

Jamie laughed softly. "God, Trev. I thought you were hot the day you moved in." He sobered. "The truth?"

"Yeah, of course." Trevor frowned in confusion.

"Sage made me think my body was only worth as much as he said it was. You had all this confidence. And..." This was the really hard thing to say. "I've always liked fat guys, Trev. It's all mixed up in my head with some of the other stuff. I can't—"

"Hey." Trevor put a hand on Jamie's knee, and he flinched, so Trevor withdrew. "I'm not mad, and you don't need to explain."

"I get like that, like everyone's gonna be so pissed if they know stuff." He sighed. "I think that's what I wanted. You never said anything—not about Sage or what I was eating or even all the times I showed up with a new piercing."

Trevor frowned. "I don't understand."

"You didn't make me talk about shit. Mack always thinks he's being helpful, and maybe he is. He doesn't let me get away with things. Cian..." Jamie trailed off, trying to find the right words. "He pushes. Not in a bad way, but he's direct. You gave me space to breathe."

Trevor snorted. "Sounds like Marlie. She says ninety percent of our problems can be solved by talking about them like grown-ups."

A dry laugh caught in Jamie's throat. "She's probably right, but sometimes I need the quiet."

"So." Trevor cleared his throat. "Let me make sure I've got this. You liked me because you have a thing for fat guys who don't pressure you to talk."

Jamie couldn't read his expression or his tone of voice. "I guess so, yeah. Are you mad?"

"No, not really." He paused. "You were wrong about one thing you said, though."

"What's that?"

"I'm not the confident guy you think I am. Jay, a lot of us have stuff we manage around food and our bodies."

Jamie tilted his head and studied Trevor. "Huh. Marlie said that too."

"Yeah." He smiled. "She's pretty smart. She's the one who taught me I don't have to settle for being 'tolerated.' I get to have love just like anyone." His smile faded, and he put his hand on Jamie's knee. "I think what's between us now is better than that, right?"

"Yeah." Jamie swallowed the lump rising in his throat. "The

music."

"Music?"

"The night we played at the church. You filled in a missing piece. After we stopped...whatever it was, Mack noticed. He said I was off. I can't do that with Cian, and it's not the same with the band."

"I...wow." Trevor sat in silence for almost a full minute. When he spoke again, it was hushed. "I wanted to do that again, you know. It meant something to me too."

"We will," Jamie assured him. "We have to figure out what's going on between us, but right now, I need to work on my shit." He glanced at the baby, who was mercifully still sleeping. "Including watching my mouth around your kid."

Trevor chuckled. "You're good. And yeah, we'll talk for real this time before we start something, okay?"

"If things work out with Cian, he has to be part of it too. And Marlie and Andre."

"I know. But what do you mean, 'if'?"

"We're still working on it. I broke his trust, and I gotta earn it back."

Trevor nodded. Since there didn't seem to be a whole lot more to say, they watched in silence as Aidan stirred. Jamie knew now what drew him to Aidan and even Skye's kids. There was hope there, hope that the future held better things than it had for Jamie at their age. He wanted more for them than a lifetime of clinging to the wrong people and the wrong things.

He stood and picked Aidan up. Giving the baby a kiss on the top of his head, Jamie handed him back to his daddy. Trevor stepped closer, and Jamie nodded. They closed the gap and enjoyed a brief press of their lips before parting. Like with Cian, the kiss suggested agreement. Jamie prayed the weeks apart would do them both some good. With one last glance, he stepped outside and pulled the door shut.

###

The summer dance performance went off beyond Cian's expectations. Beforehand, he'd peeked out at the audience. His family was there, of course. Not only his father, stepmother, and youngest two sisters but Eric, Nell, and Skye as well. He'd looked again and spotted Jamie, seated between Mack and Trevor. Jamie's other friends were there too, which surprised and pleased Cian.

Jomari had been beyond wonderful, arranging publicity and

working to get people in the door. Nate had come through as well, with some last-minute advertising and theater personnel to run front of house. Between the two of them, the auditorium was nearly full. Nate was able to help Cian out with the theater's owner and manager, which meant Cian's students had a place to go afterward, at least for this year. Jamie had been right.

The dances themselves were created by the students. Instead of a folklore or historical theme, they'd gone with a multicultural one. His students came from all different backgrounds, and he'd given them the flexibility to work their own families' traditions into the production. The result was like a patchwork quilt, all woven together by the steps and the patterns of the reels. It reminded Cian of his own family of choice.

At the end, Cian was pleased to see the audience on their feet for his students. He was proud of them and all the hard work they'd done in only two months. As the house emptied out afterward, he was so caught up in the moment and in congratulating his classes that he didn't notice at first when Jamie came backstage.

After saying goodbye to a few people, he felt the gentle tap on his shoulder and turned around. He sucked in his breath at the sight. They hadn't seen each other since Cian talked to him about going to stay in Springfield, and he'd forgotten how it felt to be up close and personal. All the things he'd begun to feel over the summer—the love and affection and desire—came back in a flood. It was powerful, and he didn't quite know how to handle it without overwhelming Jamie.

Fortunately, he didn't need to worry. Jamie stepped closer and put his arms around Cian. "Brilliant," he said.

"They were amazing." Cian pulled back to look at Jamie. *Talk somewhere quiet?* he signed. At Jamie's assent, he explained he would need to finish up with his students first.

Jamie left him there, and after another round of congratulations, he bid his students and families goodbye. Classes would start a bit late this year, in order to give him time to work out details at the theater. But they were starting, and that was the important thing. He would contact Marta at some point to let her know; she would be glad he'd found a solution.

At last he was alone, and he went in search of Jamie. He found him by the stairs. They ascended, and Jamie led him to the props room, which amused and puzzled Cian until Jamie explained.

"Nate said this was the place that changed things for him

nearly a year ago. If there's any magic in this theater, maybe it's in this room." He grinned.

It was good to see Jamie smiling, and another wave of love and longing hit Cian. "Let's hope so," he said.

Jamie's smile slid away, but he didn't have the hollow look he'd taken on the last time they spoke. "What did you want to talk about?"

"I'm not sure. I suppose I just wanted to see you alone before we go."

"That's fair."

The urge was strong to take Jamie in his arms and kiss him senseless. He wanted to press him against the wall and consume each other, even in this semi-public space. He didn't, though.

"Christ, Jamie, I didn't know I'd miss you so much. I'm sorry for everything. I don't want to lose you." His eyes stung.

"You're not." Jamie put his palm on Cian's cheek. "I'm sorry too."

They kissed then, and Cian thought it might have been one of the most wonderful experiences of his life. He didn't know what their future might hold, but he knew he wanted Jamie in it for as long as possible. Being with him was everything he'd wanted. They had their other families too; there was plenty of love on both sides to hold them.

Jamie suddenly let go of him, and Cian turned to see what had interrupted them. Nate was in the doorway of the props room, badly disguising a smile behind his fist.

"Sorry to bother you. Jamie, you ready to get your stuff out of Mack's van?"

Jamie glanced at Cian. "Yeah. Be down in a sec."

"Sure." Nate fake-coughed to cover his amusement. "Take however long you need. God knows I have a time or two."

Cian stared at him, but Jamie shook with laughter. "I think we're all aware. You should write a book—The Five Unusual Uses of a Props Room."

Nate gave him the finger as he disappeared back down the hallway. Jamie turned back to Cian.

I'll miss you, he signed.

Me too. Cian couldn't have spoken just then. All the emotions had caught back up to him. *I'll see you when you get back.*

Jamie took his hand, and together they walked back toward the stairs. They had the drive to Springfield and the rest of the weekend with Cian's partners, and then they wouldn't see each other until Nell had the baby. They'd both agreed. No calls, no texts, no visits in order to give Jamie the chance to focus only on his recovery. It was going to feel like forever.

But that kiss. It was different from the last one they'd shared. That had been full of the uncertainty they both had about their relationship. Today, they'd made a commitment to working through everything. At least, that was how Cian chose to read it.

At the top of the stairs, he stopped and let go of Jamie's hand. When Jamie turned to face him, Cian signed, *I love you*. And when Jamie signed it right back, Cian thought his heart might burst from the joy of it all.

ABOUT THE AUTHOR

A.M. Leibowitz is a queer spouse, parent, feminist, and book-lover falling somewhere on the Geek-Nerd Spectrum. They keep warm through the long, cold western New York winters by writing about life, relationships, hope, and happy-for-now endings. Their published fiction includes several novels as well as a number of short works, and their stories have been included in multiple anthologies.

In between noveling and editing, they blog coffee-fueled, quirky commentary on faith, culture, writing, books, and their family at amleibowitz.com.